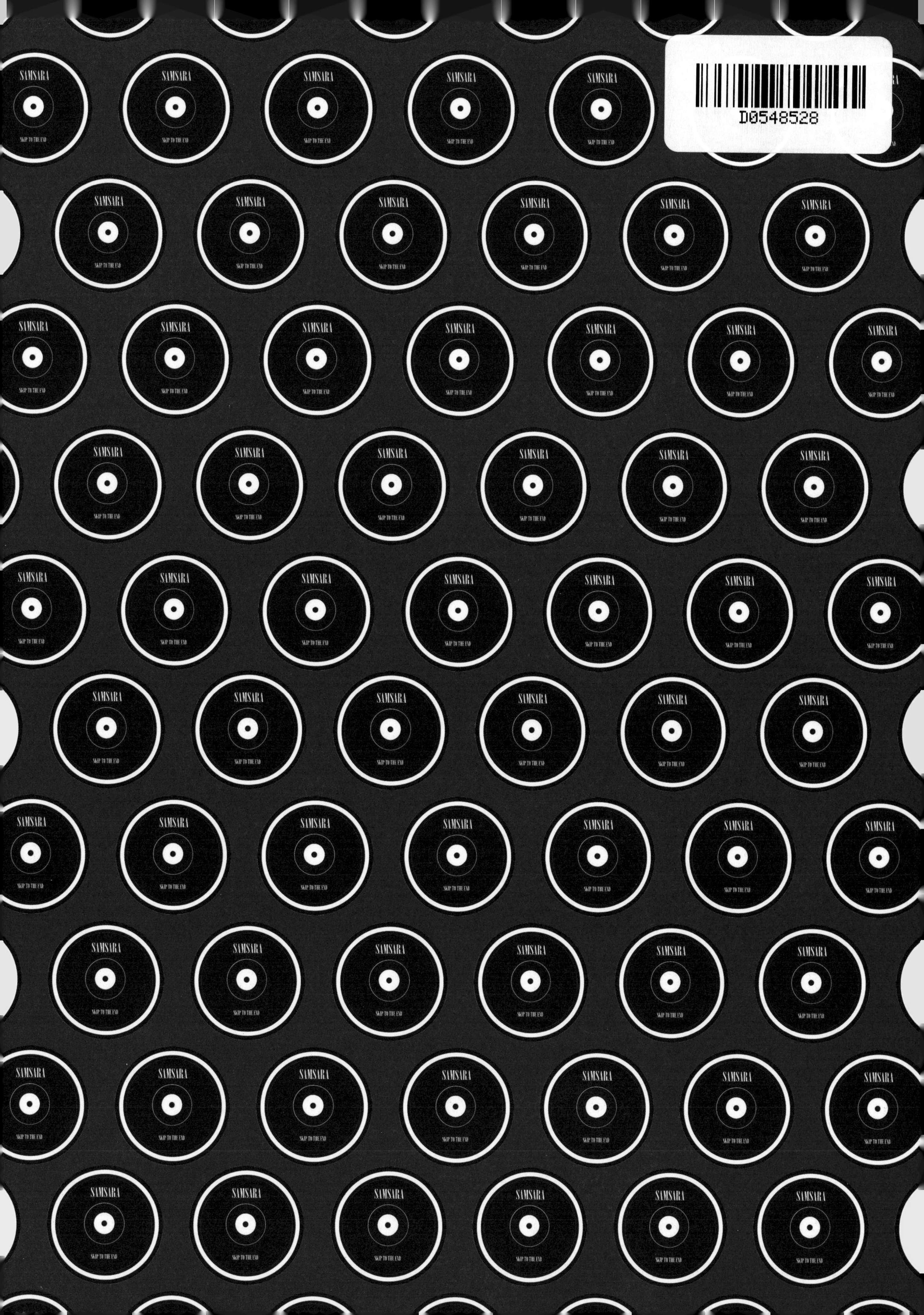
SAMSARA
SKIP TO THE END

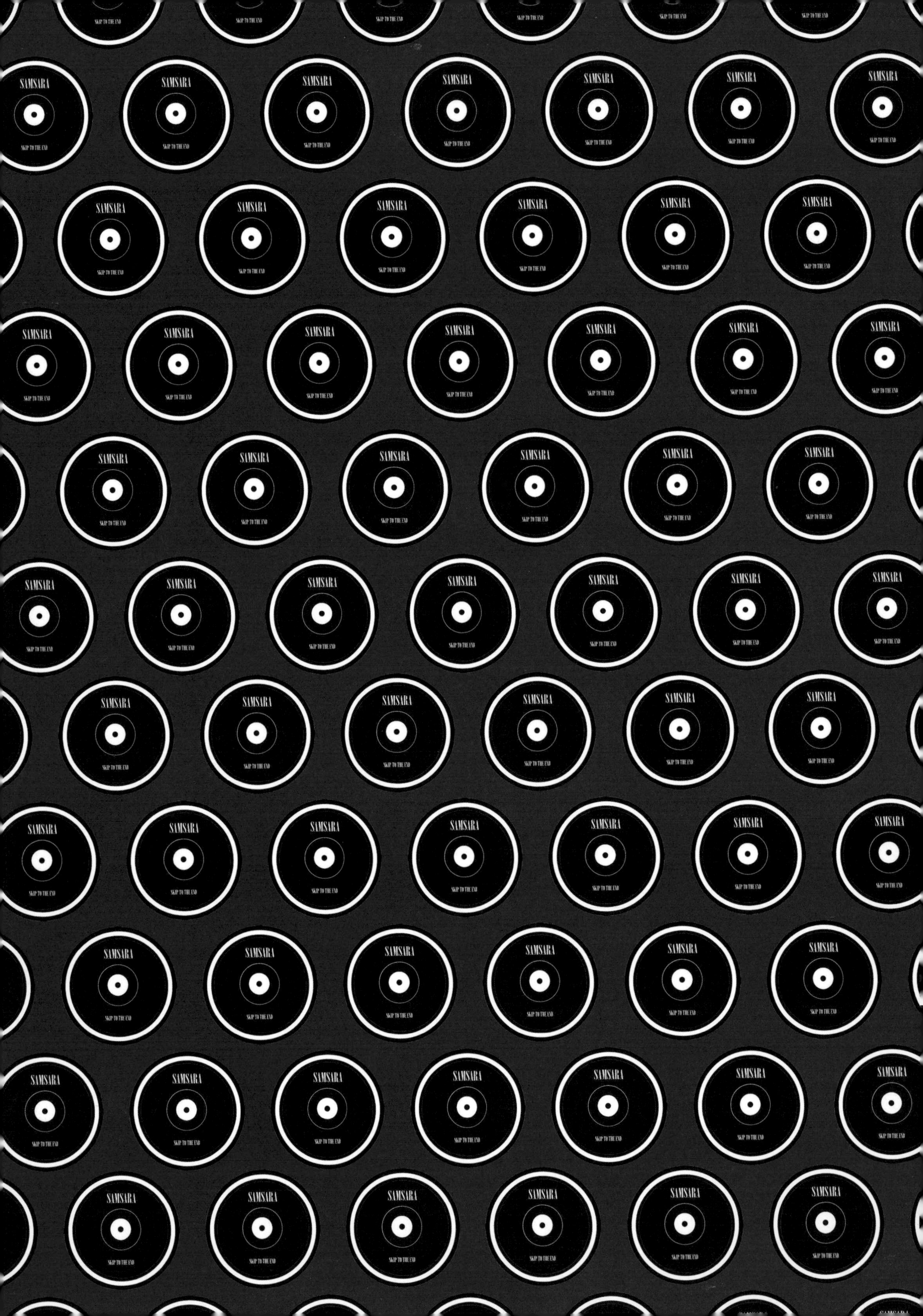
SAMSARA
SKIP TO THE END

SKIP TO THE END

SKIP TO THE END

JEREMY
HOLT

ALEX
DIOTTO

RENZO
PODESTA

ADAM
WOLLET

TIM
DANIEL

INSIGHT
COMICS

San Rafael, California

SKIP TO THE END

SCRIPT	JEREMY HOLT
ART	ALEX DIOTTO
COLORS	RENZO PODESTA
LETTERS	ADAM WOLLET
COVERS	ALEX DIOTTO & TIM DANIEL
LYRICS	JOHN MERCHANT

WRITING FUEL: CURSIVE COFFEE

TO END

SKID TO

SKIP TO THE END

THE

SKIP TO THE END

THE

mother's milk turns sour
summer turns to fall
wasting my last hour
too tired to call it out

turn the page, my friend
skipping to the end
it all comes back around
six feet underground
life was just a flirt
buried under doubt
digging out from dirt

too tired to shout it out

mother

Something about urgency.

No future in comics or punk rock.

There's something about urgency.

I'm writing this a week after I told Jeremy that he'd have it. I don't plan ahead well. And after I send it to him, I probably won't think about it again. I try not to spend too much time looking back. There are always fires that need to be put out, always things that need attention now. So I focus on those things to the detriment of all else.

We all do it. You eat gross food that will kill you later because you're hungry now. You spend your last few dollars on unimportant bullshit that you must have, knowing you won't make rent later. You go out partying all night to unwind, even though you have an important test the next day. And you do all of this because you don't think about the future. And if you did think about the future, you'd know that, when you get there, you won't spend too much time regretting what you did in the past. That is how you embrace urgency.

I don't think my desire for urgency is unusual. I think the amount that I let it shape my life might be. My need for urgency probably explains my two greatest passions in life: punk rock and comic books. They have a lot in common. Both comics and punk rock are raw. They don't pass through a lot of filters before they reach their audience. Listen to a band's demo tape or read a person's mini-comic. That is honest art with no aspirations to be anything else. Both comics and punk rock come from the underground. Record shops and comic shops, basement shows and comic cons, diving through record crates and digging through longboxes, bands in vans and artists in coffee shops, it's all basically the same thing. Sure, you can point to the superhero movie making billions of dollars or the band doing the arena tour, but that's not comics and that's not punk rock. Comics and punk rock are made knowing a few thousand people, maybe a few hundred even, are ever going to know about it. And that's really beautiful, by the way. Don't let anyone tell you otherwise.

But, most of all, I think comics and punk rock are about urgency. Short songs. Quick stories. We don't have time for guitar solos, and we don't have space for pointless dialogue. Only having seven inches of vinyl and twenty pages of paper means we need to be as honest as we can. Songs are written and pressed and performed in front of rooms full of sweaty bodies before anyone knows how to play their instruments. Comics are written, drawn, colored, and lettered by creators hunched over tables and desks all night, racing to get them out before we even know where they go. Anyone who plays in punk bands or makes comics can tell you that urgency is a big part of why we do it. And if you've ever screamed along to a band in a basement or raced to the comic shop on a Wednesday, you already know that urgency bleeds through into the work. It's what makes it honest, what makes it good, what makes it matter.

There's no glory, almost no money, and no future in comics or punk rock. We work our asses off, we sell our wares for cheap, and we move on to the next thing. That's urgency.

This comic you are about to read is about a lot of things. It's about the paths our lives take. It's about regret. It's about a punk band. It's about things that I'm not going to spoil for you. But, more than anything, I think it's about what happens when we lose our sense of urgency, when we spend too much time looking back at what was and too much time thinking about what could have been. Jeremy, Alex, Renzo, and Adam created a smart, beautiful, and heartbreaking read. Watching Jonny struggle with his life is painful and honest. You can feel him lose that immediacy of his life, and it's almost hard to read at times. The urge to skip to the end, to hopefully see him reclaim his urgency, is palpable.

But don't do that. While our protagonist fights for his urgency, surrender yours. Savor this book. Read it slow. Study the art. Reflect on the story, and think about the choices you've made in your life. Think about where the story is going and what you want your life to be. Give this book the time it deserves.

And when you finish reading this comic, take a moment to think about it.

Then go do something urgent.

Matthew Rosenberg
New York City
1/22/2017

[After spending most of his life chasing music in cramped basements, empty warehouses, dirty clubs, and death-defying tour vans, Matthew now writes comic books for a living. Weird.]

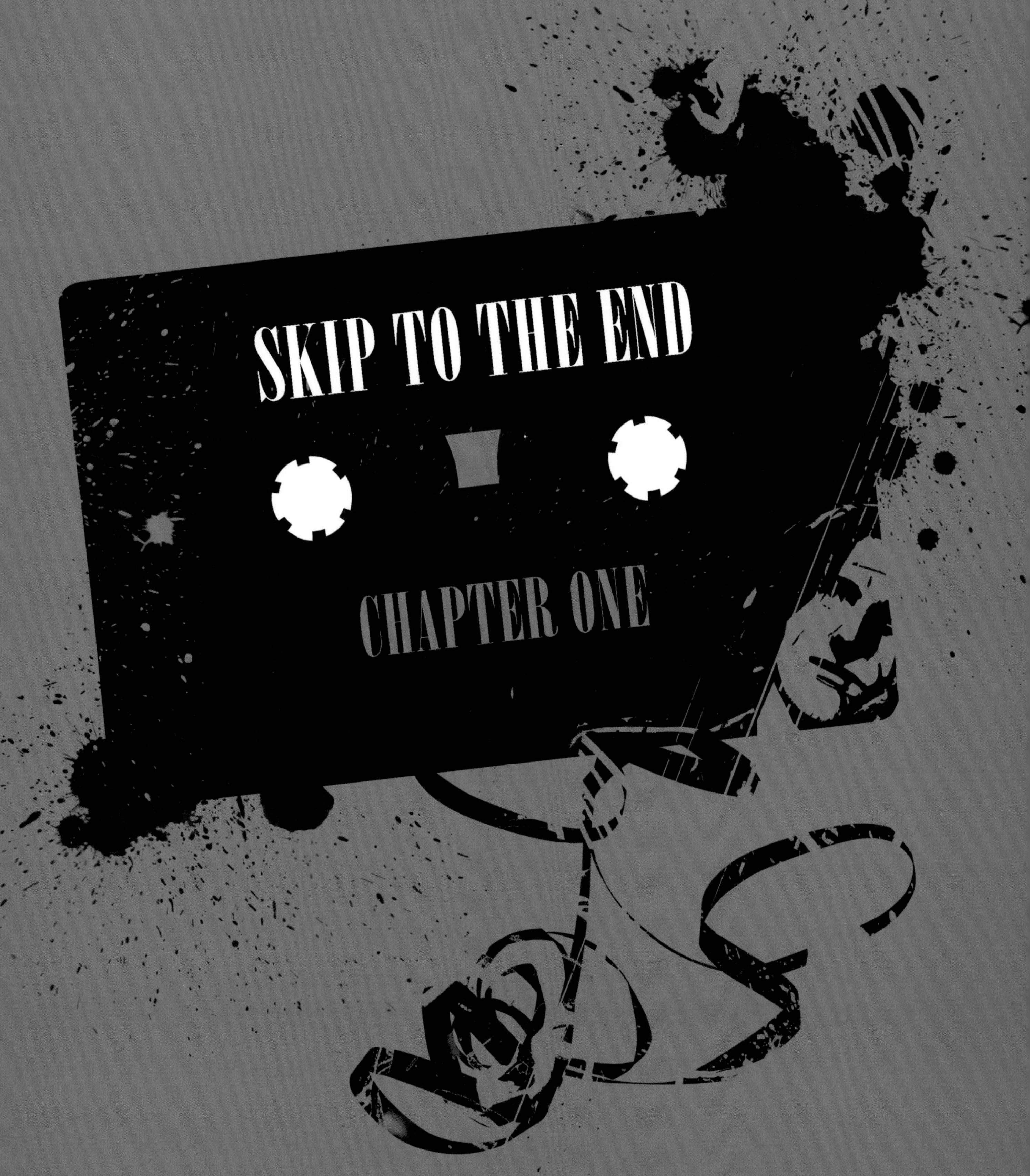
SKIP TO THE END
CHAPTER ONE

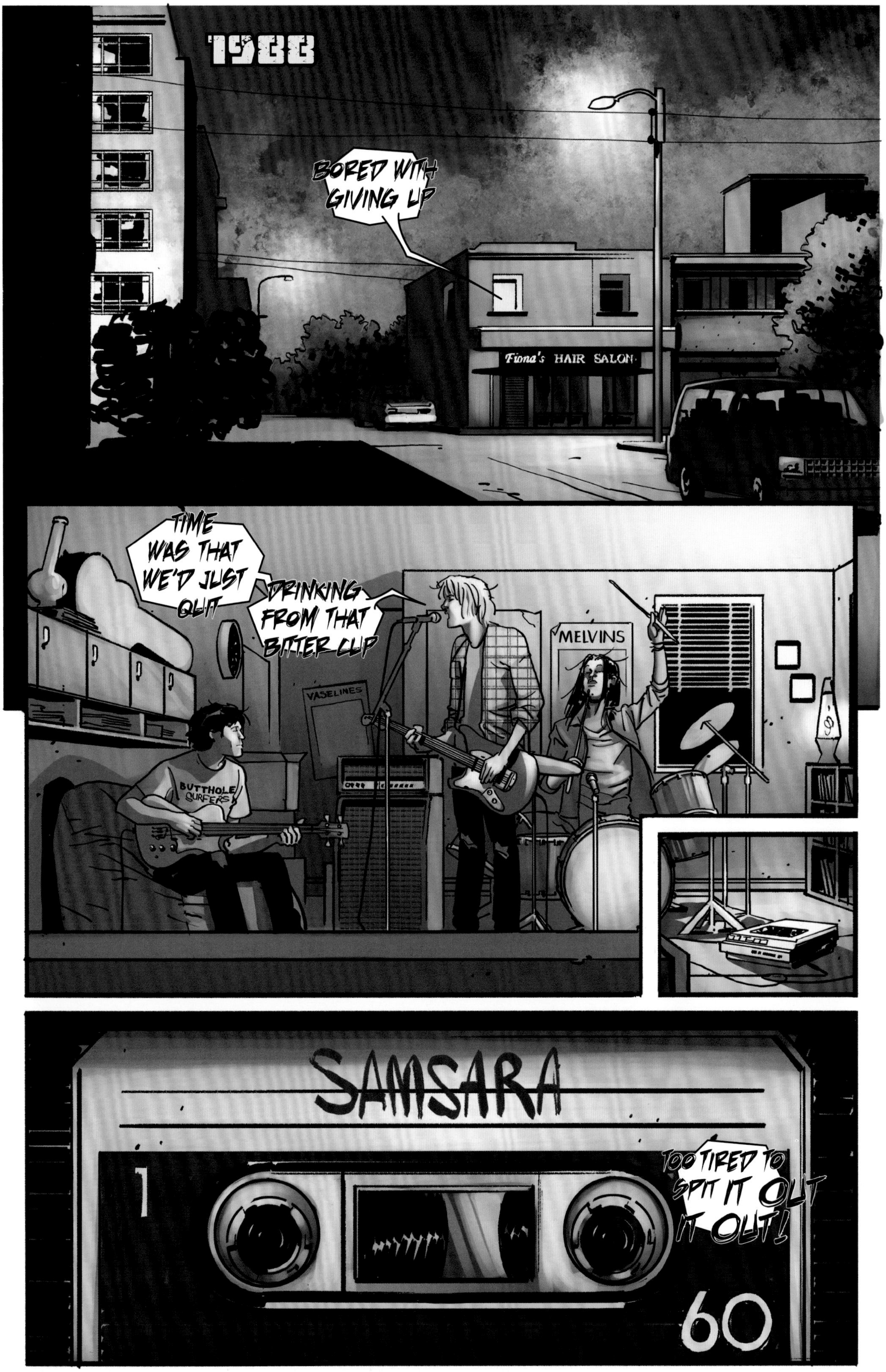
1988
BORED WITH GIVING UP
Fiona's HAIR SALON
TIME WAS THAT WE'D JUST QUIT
DRINKING FROM THAT BITTER CUP
MELVINS
VASELINES
BUTTHOLE SURFERS
SAMSARA
TOO TIRED TO SPIT IT OUT IT OUT!
1
60

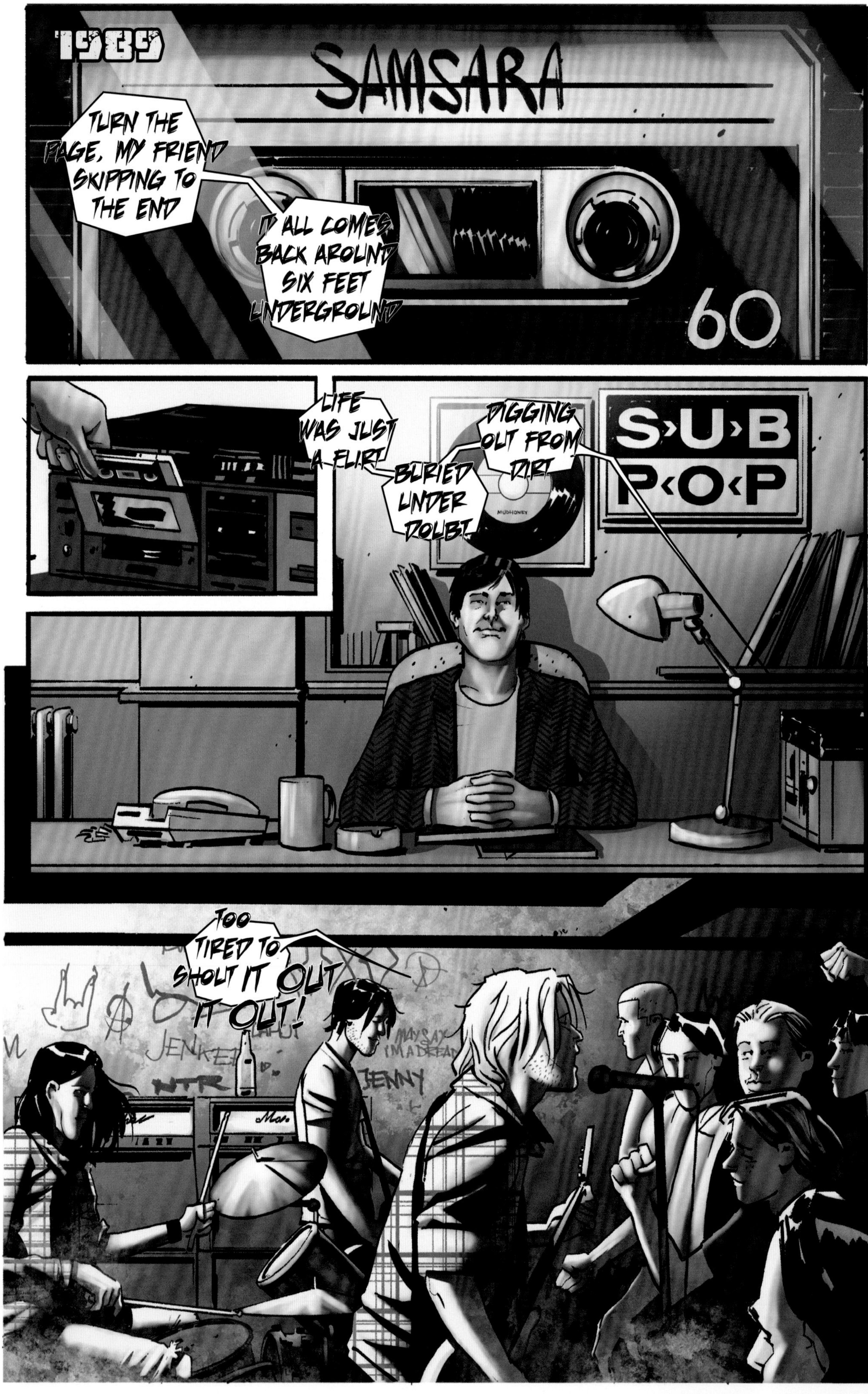
1989
SAMSARA
TURN THE PAGE, MY FRIEND SKIPPING TO THE END
IT ALL COMES BACK AROUND SIX FEET UNDERGROUND
60
LIFE WAS JUST A FLIRT
BURIED UNDER DOUBT
DIGGING OUT FROM DIRT
S·U·B P·O·P
MUDHONEY
TOO TIRED TO SHOUT IT OUT IT OUT!
NTR
JENNY

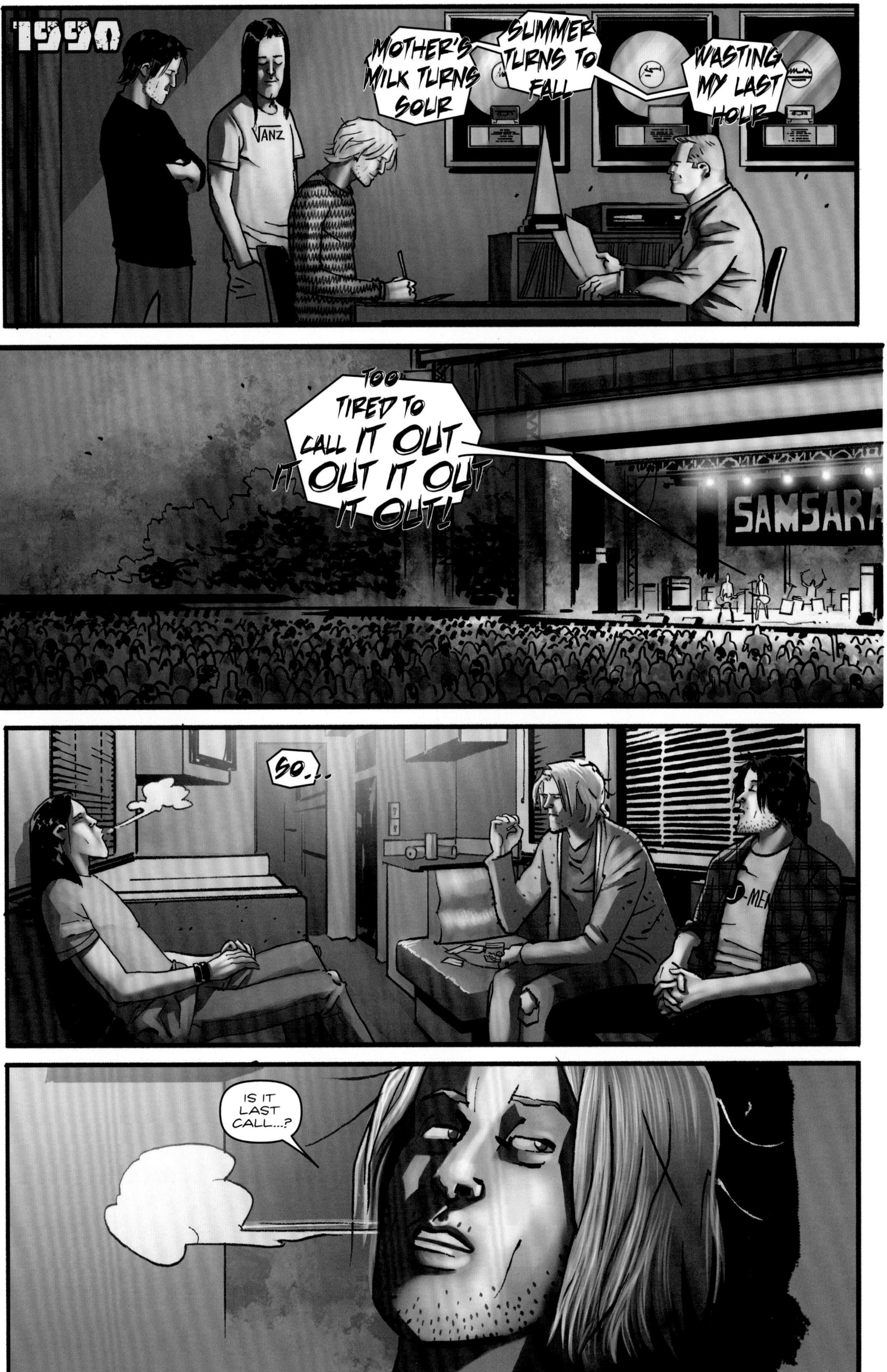
1990
MOTHER'S MILK TURNS SOUR
SUMMER TURNS TO FALL
WASTING MY LAST HOUR
VANZ
TOO TIRED TO CALL IT OUT IT OUT IT OUT IT OUT!
SAMSARA
SO...
IS IT LAST CALL...?

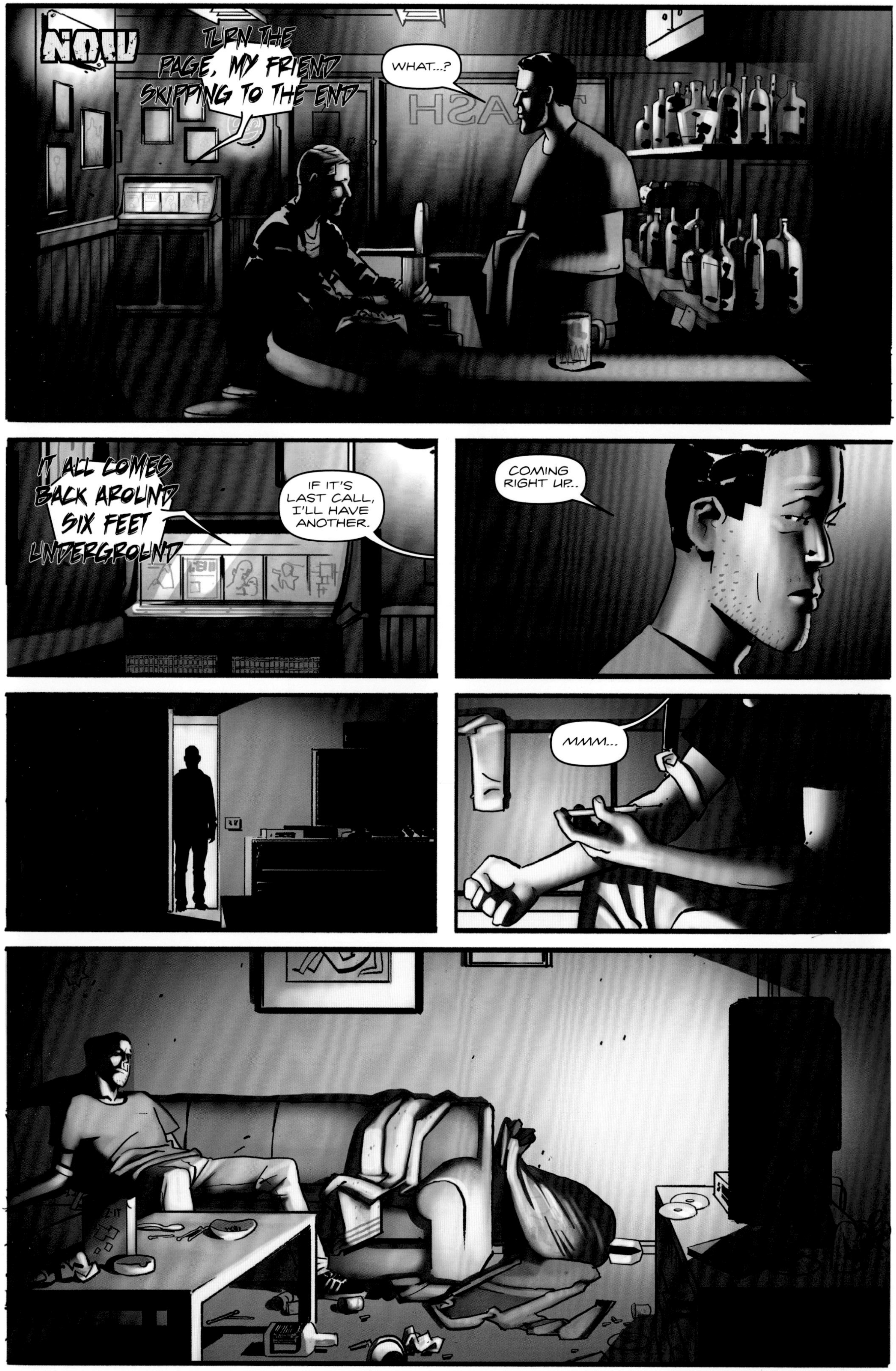
NOW
TURN THE PAGE, MY FRIEND SKIPPING TO THE END
WHAT...?
IT ALL COMES BACK AROUND SIX FEET UNDERGROUND
IF IT'S LAST CALL, I'LL HAVE ANOTHER.
COMING RIGHT UP...
MMM...

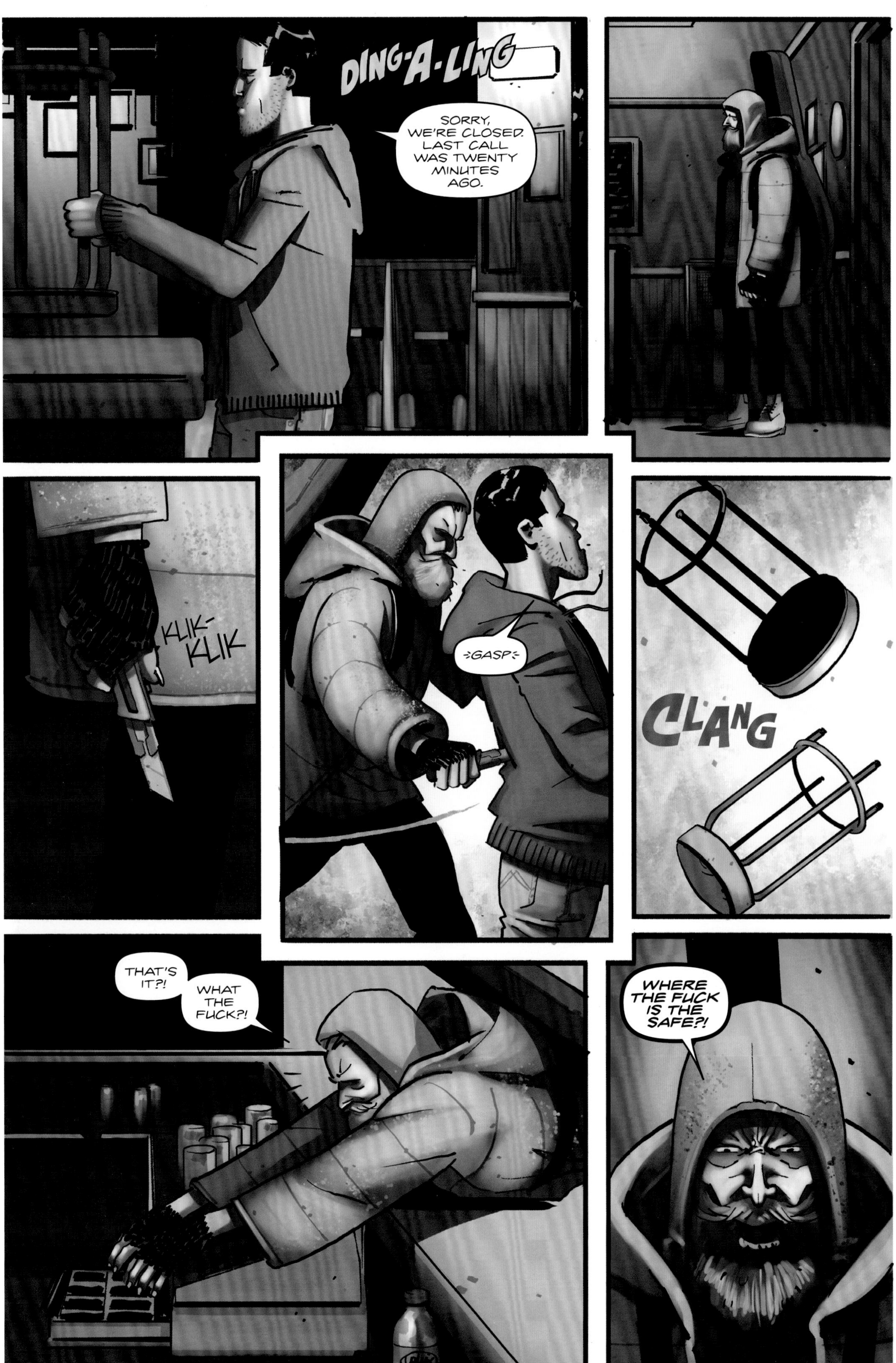
DING-A-LING
SORRY, WE'RE CLOSED. LAST CALL WAS TWENTY MINUTES AGO.
KLIK-KLIK
GASP
CLANG
THAT'S IT?!
WHAT THE FUCK?!
WHERE THE FUCK IS THE SAFE?!

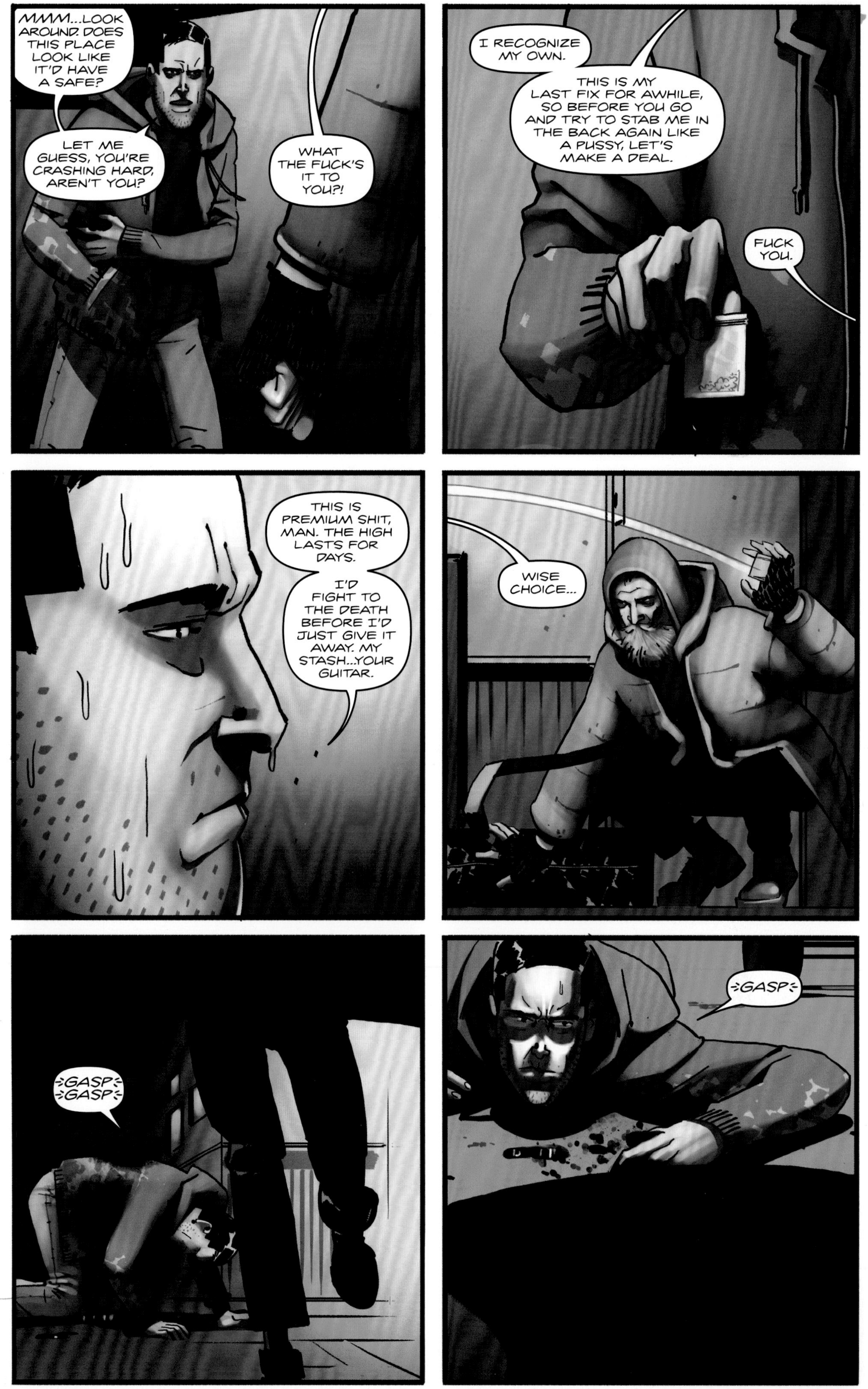
MMM...LOOK AROUND. DOES THIS PLACE LOOK LIKE IT'D HAVE A SAFE?
LET ME GUESS, YOU'RE CRASHING HARD, AREN'T YOU?
WHAT THE FUCK'S IT TO YOU?!
I RECOGNIZE MY OWN.
THIS IS MY LAST FIX FOR AWHILE, SO BEFORE YOU GO AND TRY TO STAB ME IN THE BACK AGAIN LIKE A PUSSY, LET'S MAKE A DEAL.
FUCK YOU.
THIS IS PREMIUM SHIT, MAN. THE HIGH LASTS FOR DAYS.
I'D FIGHT TO THE DEATH BEFORE I'D JUST GIVE IT AWAY. MY STASH...YOUR GUITAR.
WISE CHOICE...
GASP GASP
GASP

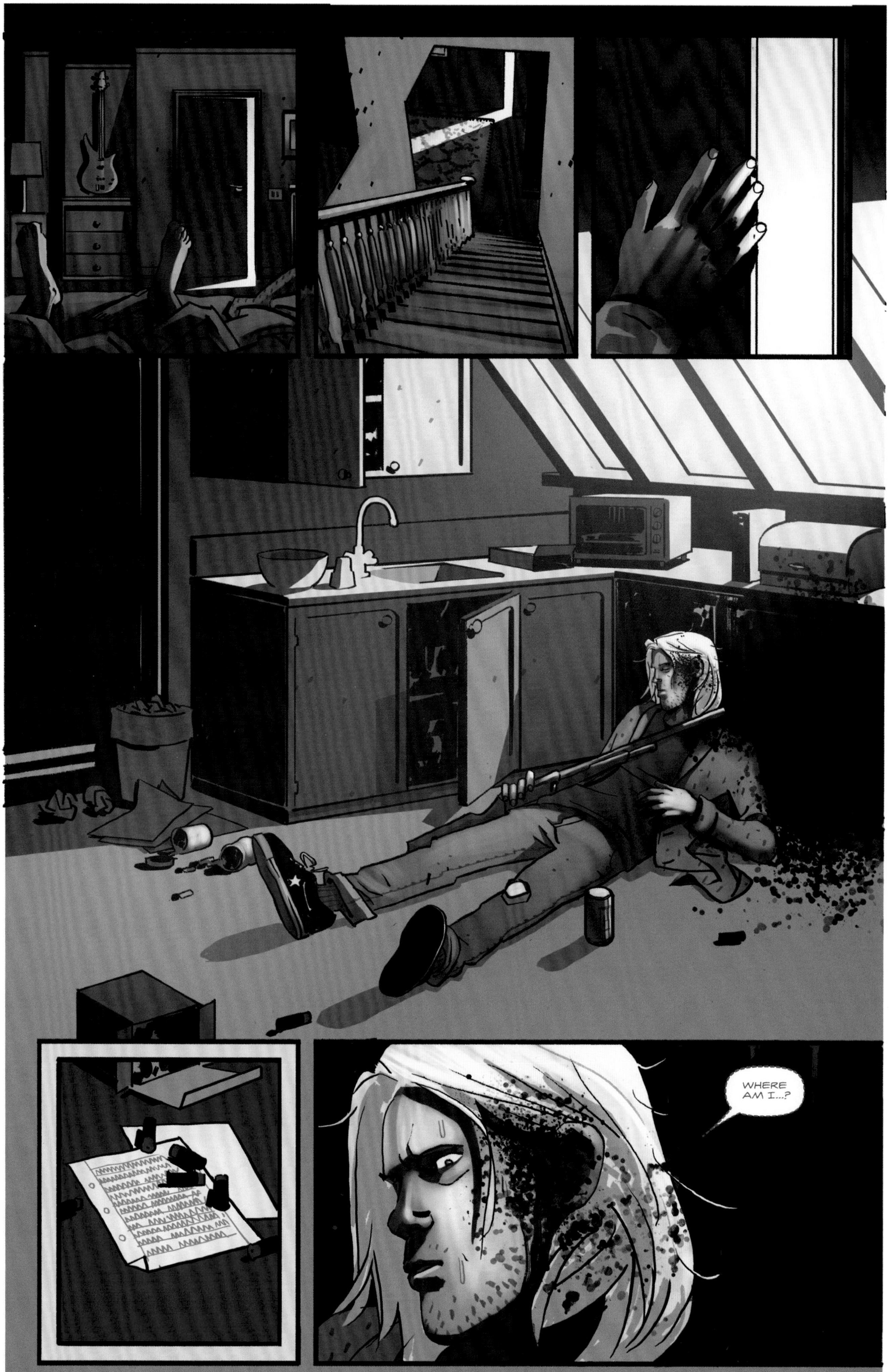
WHERE AM I...?

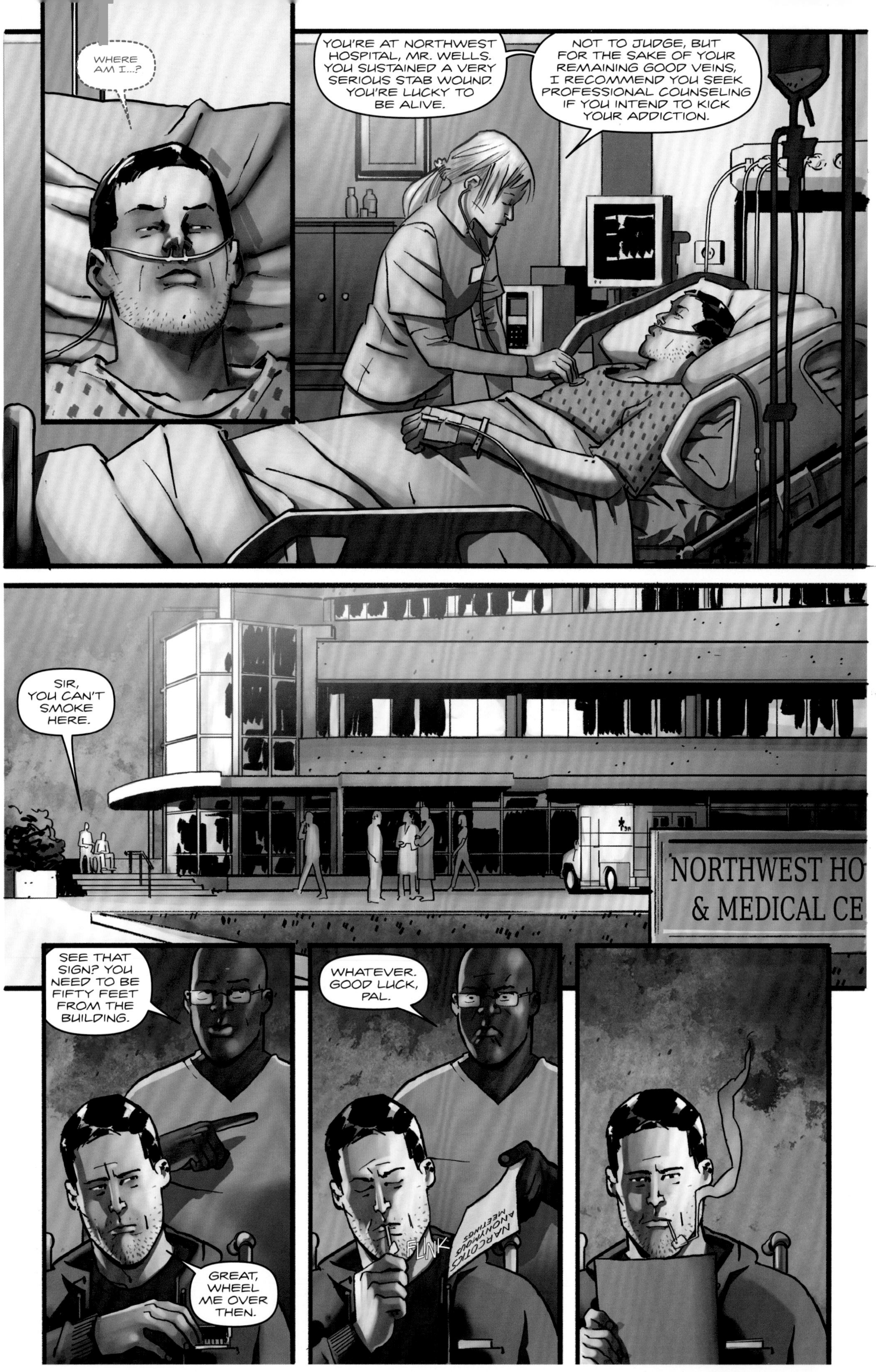
WHERE AM I...?
YOU'RE AT NORTHWEST HOSPITAL, MR. WELLS. YOU SUSTAINED A VERY SERIOUS STAB WOUND. YOU'RE LUCKY TO BE ALIVE.
NOT TO JUDGE, BUT FOR THE SAKE OF YOUR REMAINING GOOD VEINS, I RECOMMEND YOU SEEK PROFESSIONAL COUNSELING IF YOU INTEND TO KICK YOUR ADDICTION.
SIR, YOU CAN'T SMOKE HERE.
NORTHWEST HO
& MEDICAL CE
SEE THAT SIGN? YOU NEED TO BE FIFTY FEET FROM THE BUILDING.
GREAT, WHEEL ME OVER THEN.
WHATEVER. GOOD LUCK, PAL.
FLINK
NARCOTICS ANONYMOUS MEETINGS

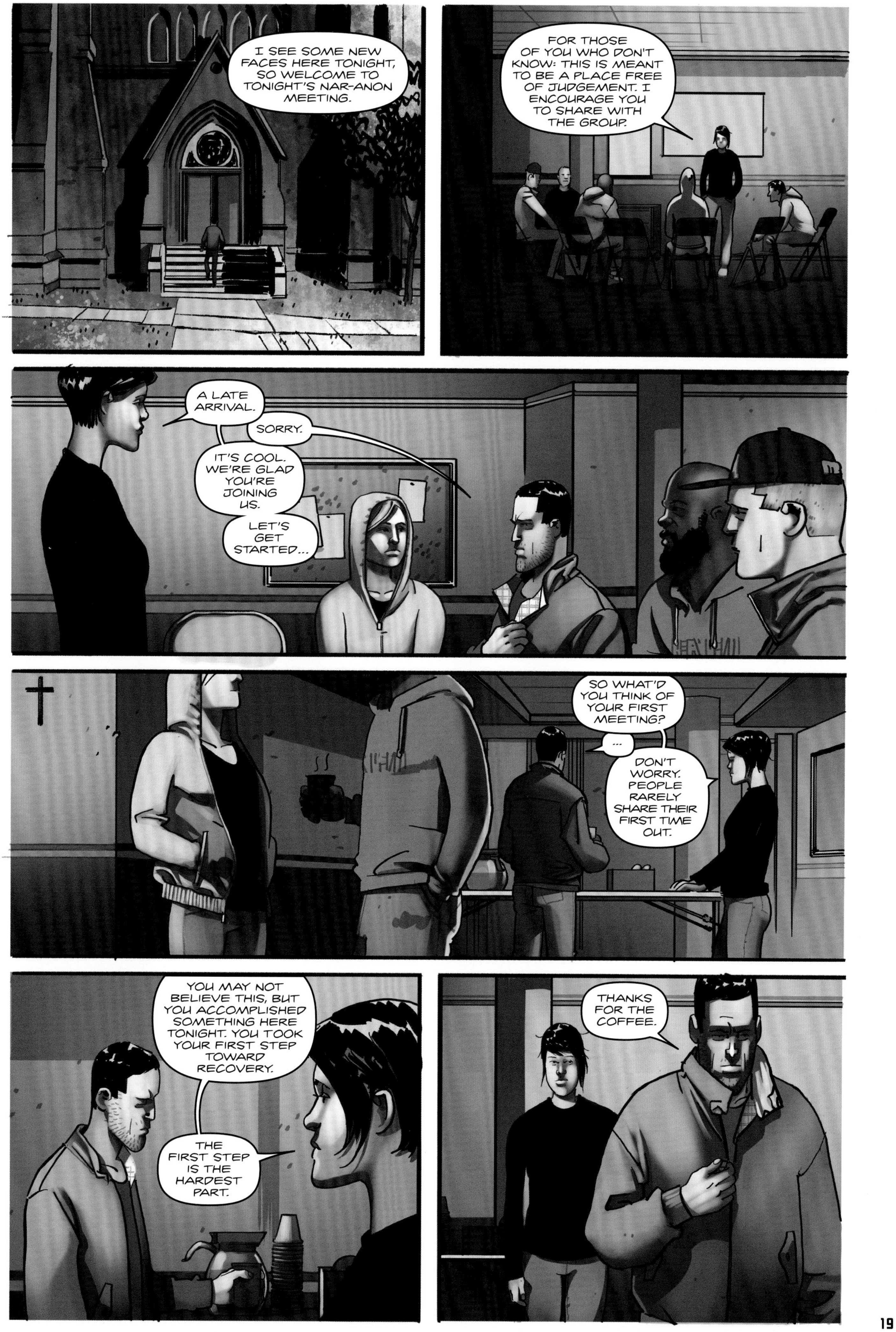
I SEE SOME NEW FACES HERE TONIGHT, SO WELCOME TO TONIGHT'S NAR-ANON MEETING.
FOR THOSE OF YOU WHO DON'T KNOW: THIS IS MEANT TO BE A PLACE FREE OF JUDGEMENT. I ENCOURAGE YOU TO SHARE WITH THE GROUP.
A LATE ARRIVAL.
SORRY.
IT'S COOL. WE'RE GLAD YOU'RE JOINING US.
LET'S GET STARTED...
SO WHAT'D YOU THINK OF YOUR FIRST MEETING?
...
DON'T WORRY. PEOPLE RARELY SHARE THEIR FIRST TIME OUT.
YOU MAY NOT BELIEVE THIS, BUT YOU ACCOMPLISHED SOMETHING HERE TONIGHT. YOU TOOK YOUR FIRST STEP TOWARD RECOVERY.
THE FIRST STEP IS THE HARDEST PART.
THANKS FOR THE COFFEE.

YOU'RE JOKING, RIGHT? YOU DIDN'T **ACTUALLY** LISTEN TO THAT CRAP?

WHAT?! IT WAS POPULAR IN HIGH SCHOOL. SORRY IF I DIDN'T HAVE SOPHISTICATED TASTE IN MUSIC WHEN I WAS **SIXTEEN**.

BUT IT WAS THE EARLY 90'S! THE ONLY STUFF WORTH LISTENING TO THEN WAS GRUNGE.

MEH, NOT A FAN.

TELL ME YOU **AT LEAST** LISTENED TO SAMSARA.

...

ARE YOU KIDDING ME?! KIRK JANSEN WAS A ROCK GOD. I REMEMBER EXACTLY WHERE I WAS THE DAY HE DIED.

I'M CORRECTING THIS COSMIC INJUSTICE RIGHT NOW. WE ARE NOT LEAVING THIS BAR UNTIL I'VE EXPOSED YOU TO HIS GENIUS.

BORED WITH GIVING UP

TIME WAS THAT WE'D JUST QUIT

DRINKING FROM THAT BITTER CUP

TOO TIRED SPIT IT OUT IT OUT

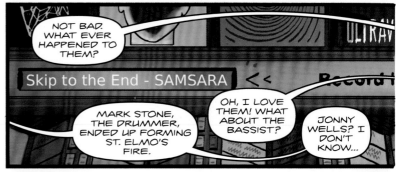

NOT BAD. WHAT EVER HAPPENED TO THEM?

Skip to the End - SAMSARA   <<

Record

ULTRAV

MARK STONE, THE DRUMMER, ENDED UP FORMING ST. ELMO'S FIRE.

OH, I LOVE THEM! WHAT ABOUT THE BASSIST?

JONNY WELLS? I DON'T KNOW...

THINK HE DIED OR SOMETHING.

THIS IS MY **FAVORITE** PART...

TURN THE PAGE, MY FRIEND SKIPPING TO THE END

IT ALL COMES BACK AROUND SIX FEET UNDERGROUND

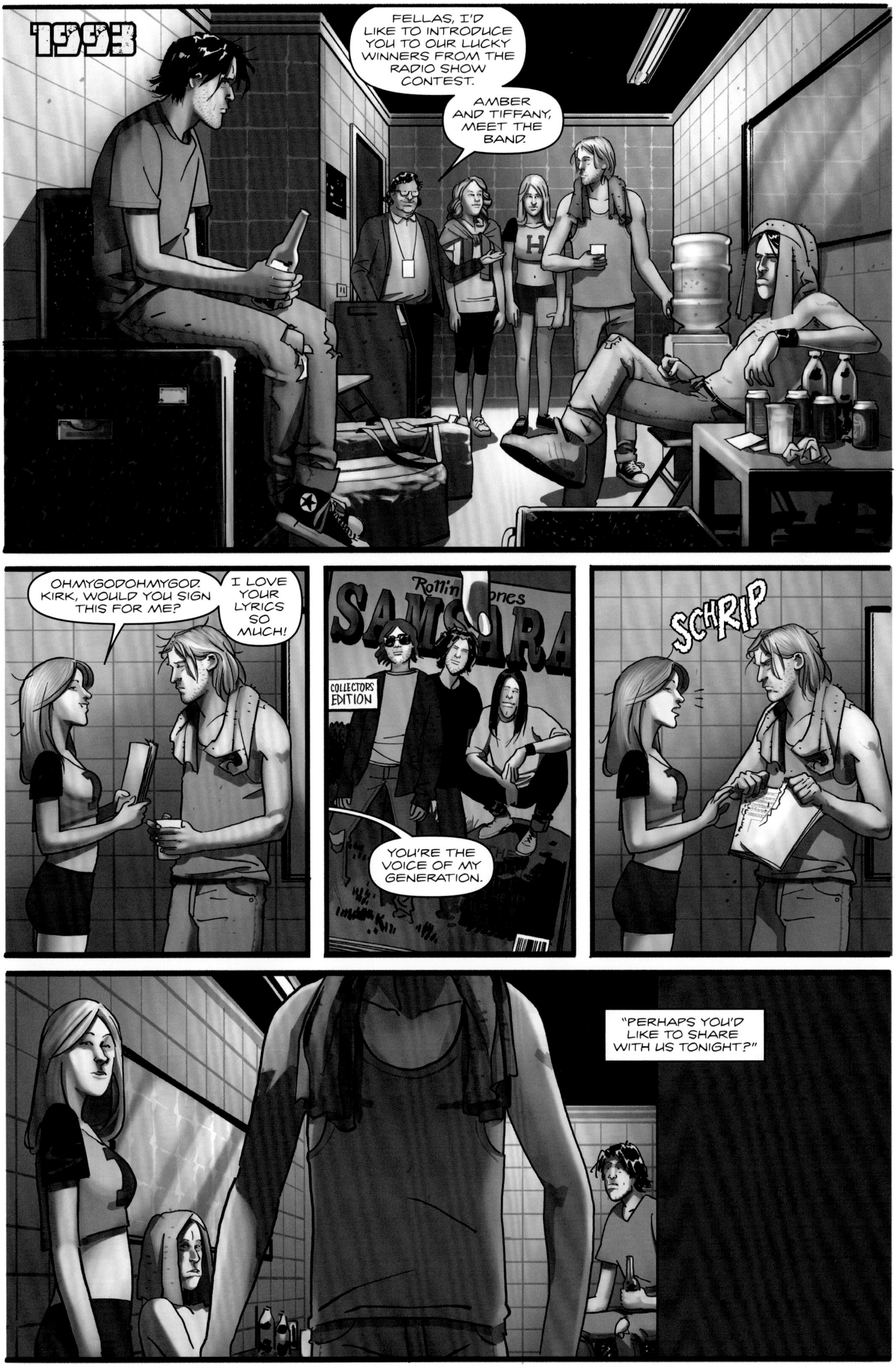
1993
FELLAS, I'D LIKE TO INTRODUCE YOU TO OUR LUCKY WINNERS FROM THE RADIO SHOW CONTEST.
AMBER AND TIFFANY, MEET THE BAND.
OHMYGODOHMYGOD. KIRK, WOULD YOU SIGN THIS FOR ME?
I LOVE YOUR LYRICS SO MUCH!
SAMSARA
COLLECTORS EDITION
YOU'RE THE VOICE OF MY GENERATION.
SCHRIP
"PERHAPS YOU'D LIKE TO SHARE WITH US TONIGHT?"

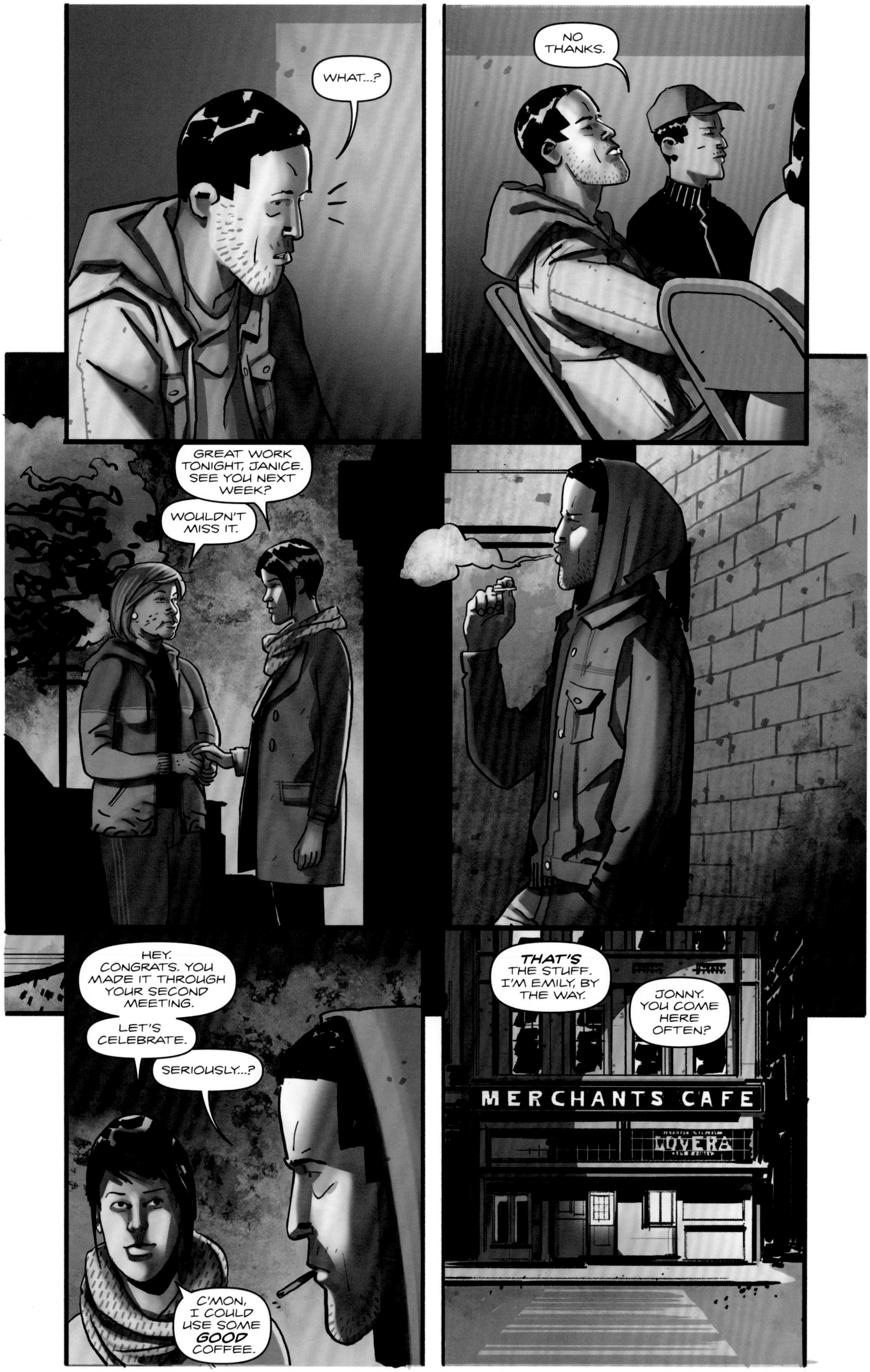
WHAT...?
NO THANKS.
GREAT WORK TONIGHT, JANICE. SEE YOU NEXT WEEK?
WOULDN'T MISS IT.
HEY. CONGRATS. YOU MADE IT THROUGH YOUR SECOND MEETING.
LET'S CELEBRATE.
SERIOUSLY...?
C'MON, I COULD USE SOME ***GOOD*** COFFEE.
THAT'S THE STUFF. I'M EMILY, BY THE WAY.
JONNY. YOU COME HERE OFTEN?
MERCHANTS CAFE
LOVERA

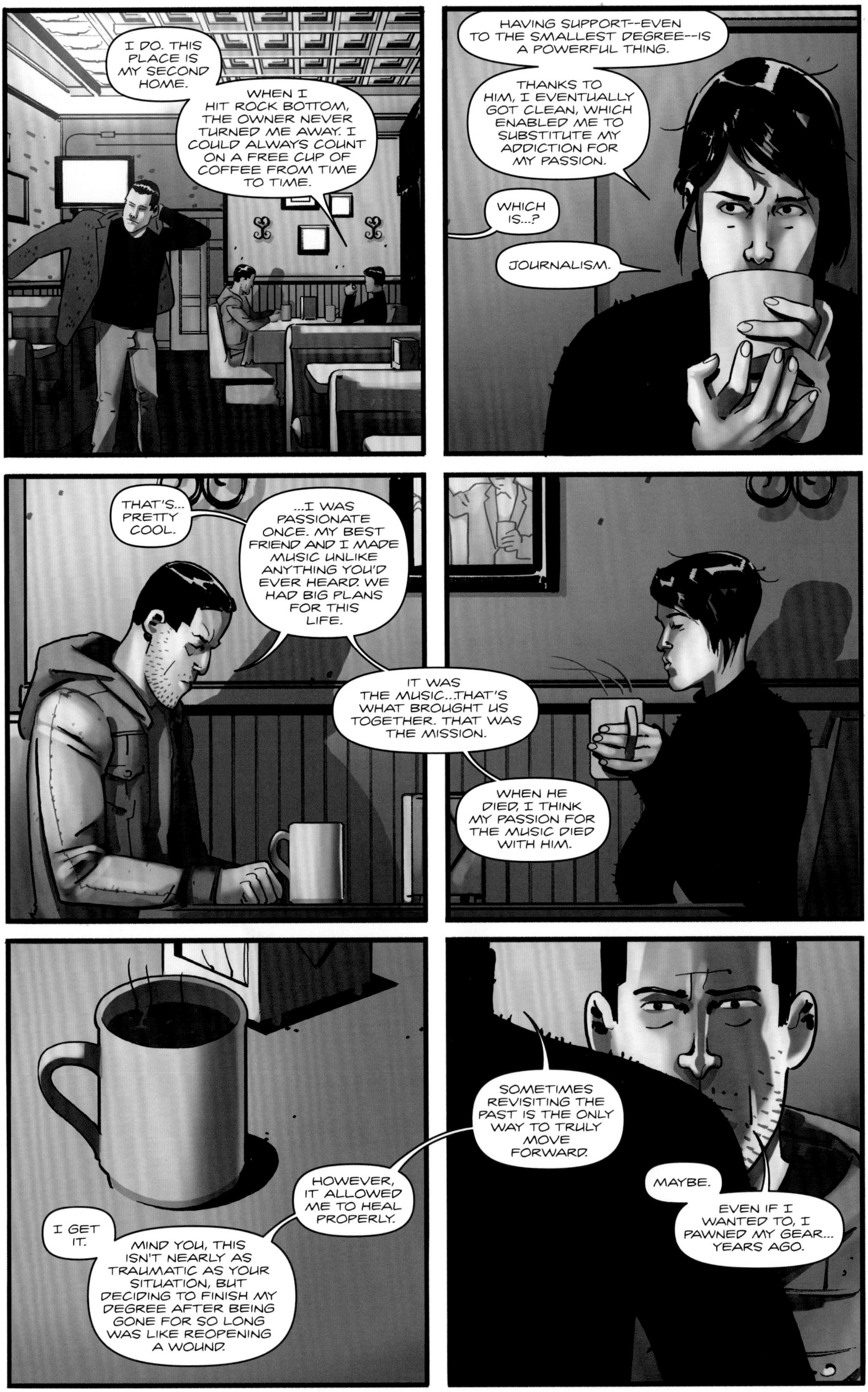
I DO. THIS PLACE IS MY SECOND HOME.
WHEN I HIT ROCK BOTTOM, THE OWNER NEVER TURNED ME AWAY. I COULD ALWAYS COUNT ON A FREE CUP OF COFFEE FROM TIME TO TIME.
HAVING SUPPORT--EVEN TO THE SMALLEST DEGREE--IS A POWERFUL THING.
THANKS TO HIM, I EVENTUALLY GOT CLEAN, WHICH ENABLED ME TO SUBSTITUTE MY ADDICTION FOR MY PASSION.
WHICH IS...?
JOURNALISM.
THAT'S... PRETTY COOL.
...I WAS PASSIONATE ONCE. MY BEST FRIEND AND I MADE MUSIC UNLIKE ANYTHING YOU'D EVER HEARD. WE HAD BIG PLANS FOR THIS LIFE.
IT WAS THE MUSIC...THAT'S WHAT BROUGHT US TOGETHER. THAT WAS THE MISSION.
WHEN HE DIED, I THINK MY PASSION FOR THE MUSIC DIED WITH HIM.
I GET IT.
MIND YOU, THIS ISN'T NEARLY AS TRAUMATIC AS YOUR SITUATION, BUT DECIDING TO FINISH MY DEGREE AFTER BEING GONE FOR SO LONG WAS LIKE REOPENING A WOUND.
HOWEVER, IT ALLOWED ME TO HEAL PROPERLY.
SOMETIMES REVISITING THE PAST IS THE ONLY WAY TO TRULY MOVE FORWARD.
MAYBE.
EVEN IF I WANTED TO, I PAWNED MY GEAR... YEARS AGO.

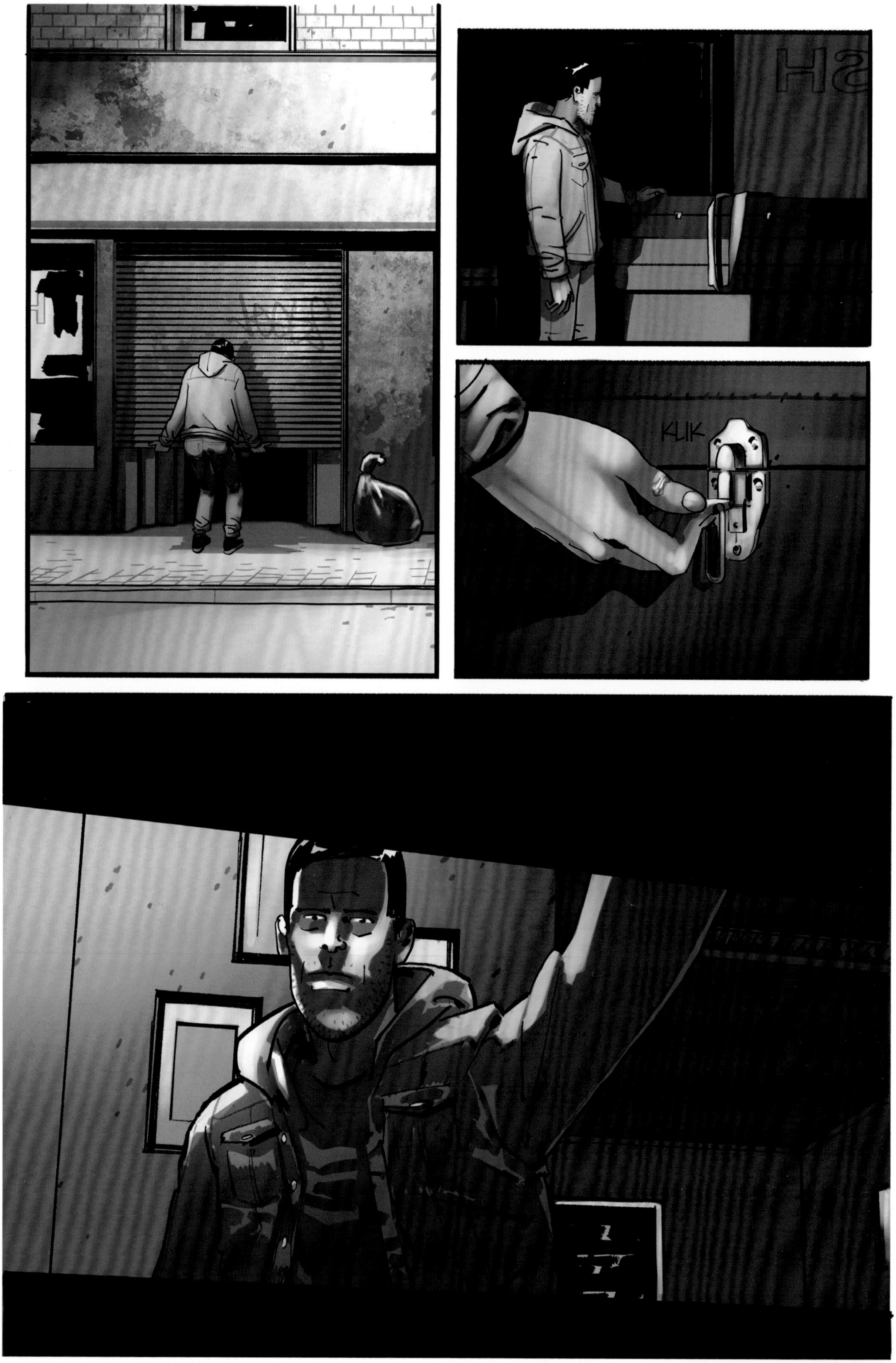
KLIK

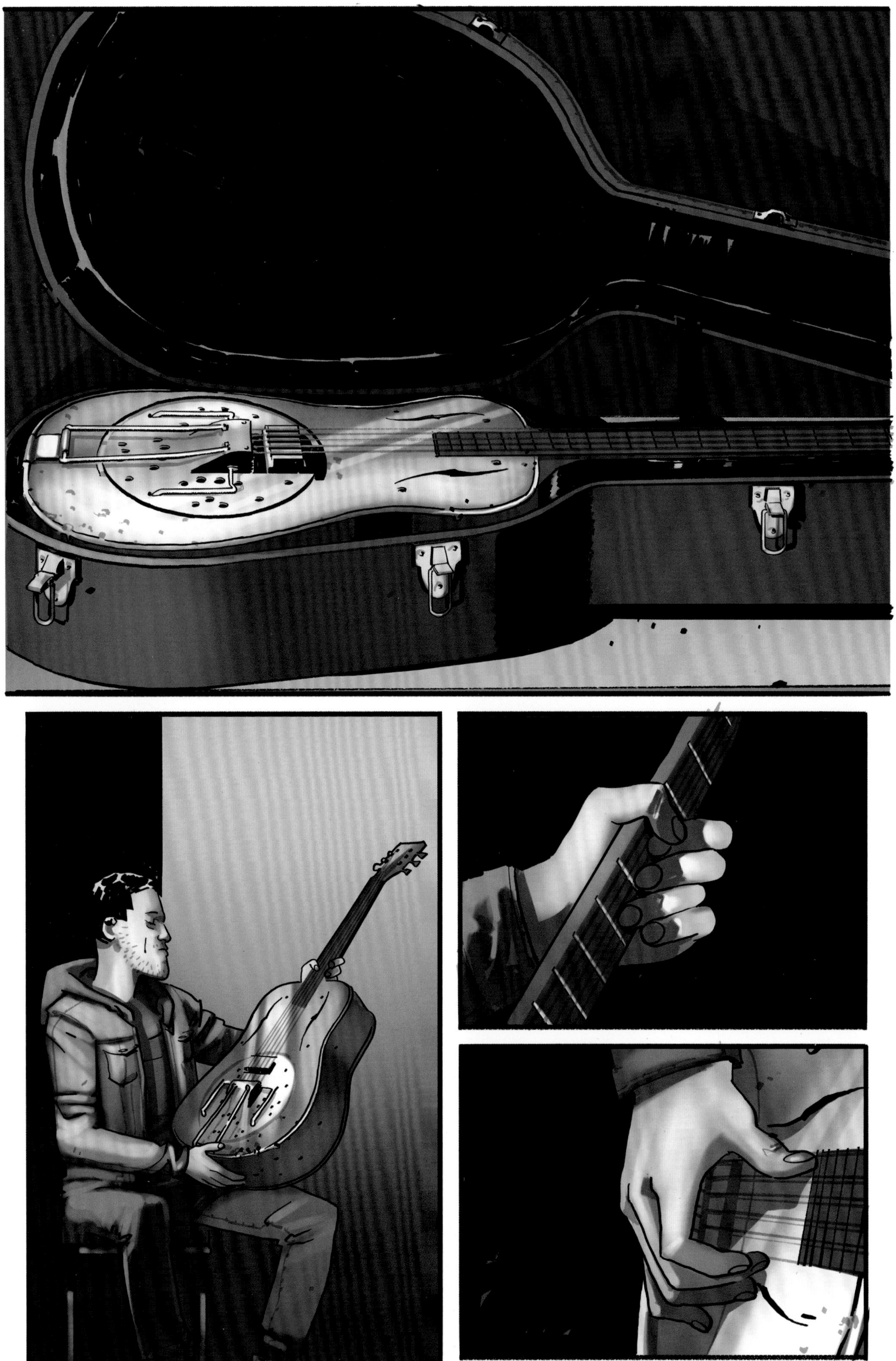

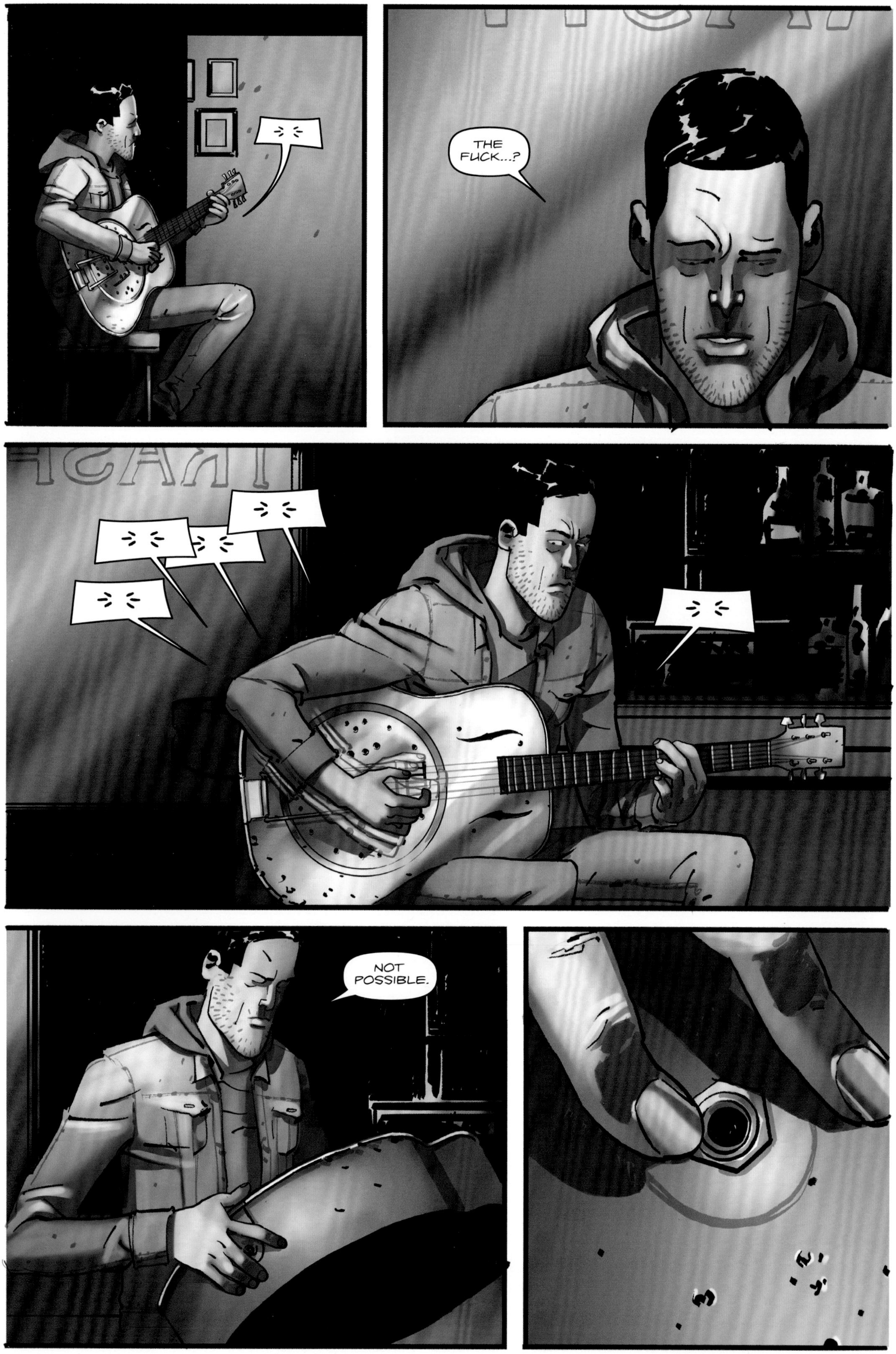
THE FUCK...?
NOT POSSIBLE.

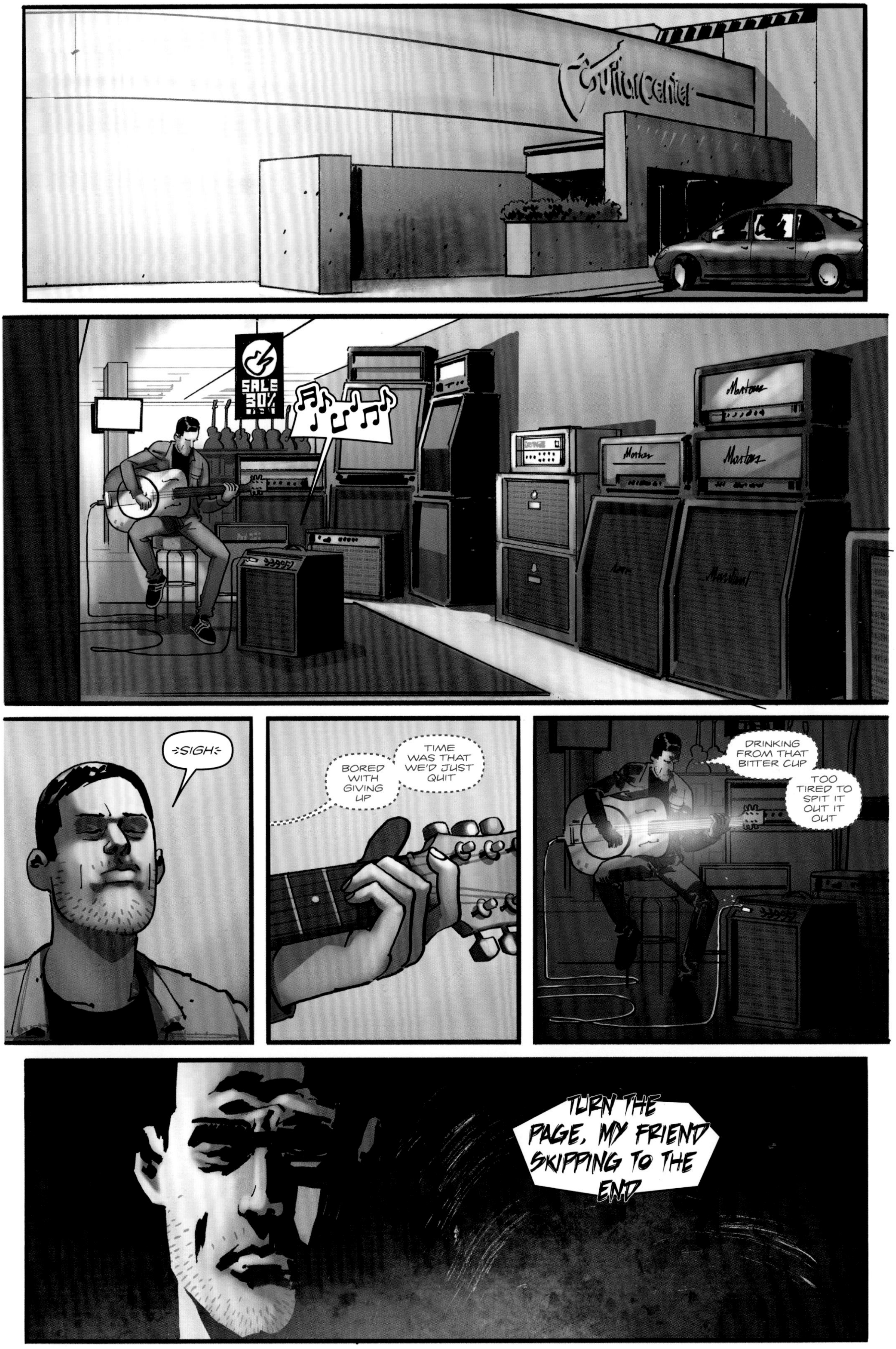
GuitarCenter
SALE 30%
~SIGH~
BORED WITH GIVING UP
TIME WAS THAT WE'D JUST QUIT
DRINKING FROM THAT BITTER CUP
TOO TIRED TO SPIT IT OUT IT OUT
TURN THE PAGE, MY FRIEND SKIPPING TO THE END

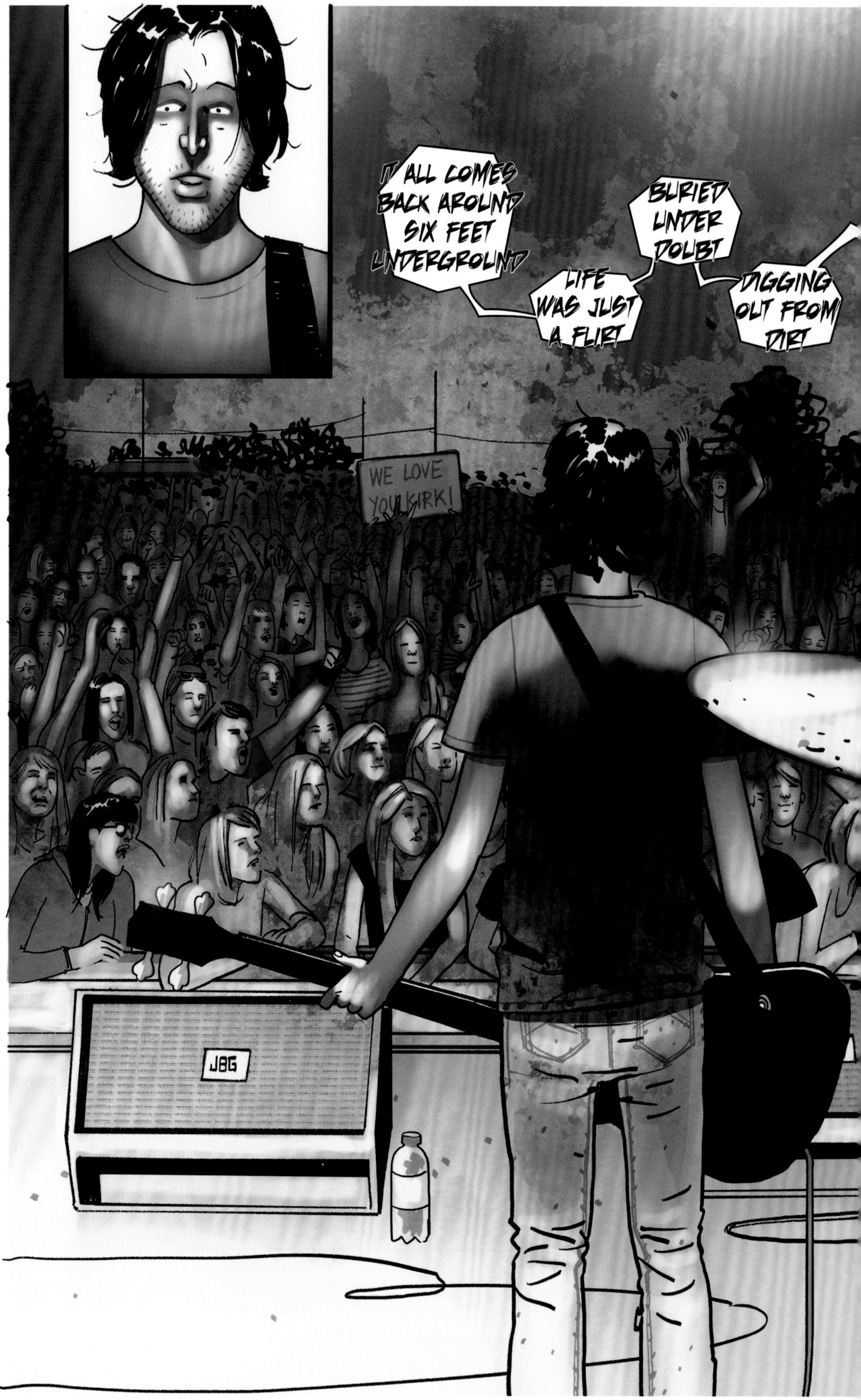
IT ALL COMES BACK AROUND SIX FEET UNDERGROUND
LIFE WAS JUST A FLIRT
BURIED UNDER DOUBT
DIGGING OUT FROM DIRT
WE LOVE YOU KIRK!
JBG

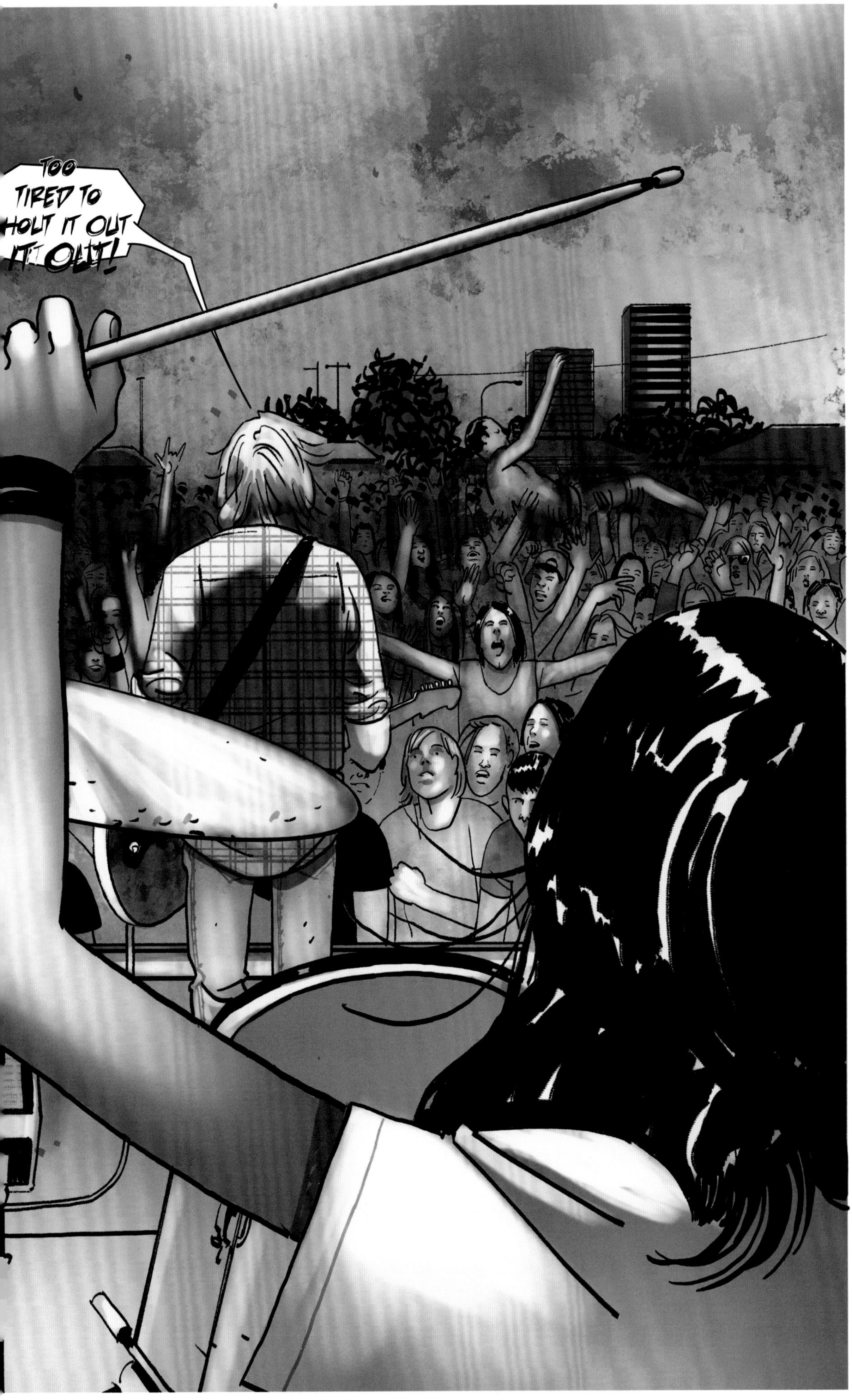
TOO
TIRED TO
HOUT IT OUT
IT OUT!

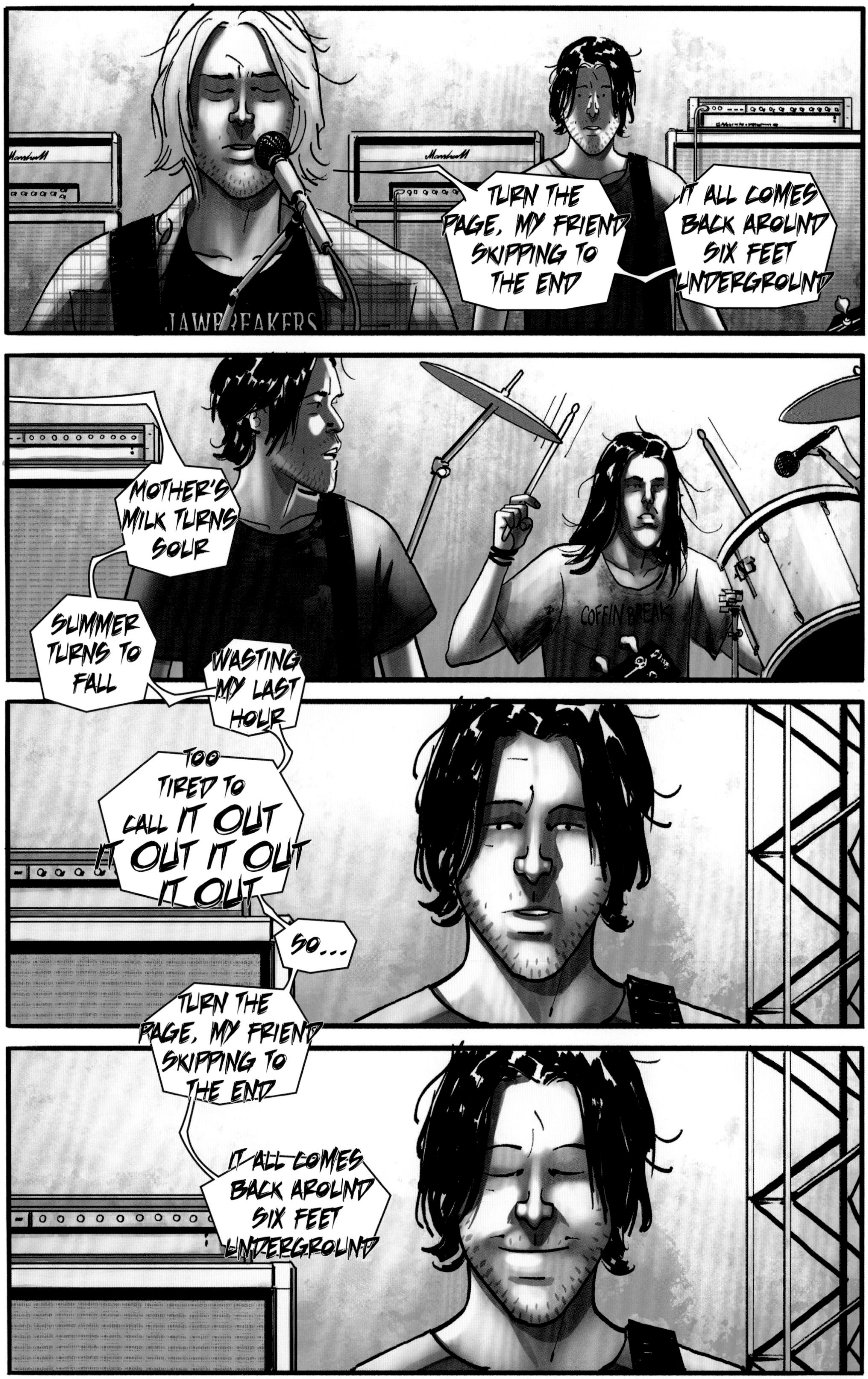
JAWBREAKERS
TURN THE PAGE, MY FRIEND SKIPPING TO THE END
IT ALL COMES BACK AROUND SIX FEET UNDERGROUND
MOTHER'S MILK TURNS SOUR
SUMMER TURNS TO FALL
WASTING MY LAST HOUR
COFFIN BREAK
TOO TIRED TO CALL IT OUT IT OUT IT OUT IT OUT
SO...
TURN THE PAGE, MY FRIEND SKIPPING TO THE END
IT ALL COMES BACK AROUND SIX FEET UNDERGROUND

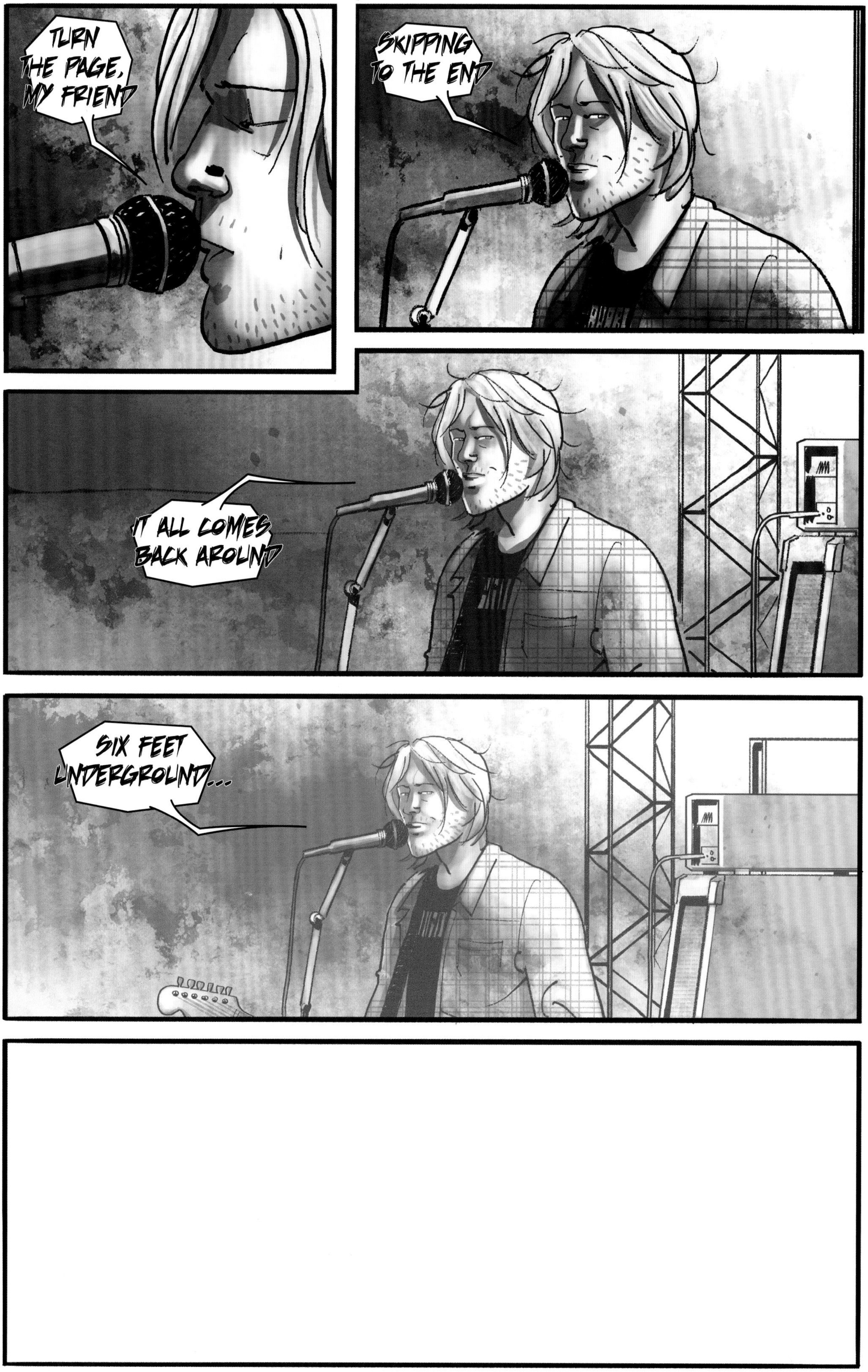
TURN THE PAGE, MY FRIEND
SKIPPING TO THE END
IT ALL COMES BACK AROUND
SIX FEET UNDERGROUND...

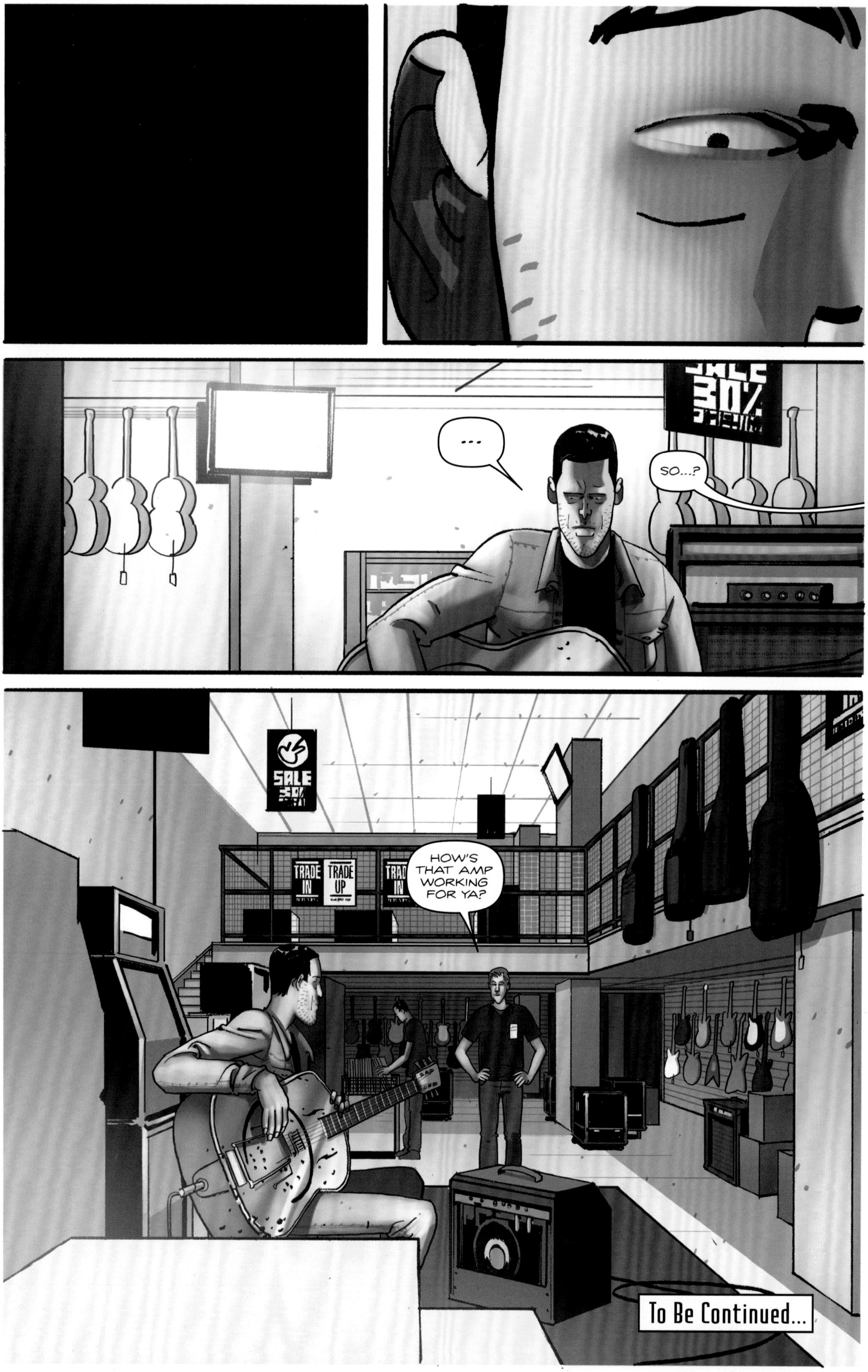
...
SO...?
SALE
TRADE IN
TRADE UP
HOW'S THAT AMP WORKING FOR YA?
To Be Continued...

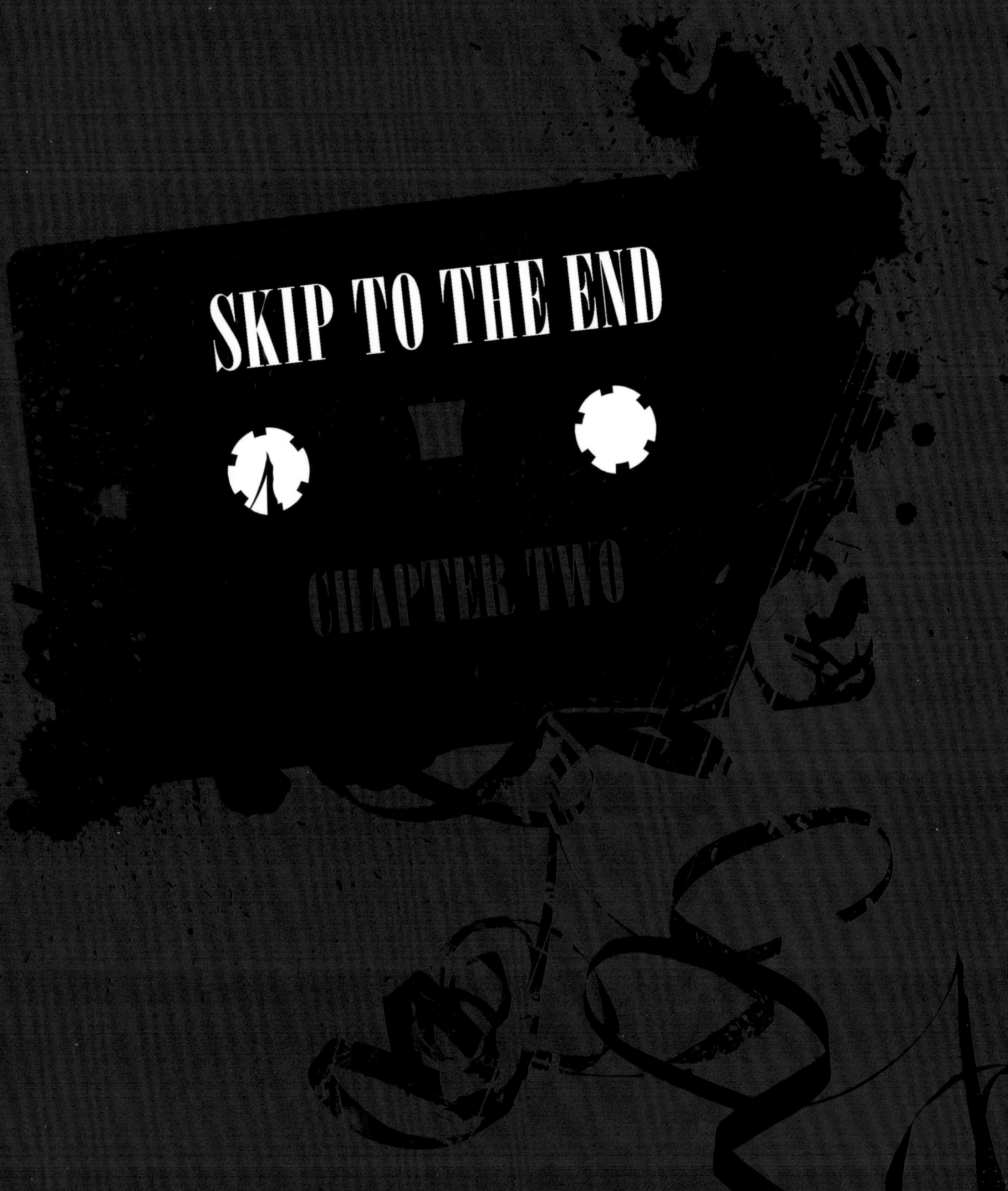
SKIP TO THE END
CHAPTER TWO

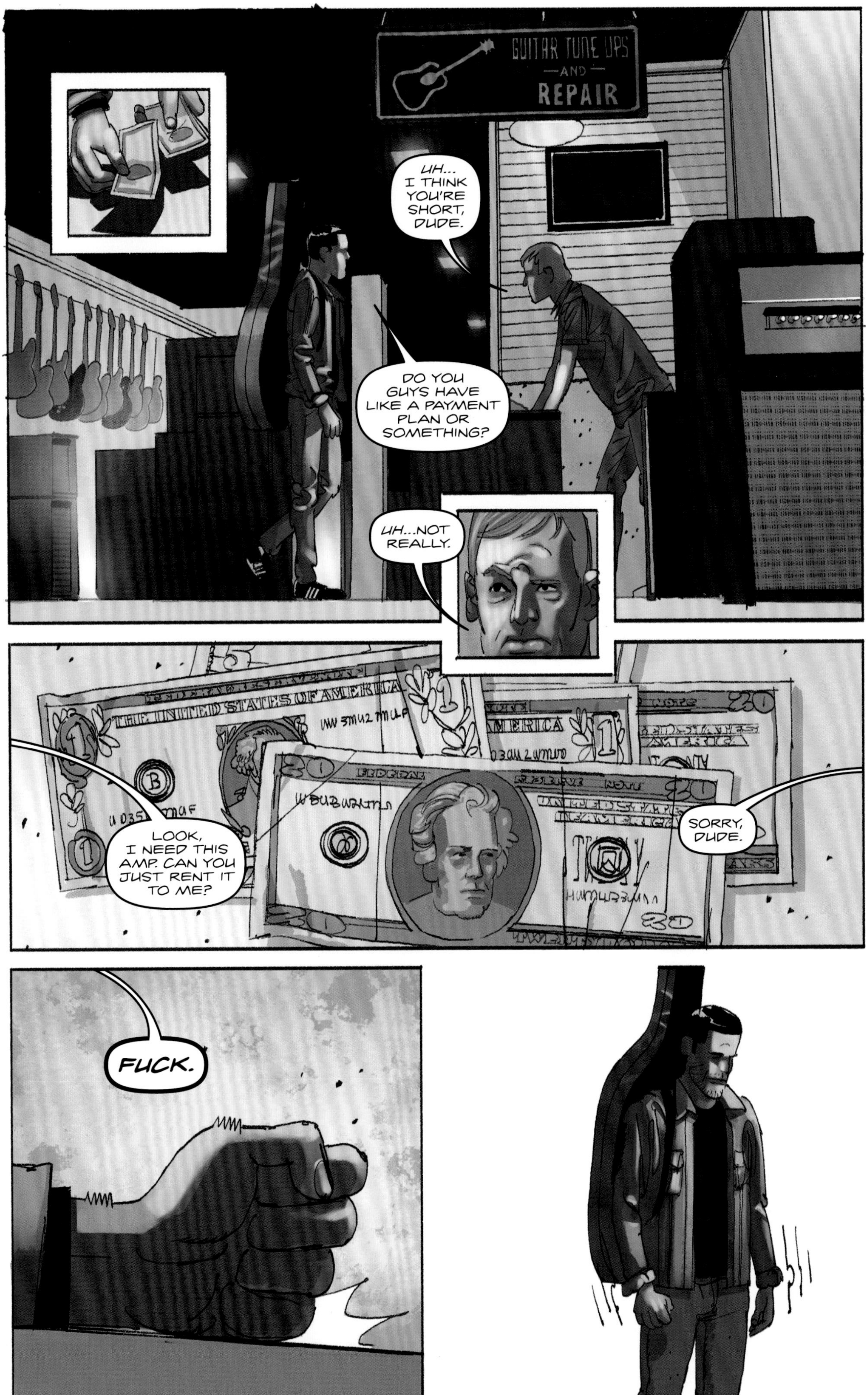
GUITAR TUNE UPS
AND
REPAIR
UH... I THINK YOU'RE SHORT, DUDE.
DO YOU GUYS HAVE LIKE A PAYMENT PLAN OR SOMETHING?
UH...NOT REALLY.
LOOK, I NEED THIS AMP. CAN YOU JUST RENT IT TO ME?
SORRY, DUDE.
FUCK.

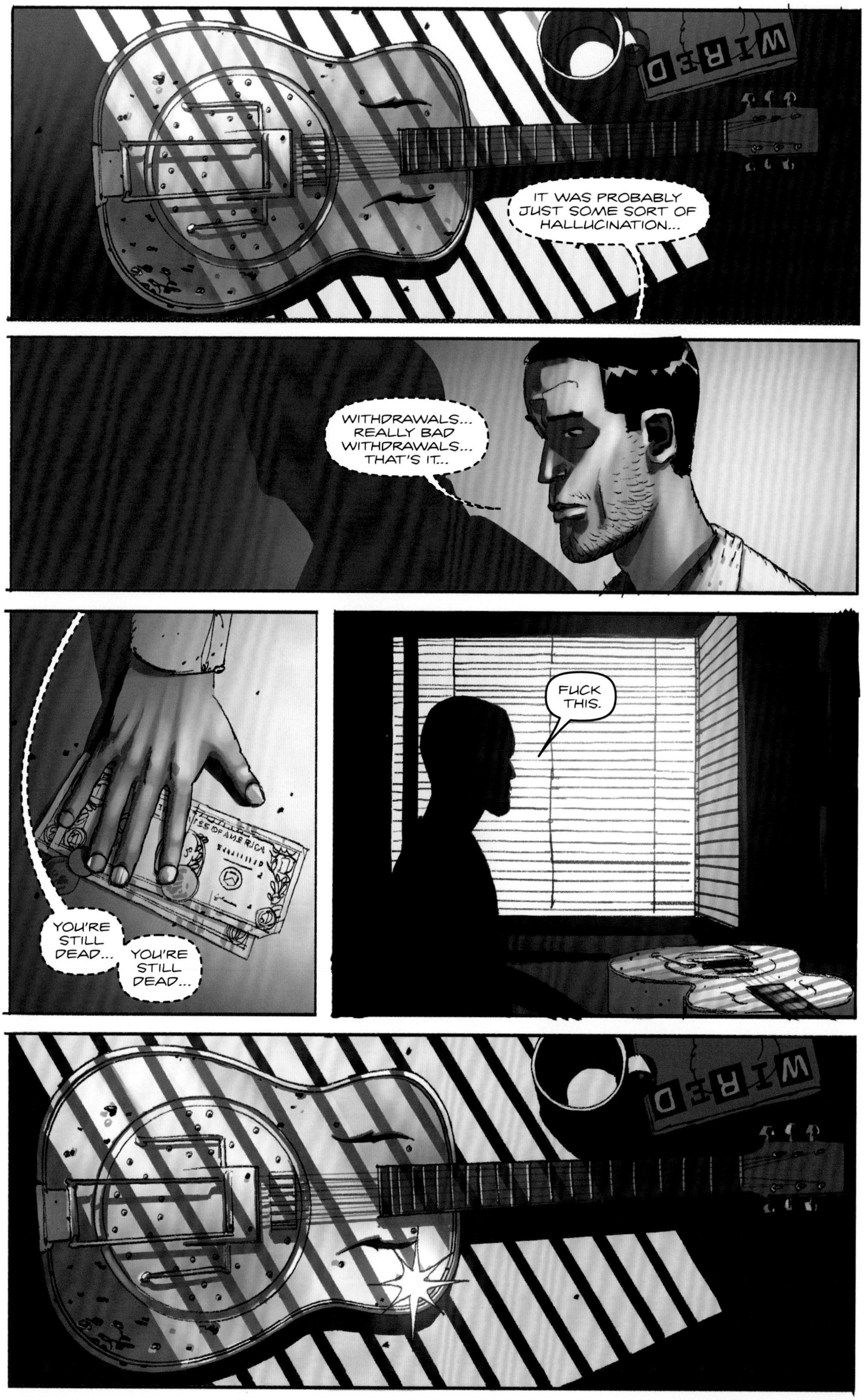
WIRED
IT WAS PROBABLY JUST SOME SORT OF HALLUCINATION...
WITHDRAWALS... REALLY BAD WITHDRAWALS... THAT'S IT...
YOU'RE STILL DEAD...
YOU'RE STILL DEAD...
FUCK THIS.
WIRED

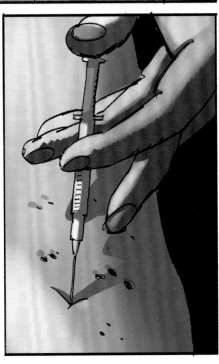

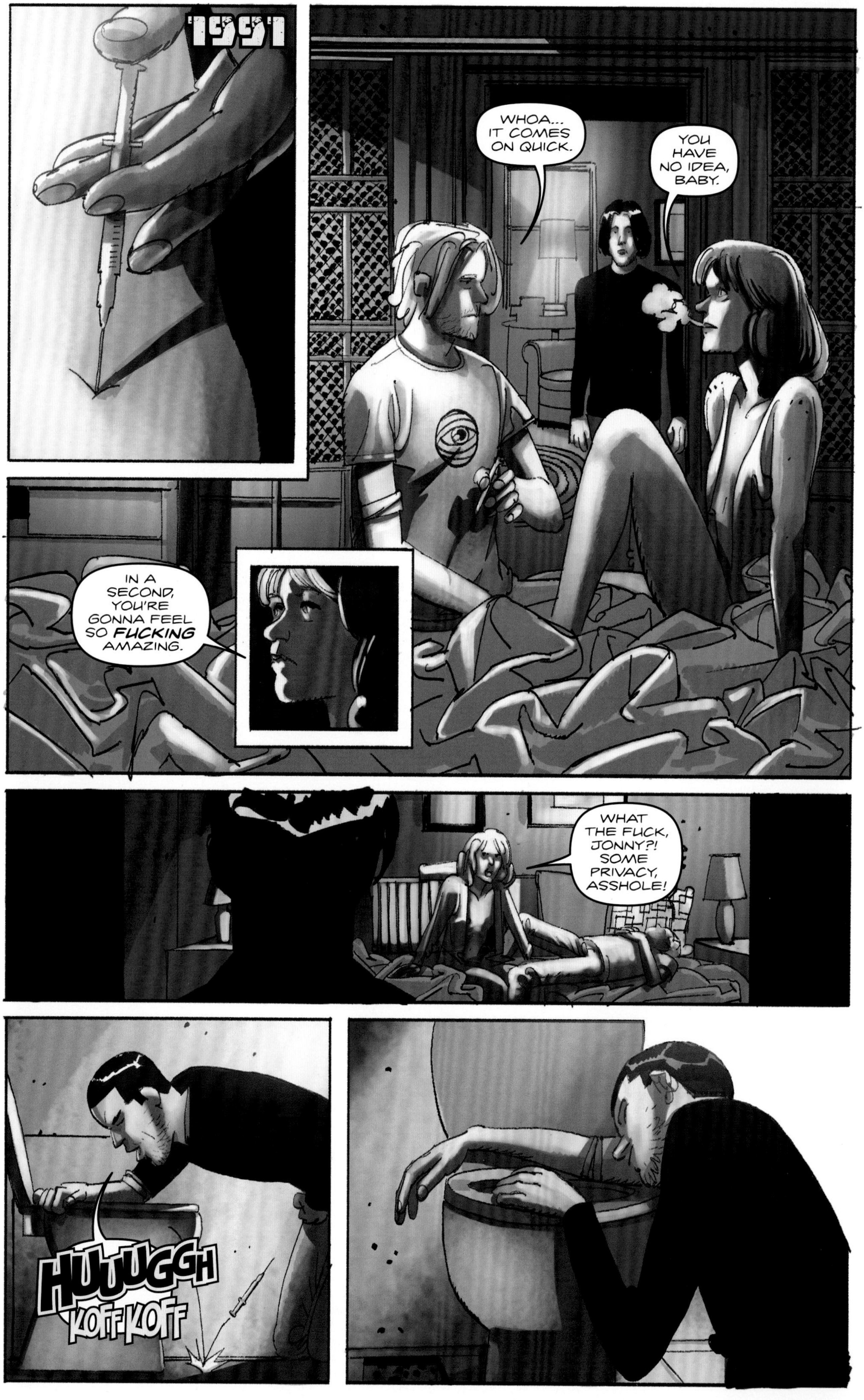

1991
WHOA... IT COMES ON QUICK.
YOU HAVE NO IDEA, BABY.
IN A SECOND, YOU'RE GONNA FEEL SO **FUCKING** AMAZING.
WHAT THE FUCK, JONNY?! SOME PRIVACY, ASSHOLE!
HUUUGGH
KOFF KOFF

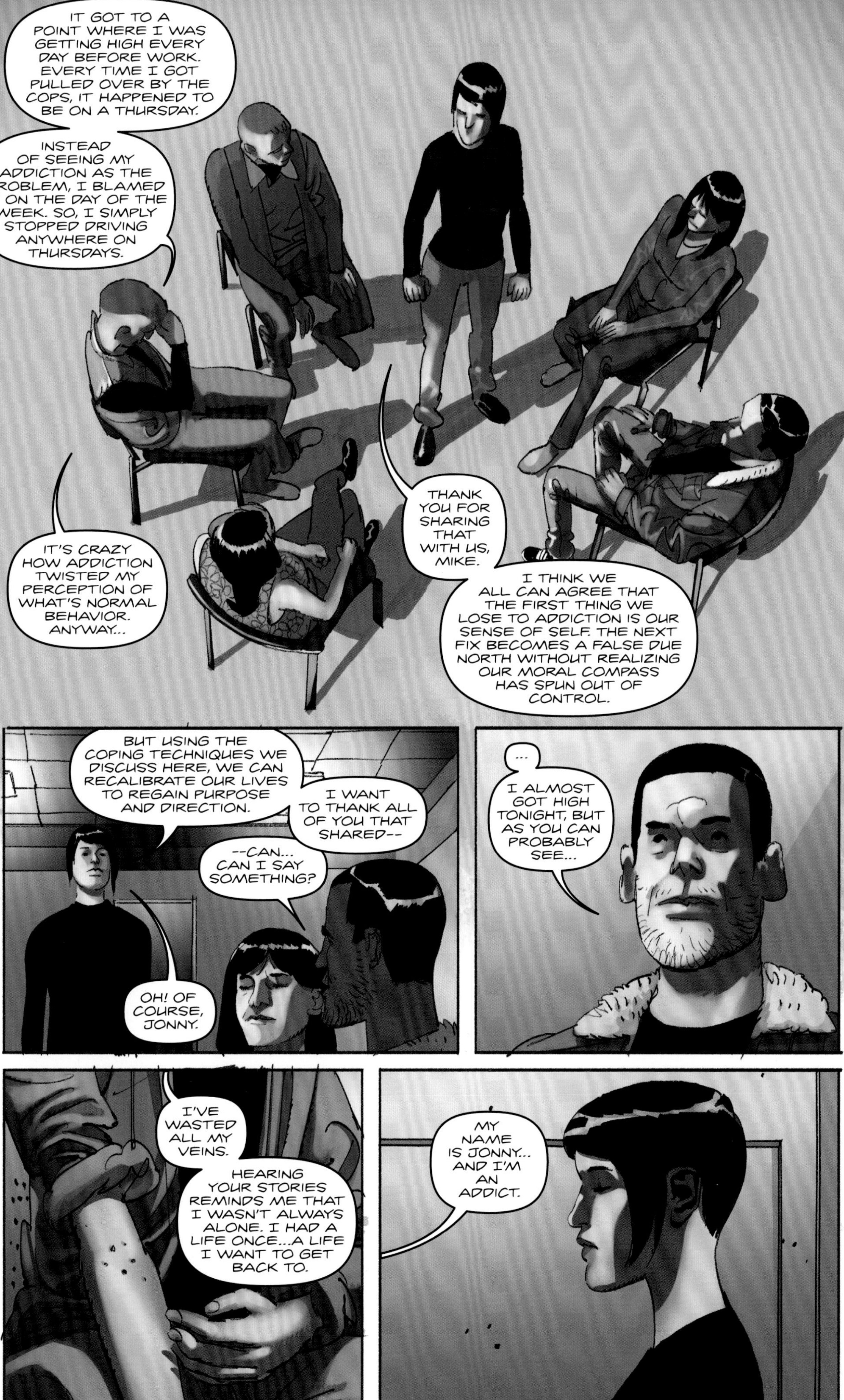
IT GOT TO A POINT WHERE I WAS GETTING HIGH EVERY DAY BEFORE WORK. EVERY TIME I GOT PULLED OVER BY THE COPS, IT HAPPENED TO BE ON A THURSDAY.
INSTEAD OF SEEING MY ADDICTION AS THE PROBLEM, I BLAMED IT ON THE DAY OF THE WEEK. SO, I SIMPLY STOPPED DRIVING ANYWHERE ON THURSDAYS.
IT'S CRAZY HOW ADDICTION TWISTED MY PERCEPTION OF WHAT'S NORMAL BEHAVIOR. ANYWAY...
THANK YOU FOR SHARING THAT WITH US, MIKE.
I THINK WE ALL CAN AGREE THAT THE FIRST THING WE LOSE TO ADDICTION IS OUR SENSE OF SELF. THE NEXT FIX BECOMES A FALSE DUE NORTH WITHOUT REALIZING OUR MORAL COMPASS HAS SPUN OUT OF CONTROL.
BUT USING THE COPING TECHNIQUES WE DISCUSS HERE, WE CAN RECALIBRATE OUR LIVES TO REGAIN PURPOSE AND DIRECTION.
I WANT TO THANK ALL OF YOU THAT SHARED--
--CAN... CAN I SAY SOMETHING?
OH! OF COURSE, JONNY.
...
I ALMOST GOT HIGH TONIGHT, BUT AS YOU CAN PROBABLY SEE...
I'VE WASTED ALL MY VEINS.
HEARING YOUR STORIES REMINDS ME THAT I WASN'T ALWAYS ALONE. I HAD A LIFE ONCE...A LIFE I WANT TO GET BACK TO.
MY NAME IS JONNY... AND I'M AN ADDICT.

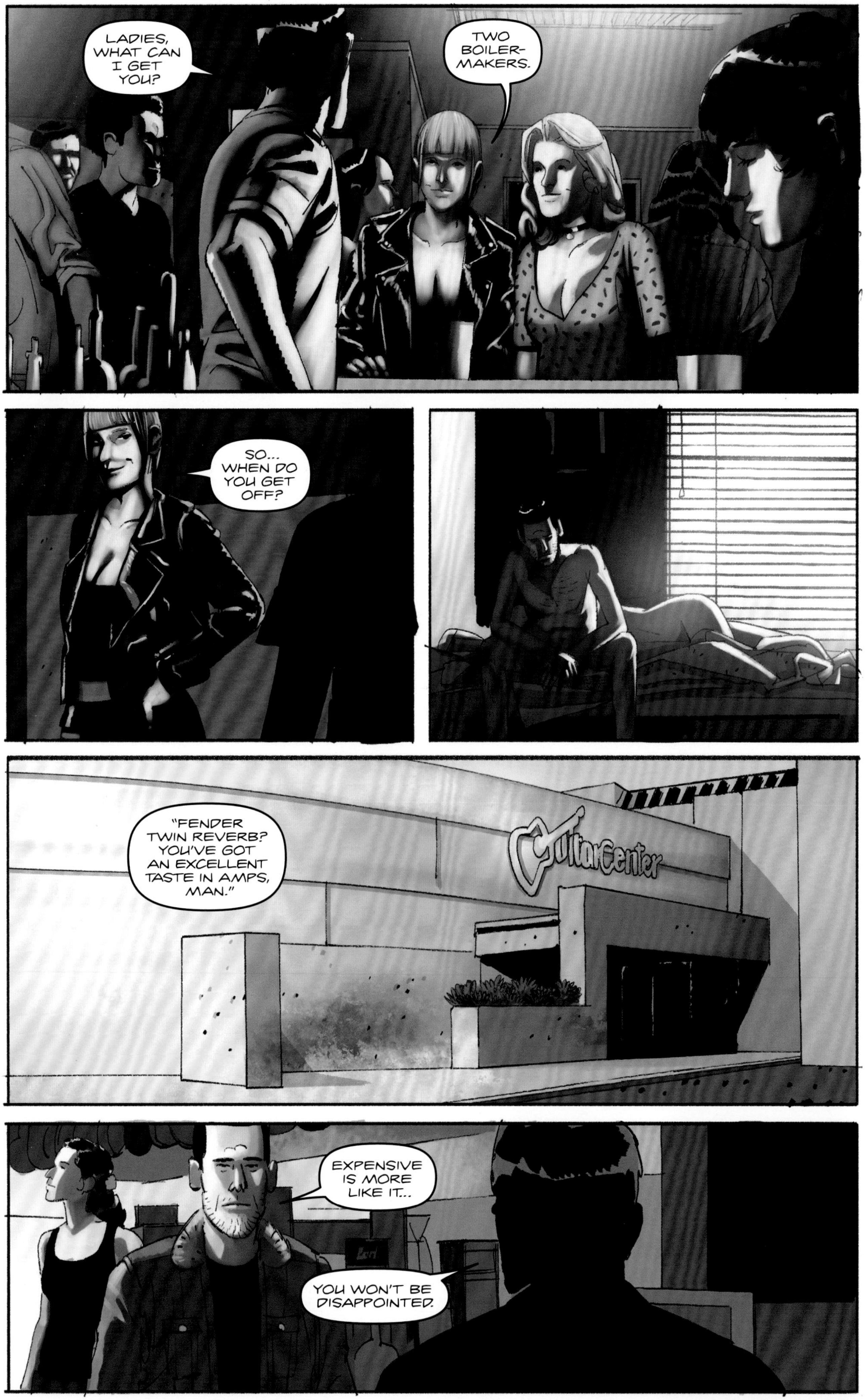
LADIES, WHAT CAN I GET YOU?
TWO BOILER-MAKERS.
SO... WHEN DO YOU GET OFF?
"FENDER TWIN REVERB? YOU'VE GOT AN EXCELLENT TASTE IN AMPS, MAN."
EXPENSIVE IS MORE LIKE IT...
YOU WON'T BE DISAPPOINTED.

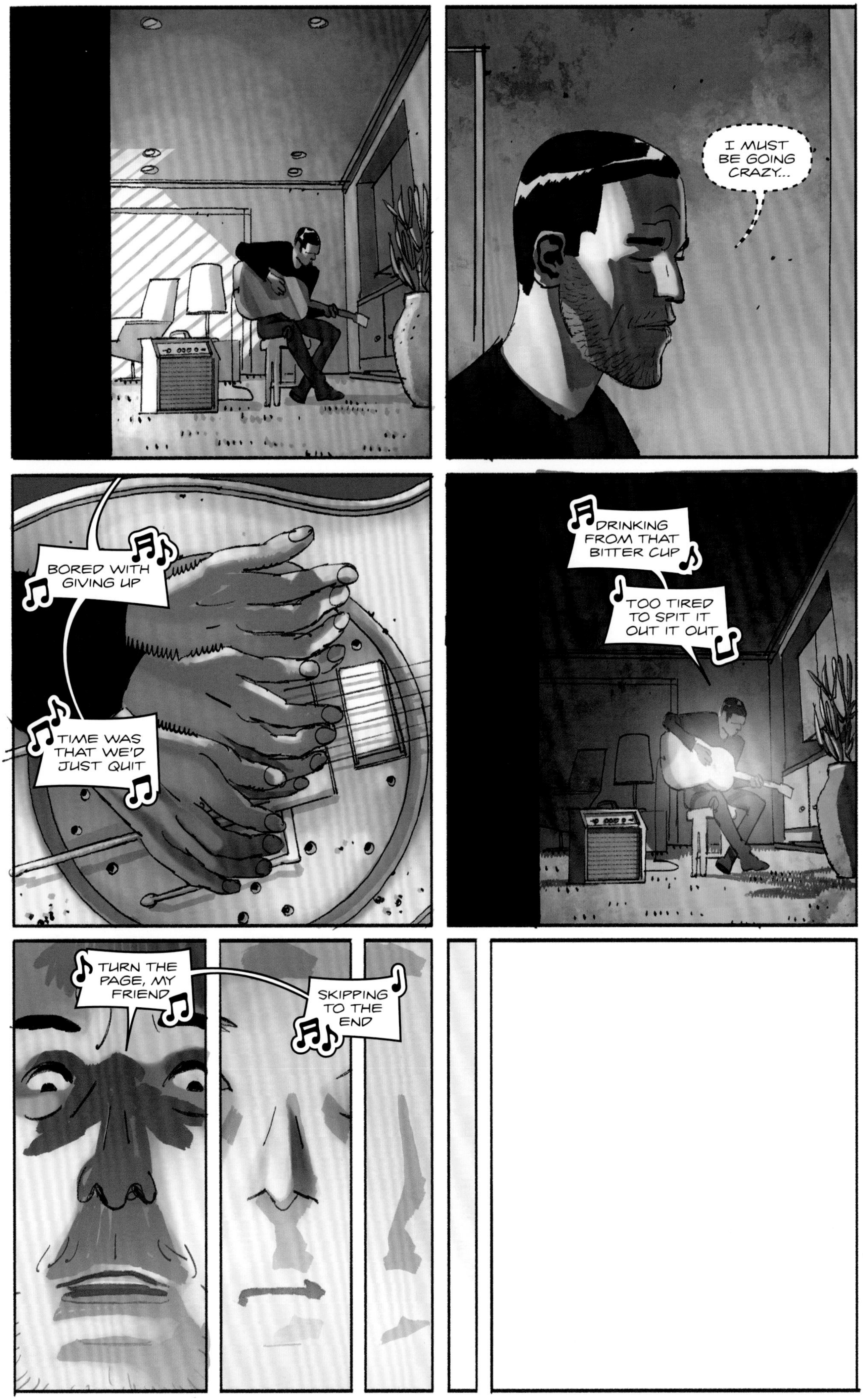
I MUST BE GOING CRAZY...
BORED WITH GIVING UP
TIME WAS THAT WE'D JUST QUIT
DRINKING FROM THAT BITTER CUP
TOO TIRED TO SPIT IT OUT IT OUT
TURN THE PAGE, MY FRIEND
SKIPPING TO THE END

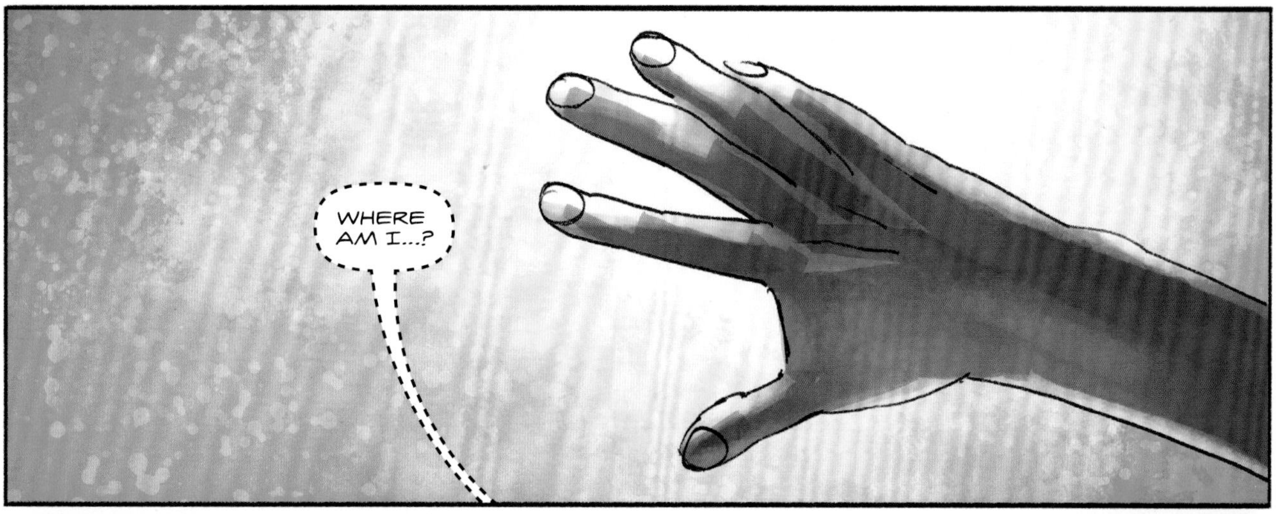
WHERE AM I...?

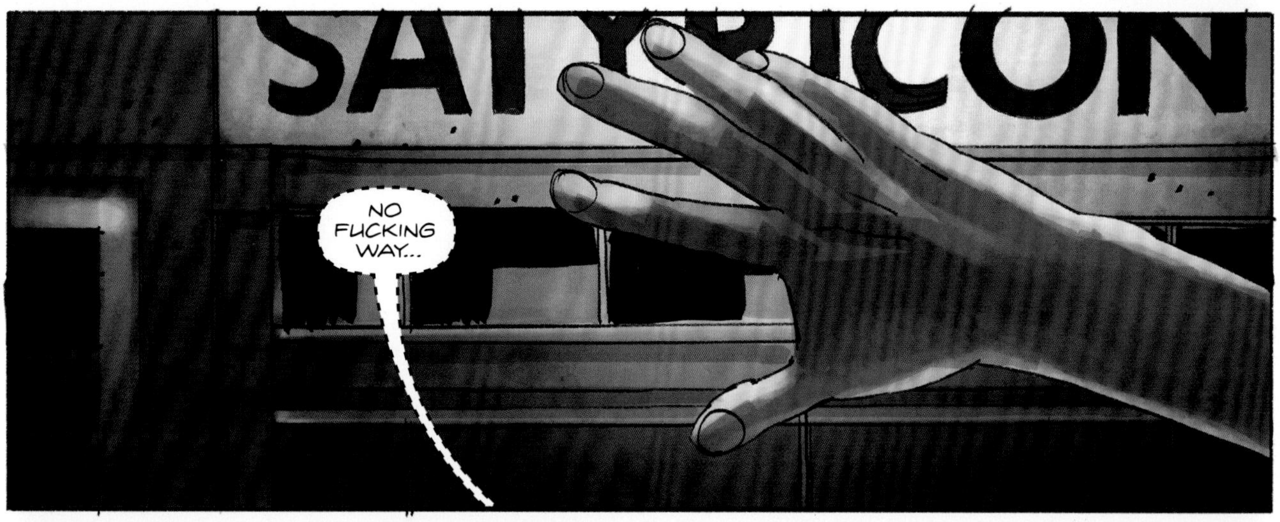
NO FUCKING WAY...

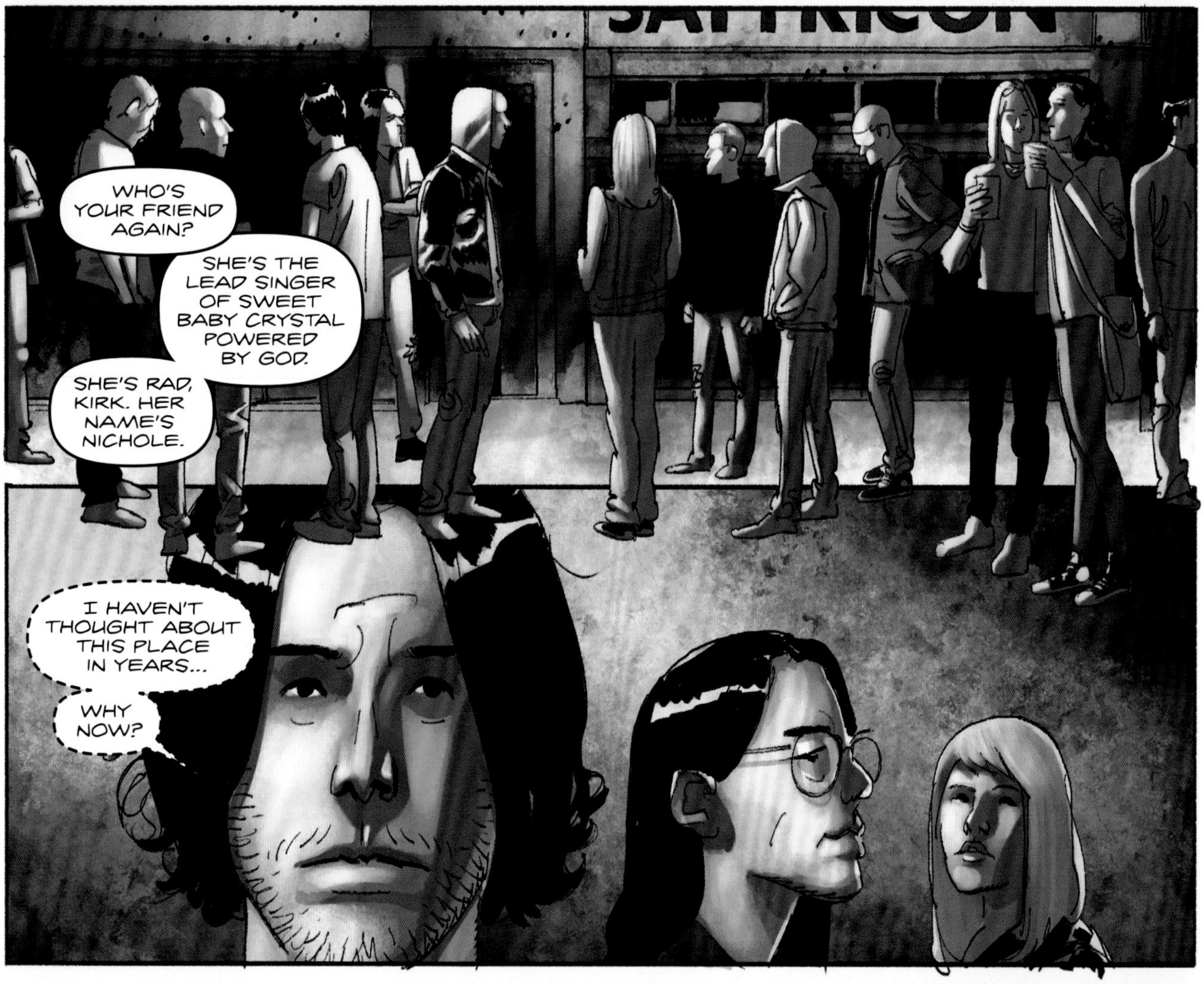
WHO'S YOUR FRIEND AGAIN?
SHE'S THE LEAD SINGER OF SWEET BABY CRYSTAL POWERED BY GOD.
SHE'S RAD, KIRK. HER NAME'S NICHOLE.
I HAVEN'T THOUGHT ABOUT THIS PLACE IN YEARS...
WHY NOW?

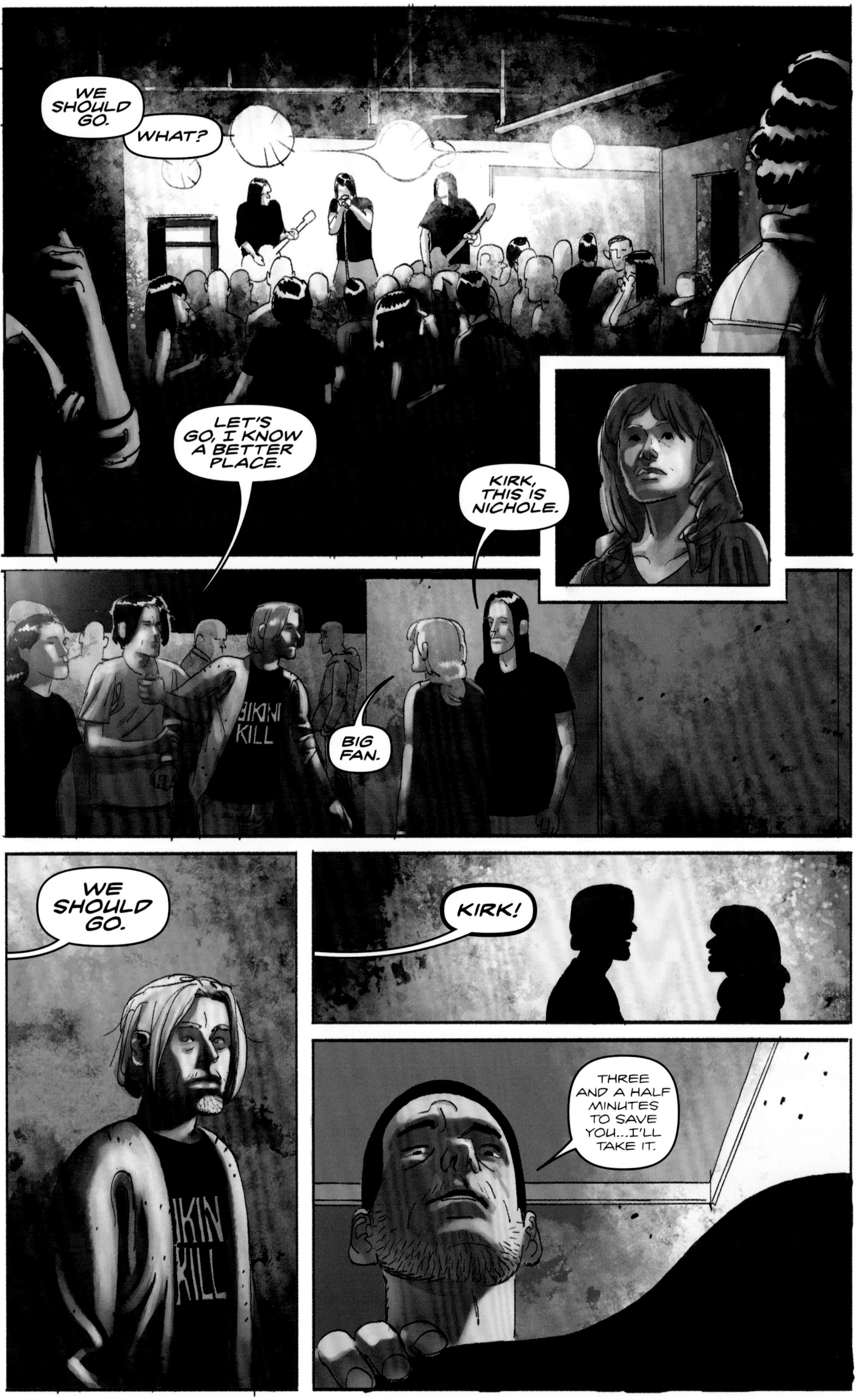
WE SHOULD GO.
WHAT?
LET'S GO, I KNOW A BETTER PLACE.
KIRK, THIS IS NICHOLE.
BIKINI KILL
BIG FAN.
WE SHOULD GO.
KIRK!
THREE AND A HALF MINUTES TO SAVE YOU...I'LL TAKE IT.

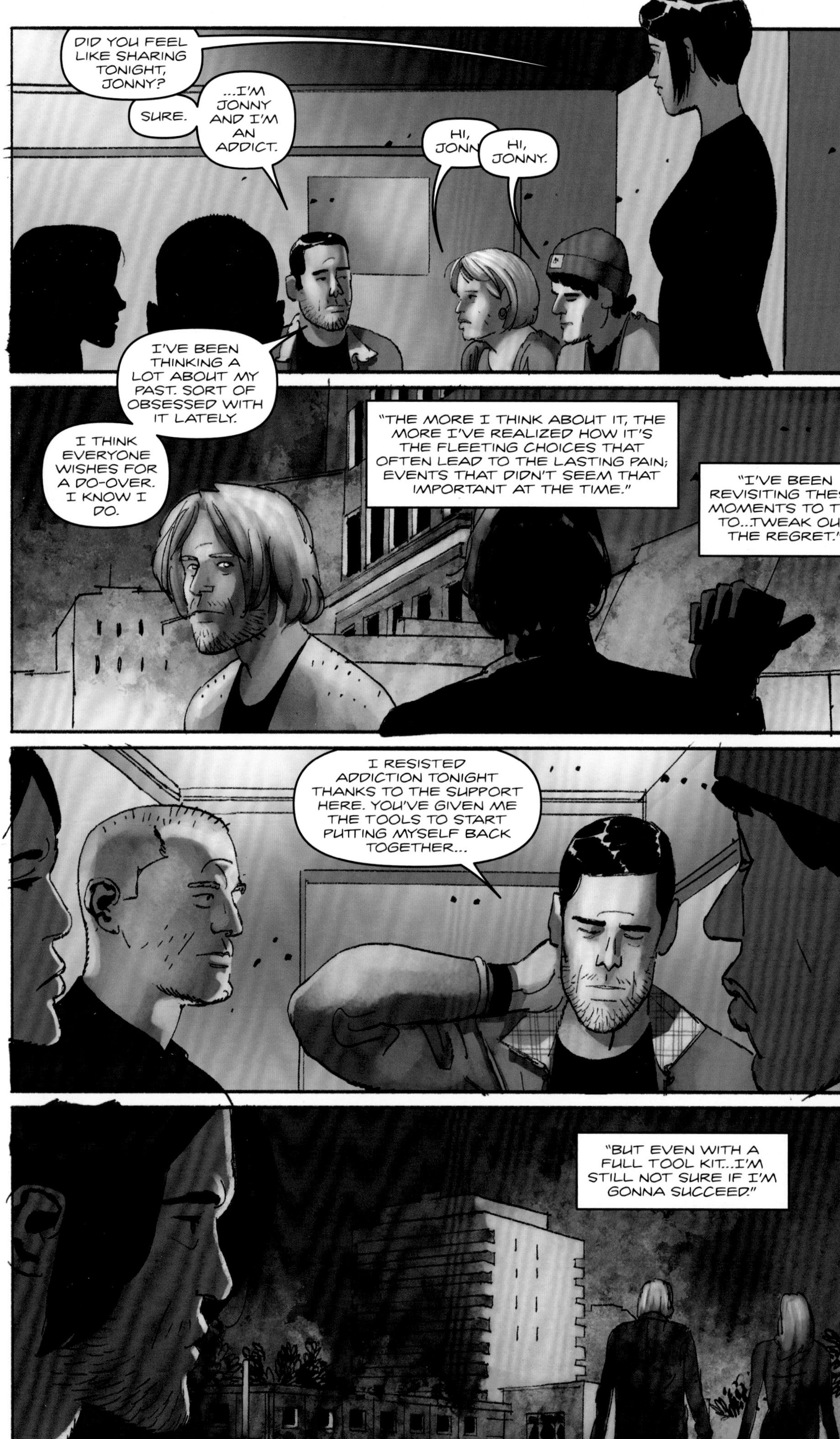
DID YOU FEEL LIKE SHARING TONIGHT, JONNY?
SURE.
...I'M JONNY AND I'M AN ADDICT.
HI, JONNY.
HI, JONNY.
I'VE BEEN THINKING A LOT ABOUT MY PAST. SORT OF OBSESSED WITH IT LATELY.
I THINK EVERYONE WISHES FOR A DO-OVER. I KNOW I DO.
"THE MORE I THINK ABOUT IT, THE MORE I'VE REALIZED HOW IT'S THE FLEETING CHOICES THAT OFTEN LEAD TO THE LASTING PAIN; EVENTS THAT DIDN'T SEEM THAT IMPORTANT AT THE TIME."
"I'VE BEEN REVISITING THESE MOMENTS TO TRY TO...TWEAK OUT THE REGRET."
I RESISTED ADDICTION TONIGHT THANKS TO THE SUPPORT HERE. YOU'VE GIVEN ME THE TOOLS TO START PUTTING MYSELF BACK TOGETHER...
"BUT EVEN WITH A FULL TOOL KIT...I'M STILL NOT SURE IF I'M GONNA SUCCEED."

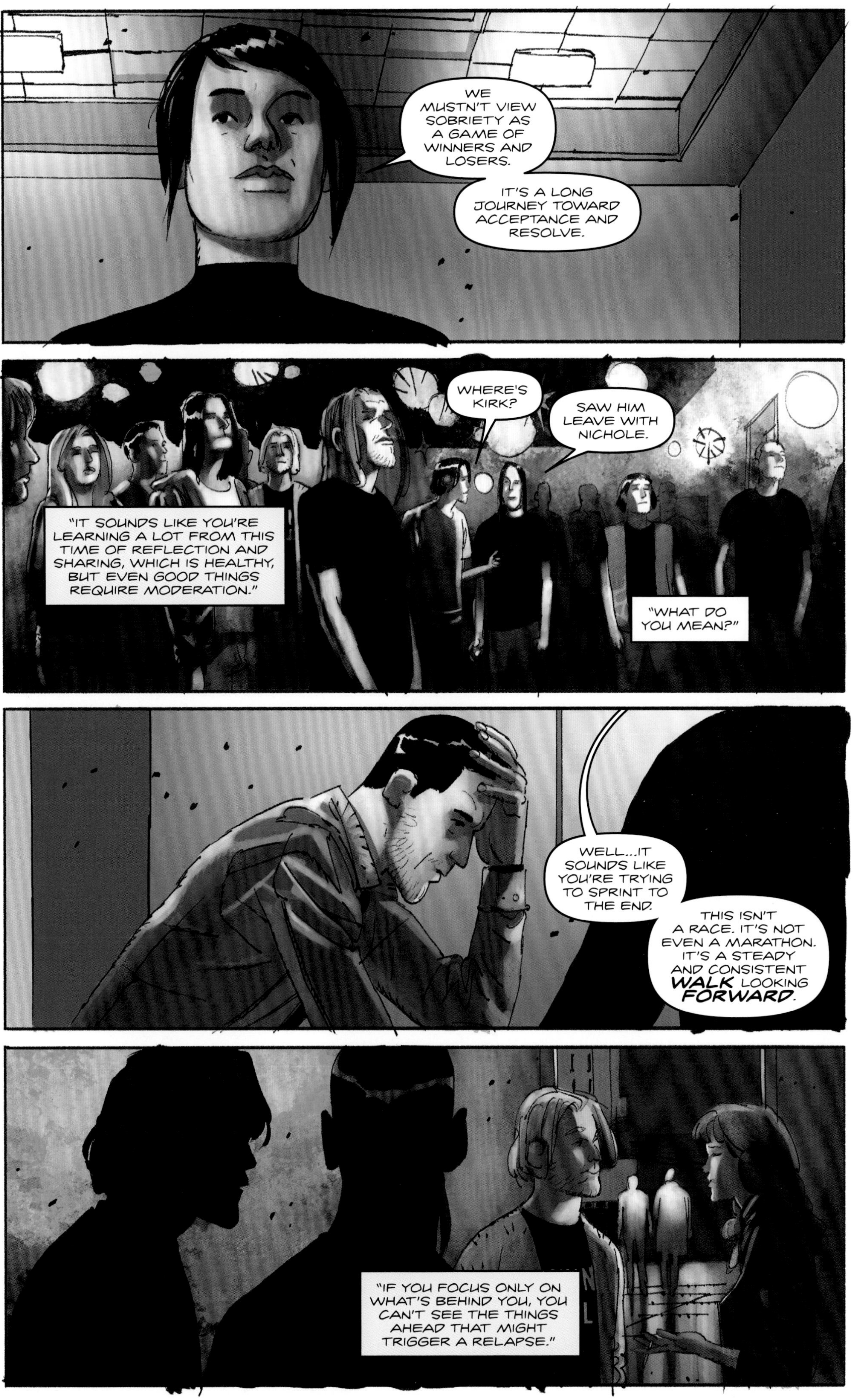
WE MUSTN'T VIEW SOBRIETY AS A GAME OF WINNERS AND LOSERS.
IT'S A LONG JOURNEY TOWARD ACCEPTANCE AND RESOLVE.
WHERE'S KIRK?
SAW HIM LEAVE WITH NICHOLE.
"IT SOUNDS LIKE YOU'RE LEARNING A LOT FROM THIS TIME OF REFLECTION AND SHARING, WHICH IS HEALTHY, BUT EVEN GOOD THINGS REQUIRE MODERATION."
"WHAT DO YOU MEAN?"
WELL...IT SOUNDS LIKE YOU'RE TRYING TO SPRINT TO THE END.
THIS ISN'T A RACE. IT'S NOT EVEN A MARATHON. IT'S A STEADY AND CONSISTENT WALK LOOKING FORWARD.
"IF YOU FOCUS ONLY ON WHAT'S BEHIND YOU, YOU CAN'T SEE THE THINGS AHEAD THAT MIGHT TRIGGER A RELAPSE."

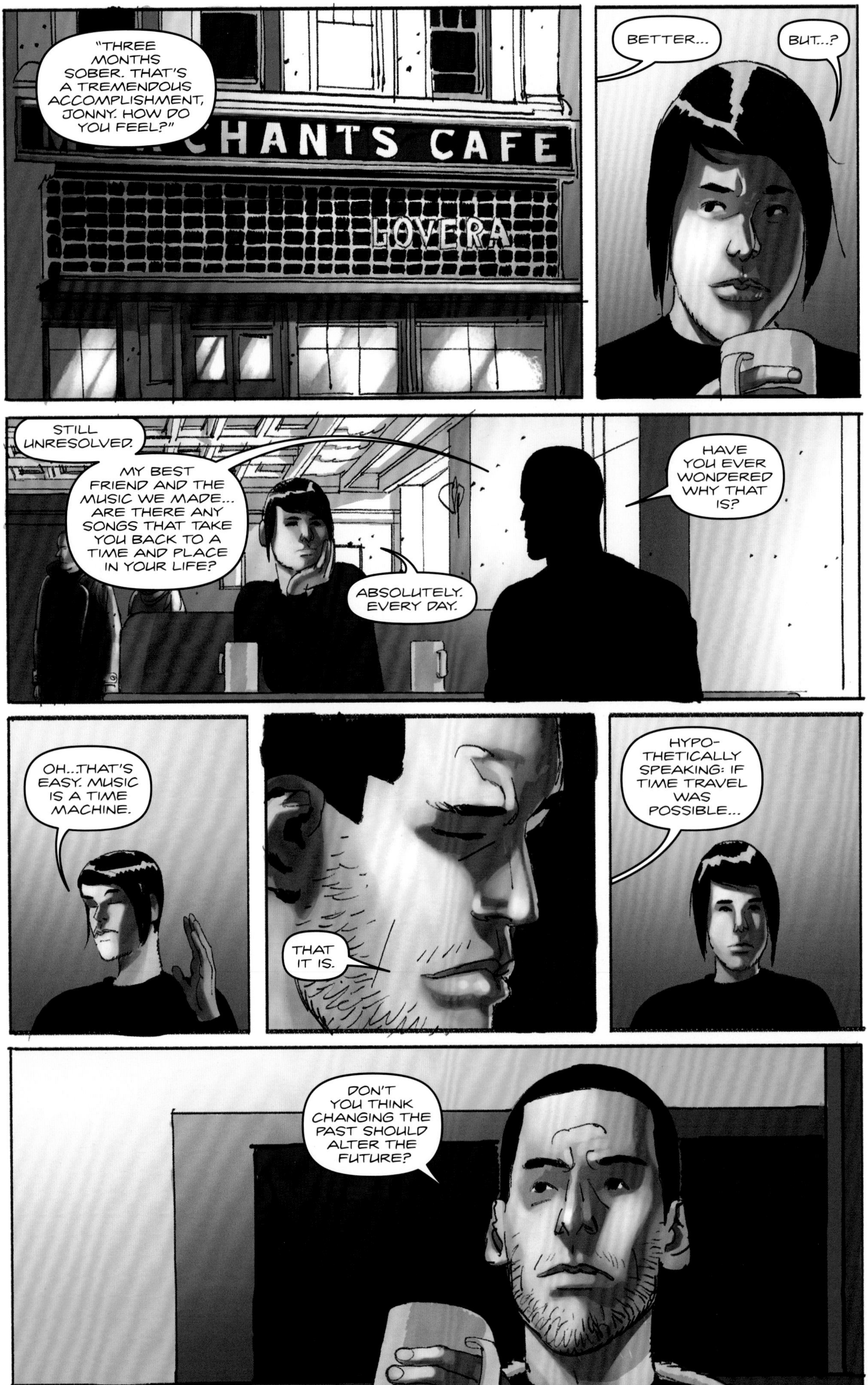
"THREE MONTHS SOBER. THAT'S A TREMENDOUS ACCOMPLISHMENT, JONNY. HOW DO YOU FEEL?"
CHANTS CAFE
LOVERA
BETTER...
BUT...?
STILL UNRESOLVED.
MY BEST FRIEND AND THE MUSIC WE MADE... ARE THERE ANY SONGS THAT TAKE YOU BACK TO A TIME AND PLACE IN YOUR LIFE?
ABSOLUTELY. EVERY DAY.
HAVE YOU EVER WONDERED WHY THAT IS?
OH...THAT'S EASY. MUSIC IS A TIME MACHINE.
THAT IT IS.
HYPOTHETICALLY SPEAKING: IF TIME TRAVEL WAS POSSIBLE...
DON'T YOU THINK CHANGING THE PAST SHOULD ALTER THE FUTURE?

WHAT, LIKE BACK TO THE FUTURE? HATE ME IF YOU MUST, BUT I NEVER LIKED THOSE MOVIES.

REALLY?

YEAH, TOO MANY PLOT HOLES IN THE TIMELINE.

HAVE YOU EVER SEEN SLIDING DOORS?

NOPE.

YOU'D LIKE IT, I THINK. WHAT YOU WERE SHARING AT TONIGHT'S MEETING ACTUALLY REMINDED ME OF IT.

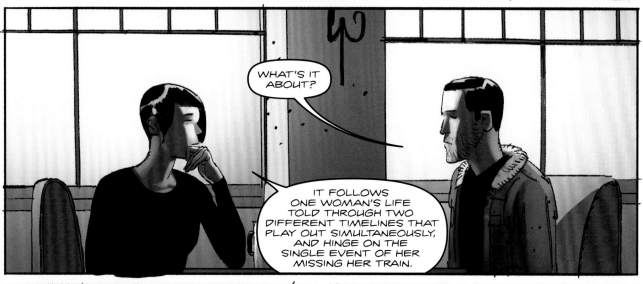

WHAT'S IT ABOUT?

IT FOLLOWS ONE WOMAN'S LIFE TOLD THROUGH TWO DIFFERENT TIMELINES THAT PLAY OUT SIMULTANEOUSLY, AND HINGE ON THE SINGLE EVENT OF HER MISSING HER TRAIN.

IT'S TECHNICALLY NOT EVEN ABOUT TIME TRAVEL, BUT I THINK THE IDEA OF A LAYERED MULTIVERSE MAKES MORE SENSE TO ME.

INTERESTING.

IT WOULD EXPLAIN THE SENSATION OF DÉJÀ VU.

YEAH... THAT'S ONE WAY OF LOOKING AT IT.

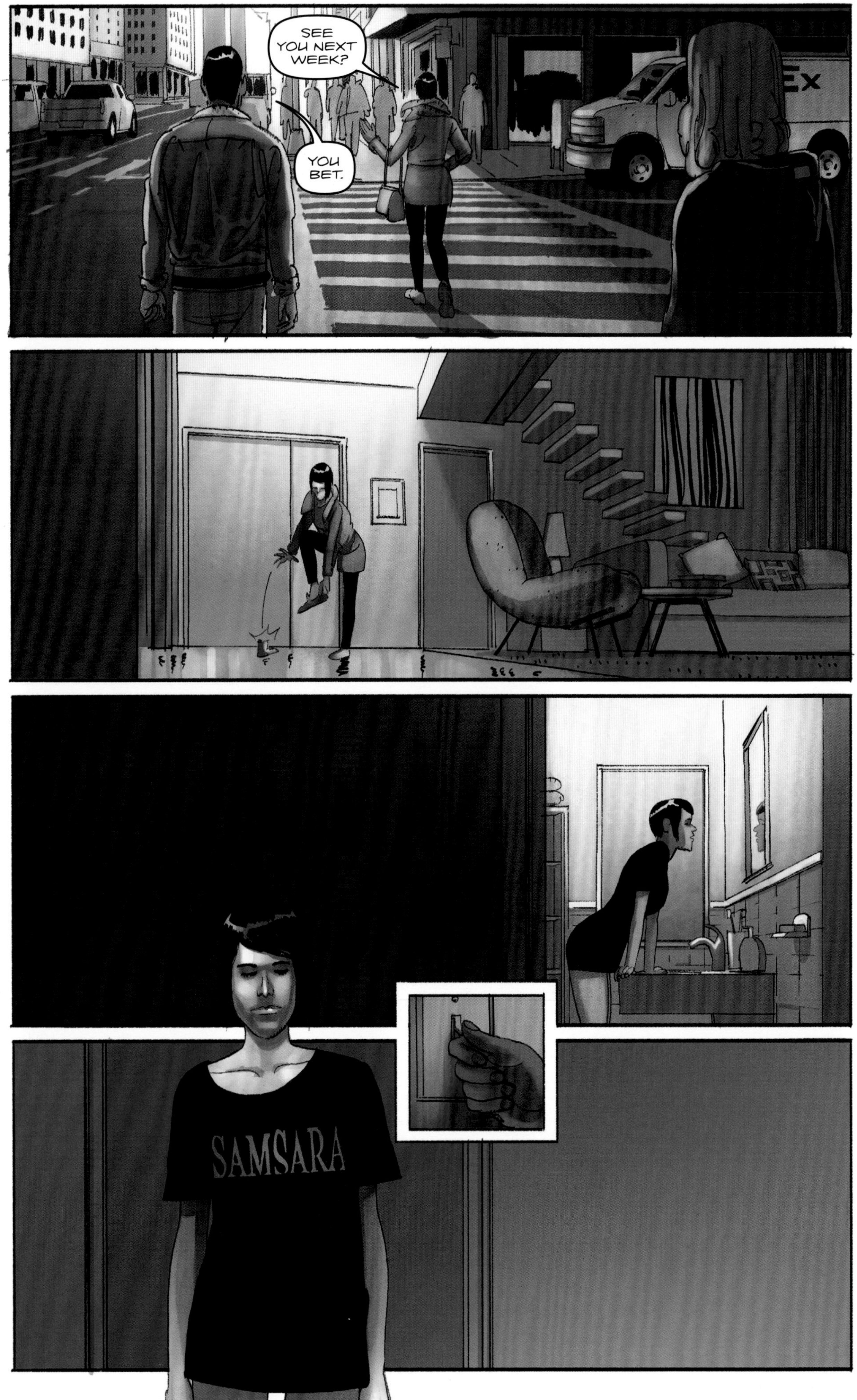
SEE YOU NEXT WEEK?
YOU BET.
SAMSARA

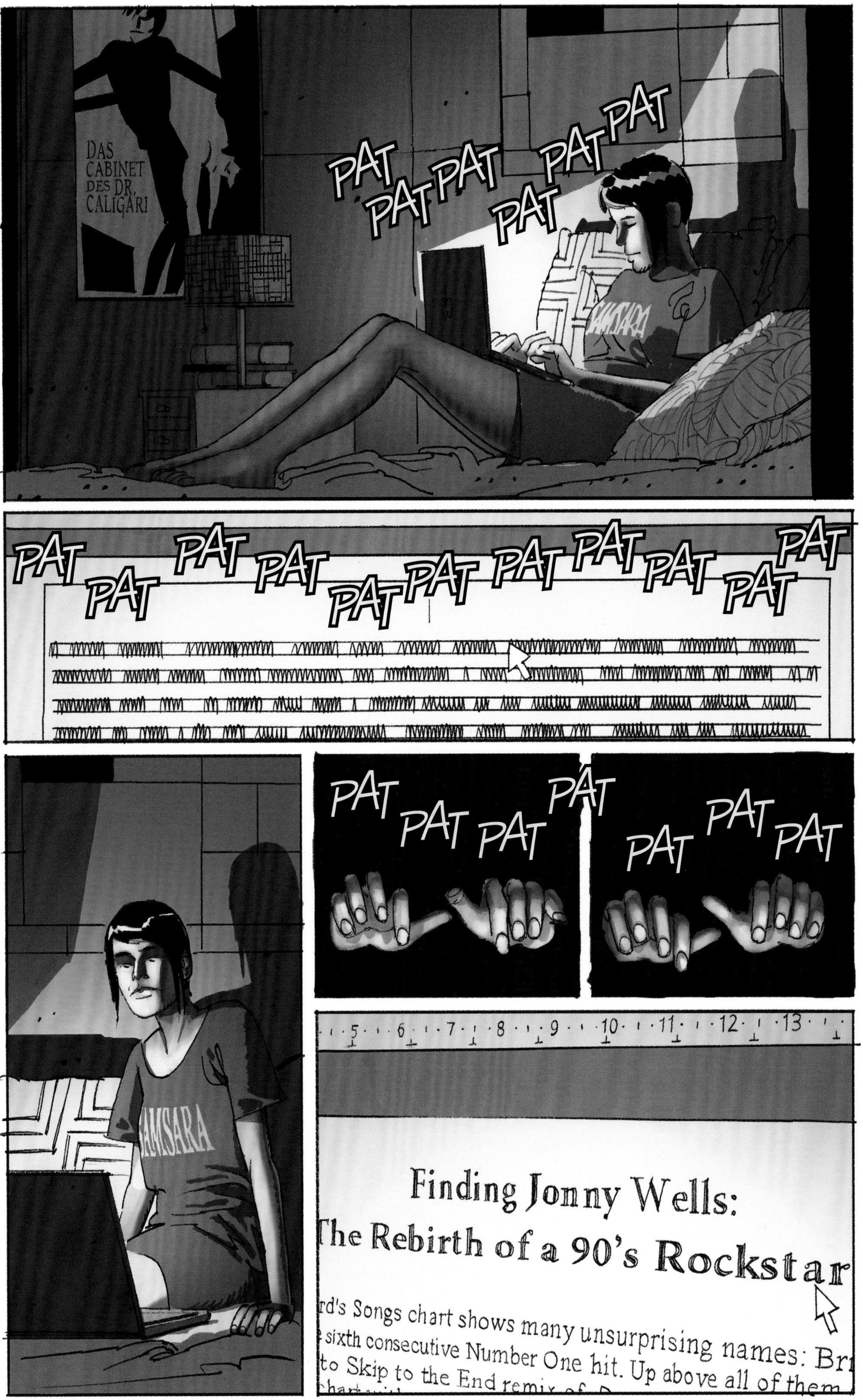
DAS CABINET DES DR. CALIGARI
PAT PAT PAT PAT PAT PAT PAT
SAMSARA
PAT PAT PAT PAT PAT PAT PAT PAT PAT PAT PAT
PAT PAT PAT PAT
PAT PAT PAT
SAMSARA
Finding Jonny Wells:
The Rebirth of a 90's Rockstar
rd's Songs chart shows many unsurprising names: Br
sixth consecutive Number One hit. Up above all of them
to Skip to the End remix of

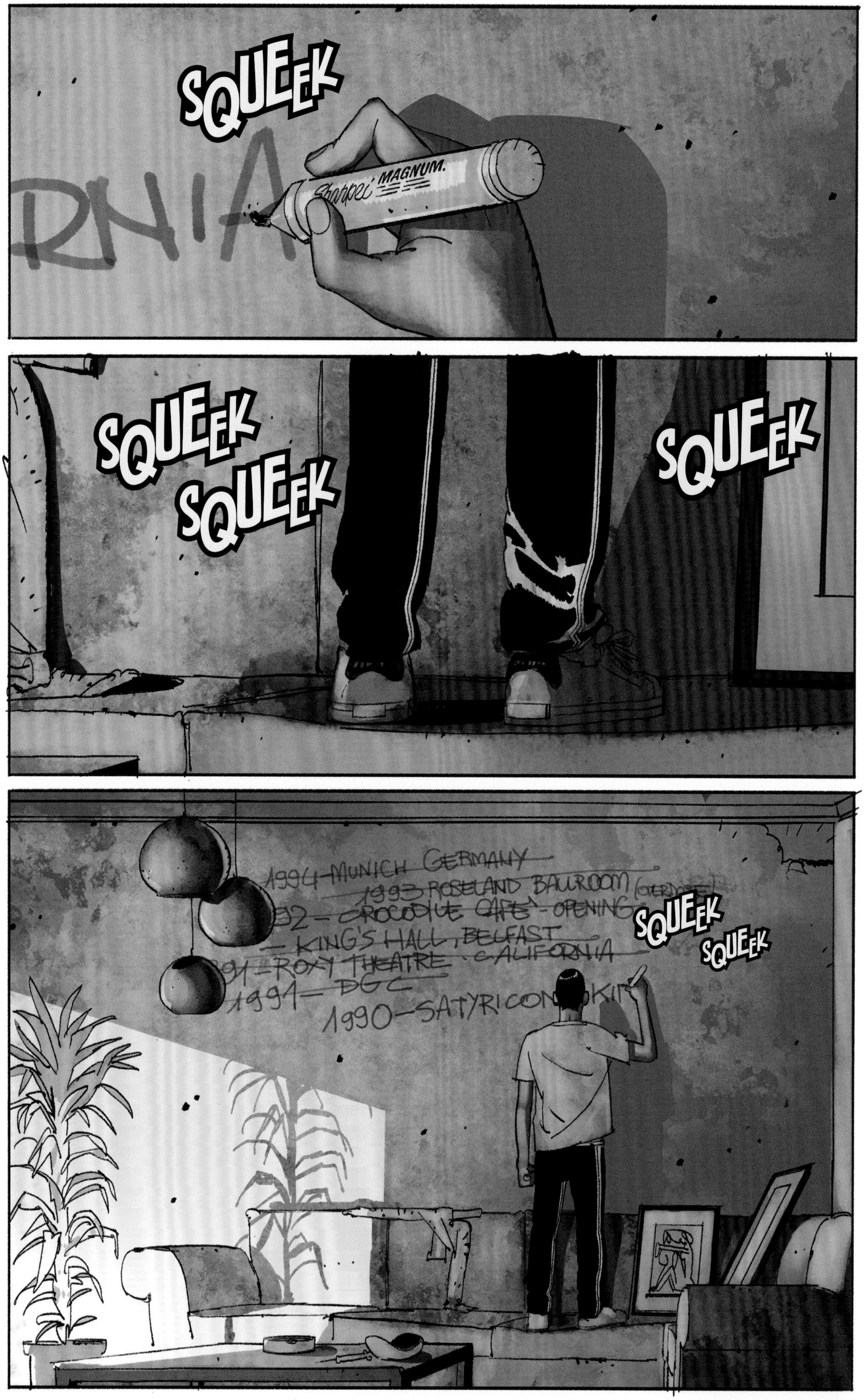
SQUEEK
Sharpie MAGNUM.
SQUEEK
SQUEEK
SQUEEK
1994-MUNICH GERMANY
1993 ROSELAND BALLROOM
92 - CROCODILE CAFE - OPENING
- KING'S HALL, BELFAST
91 - ROXY THEATRE . CALIFORNIA
1991- DGC
1990-SATYRICON
SQUEEK
SQUEEK

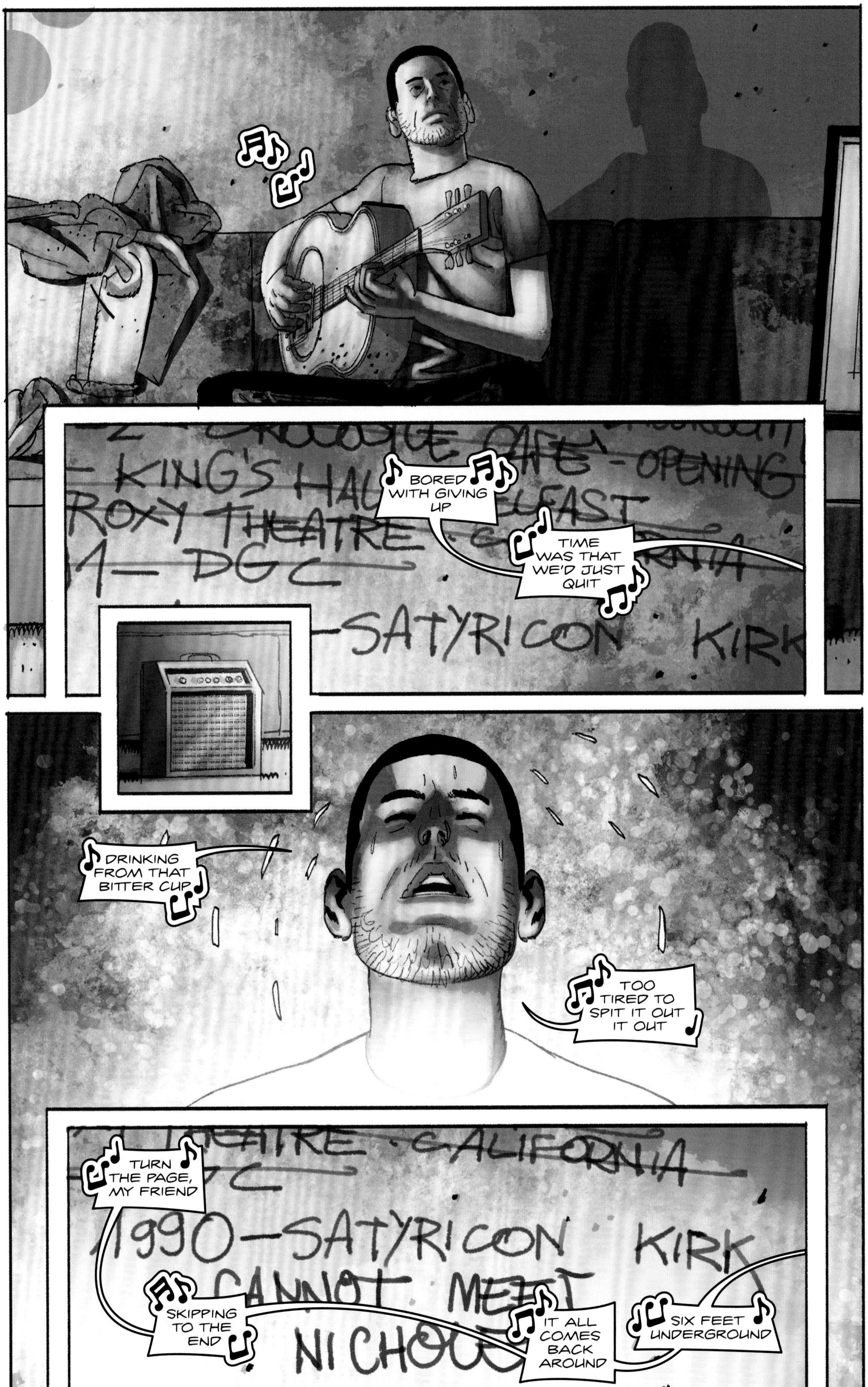
BORED WITH GIVING UP
TIME WAS THAT WE'D JUST QUIT
ROXY THEATRE
SATYRICON KIRK
DRINKING FROM THAT BITTER CUP
TOO TIRED TO SPIT IT OUT IT OUT
TURN THE PAGE, MY FRIEND
1990-SATYRICON KIRK
SKIPPING TO THE END
IT ALL COMES BACK AROUND
SIX FEET UNDERGROUND

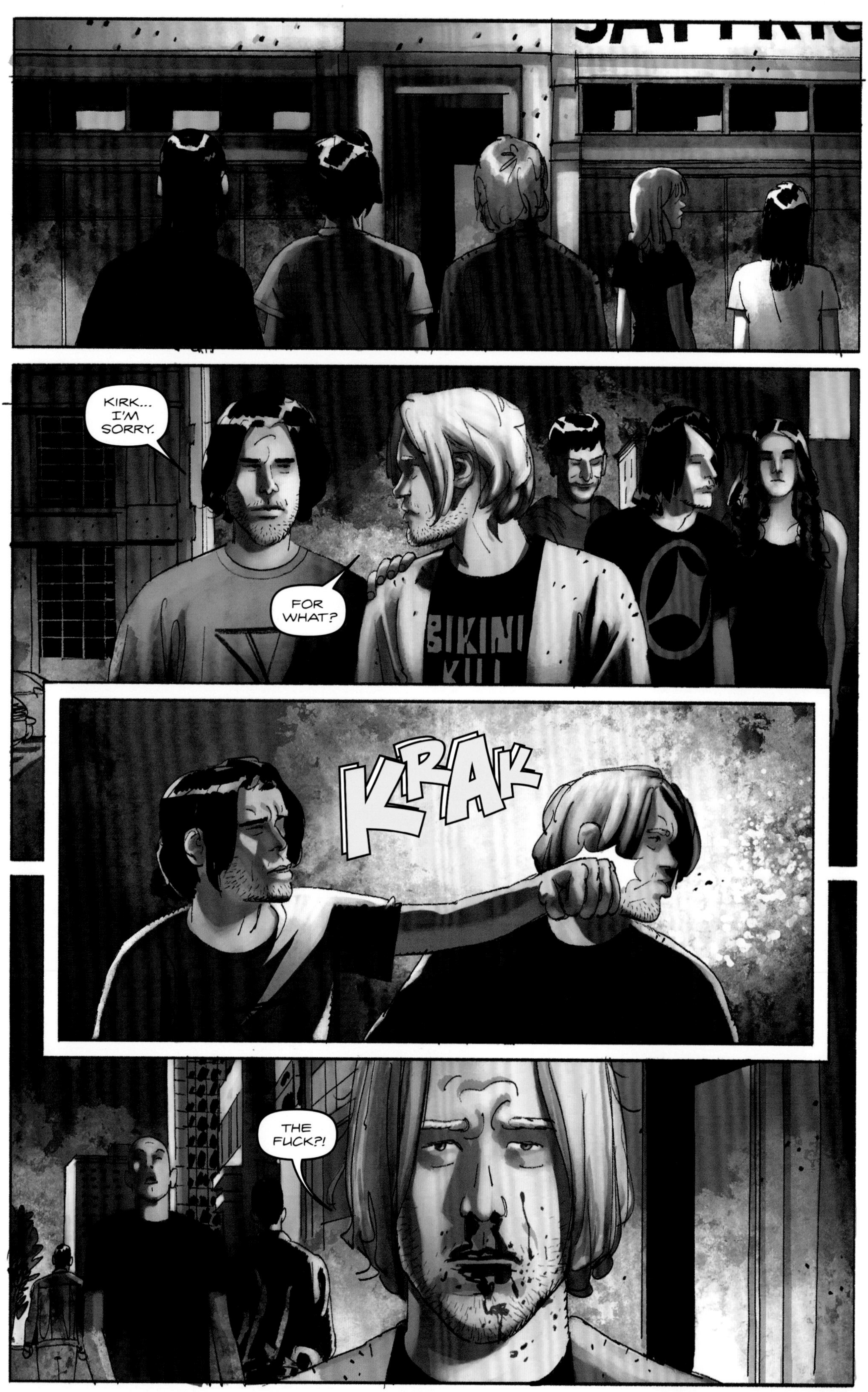
KIRK... I'M SORRY.
FOR WHAT?
KRAK
THE FUCK?!

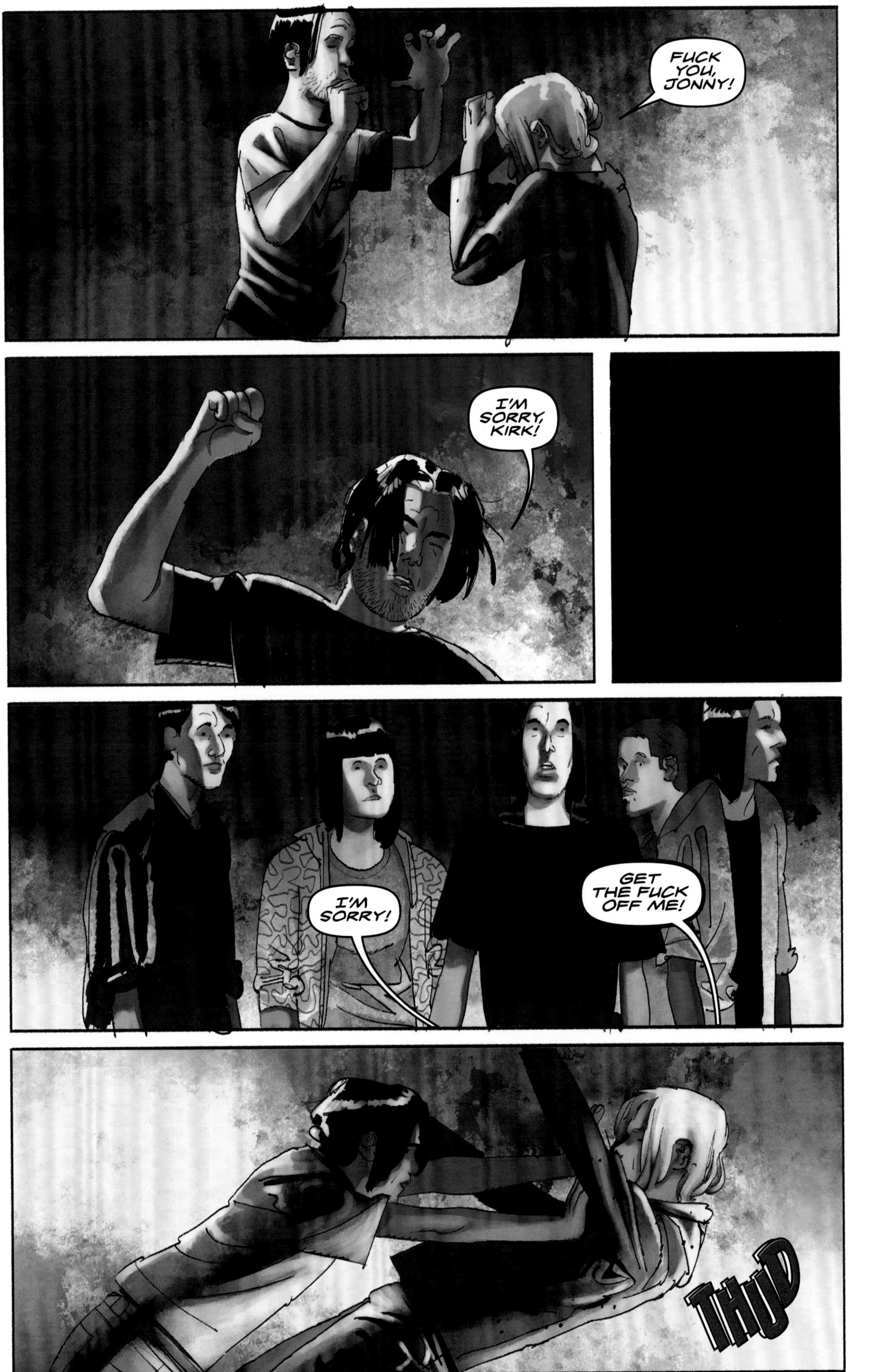
FUCK YOU, JONNY!
I'M SORRY, KIRK!
I'M SORRY!
GET THE FUCK OFF ME!
THUD

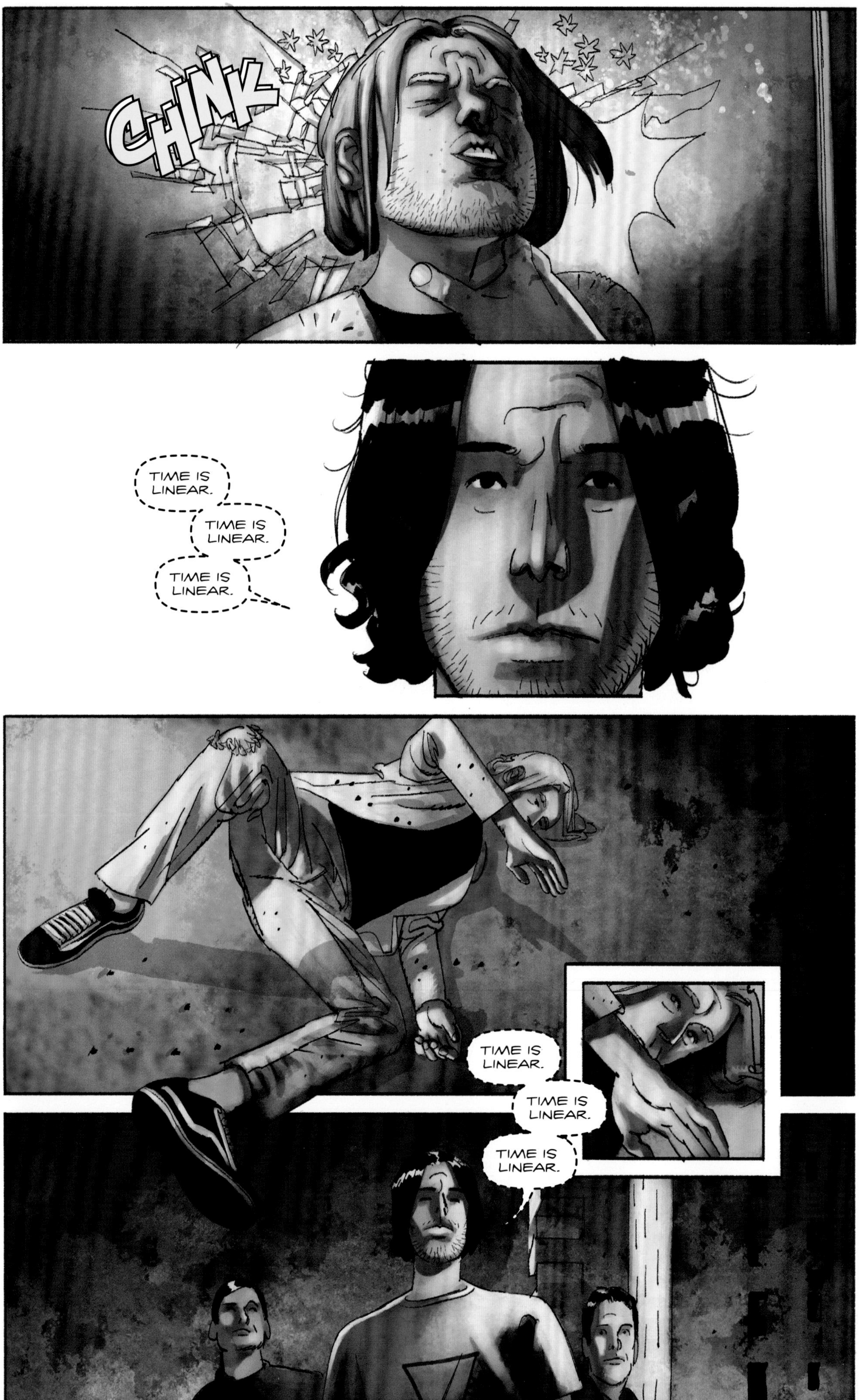
CHINK
TIME IS LINEAR.
TIME IS LINEAR.
TIME IS LINEAR.
TIME IS LINEAR.
TIME IS LINEAR.
TIME IS LINEAR.

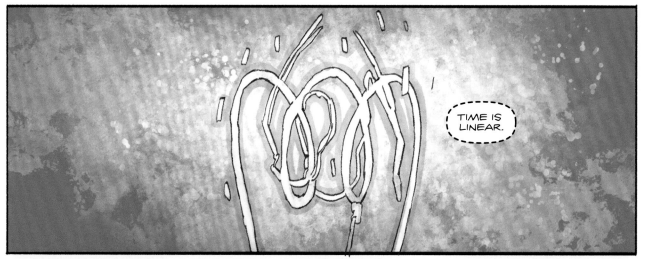

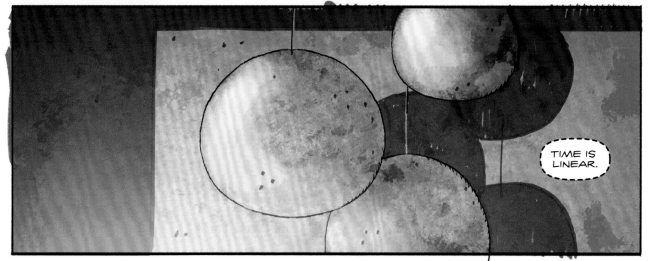

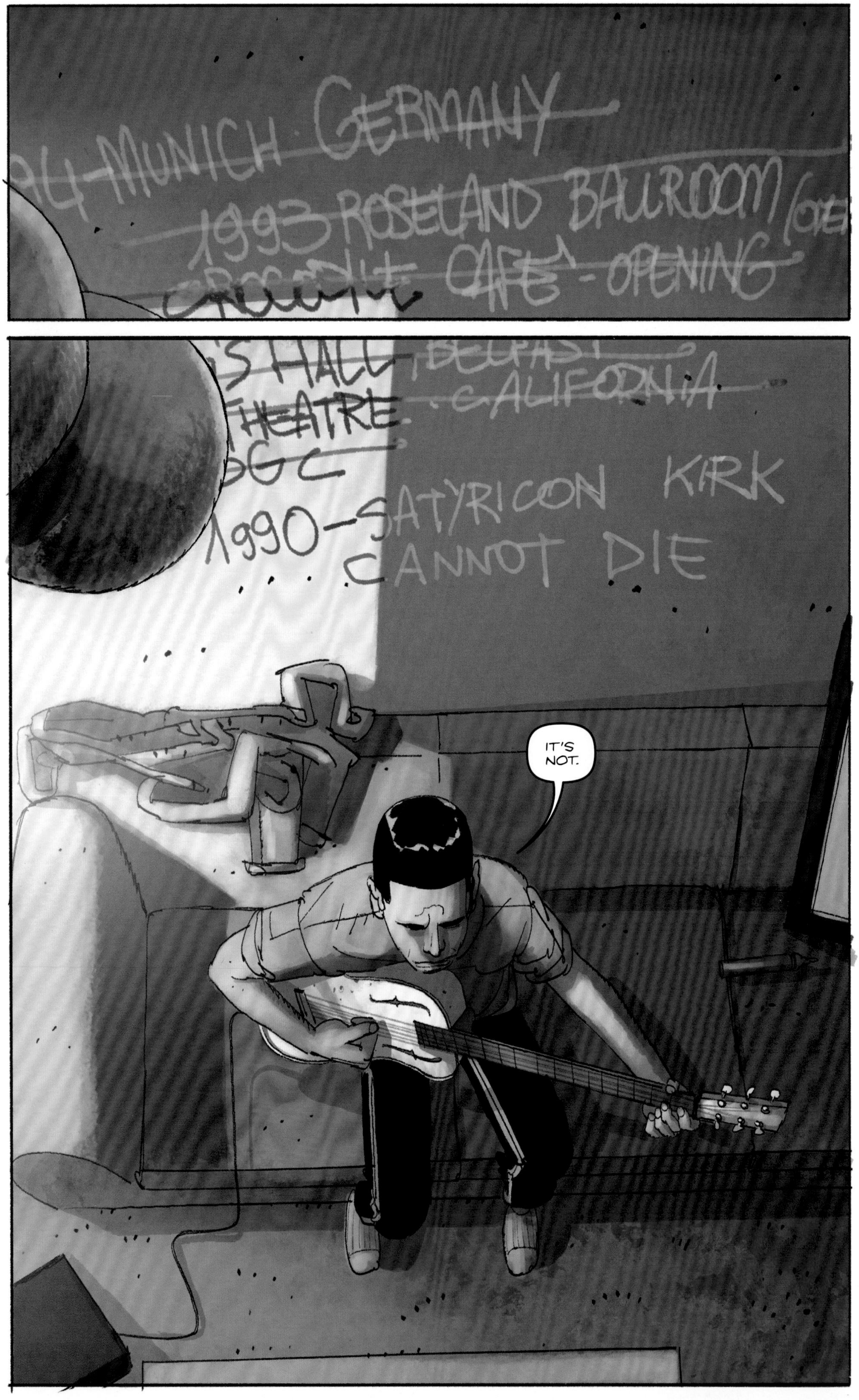

MUNICH GERMANY
1993 ROSELAND BALLROOM
CAFE - OPENING
THEATRE
CALIFORNIA
1990-SATYRICON
KIRK CANNOT DIE
IT'S NOT.

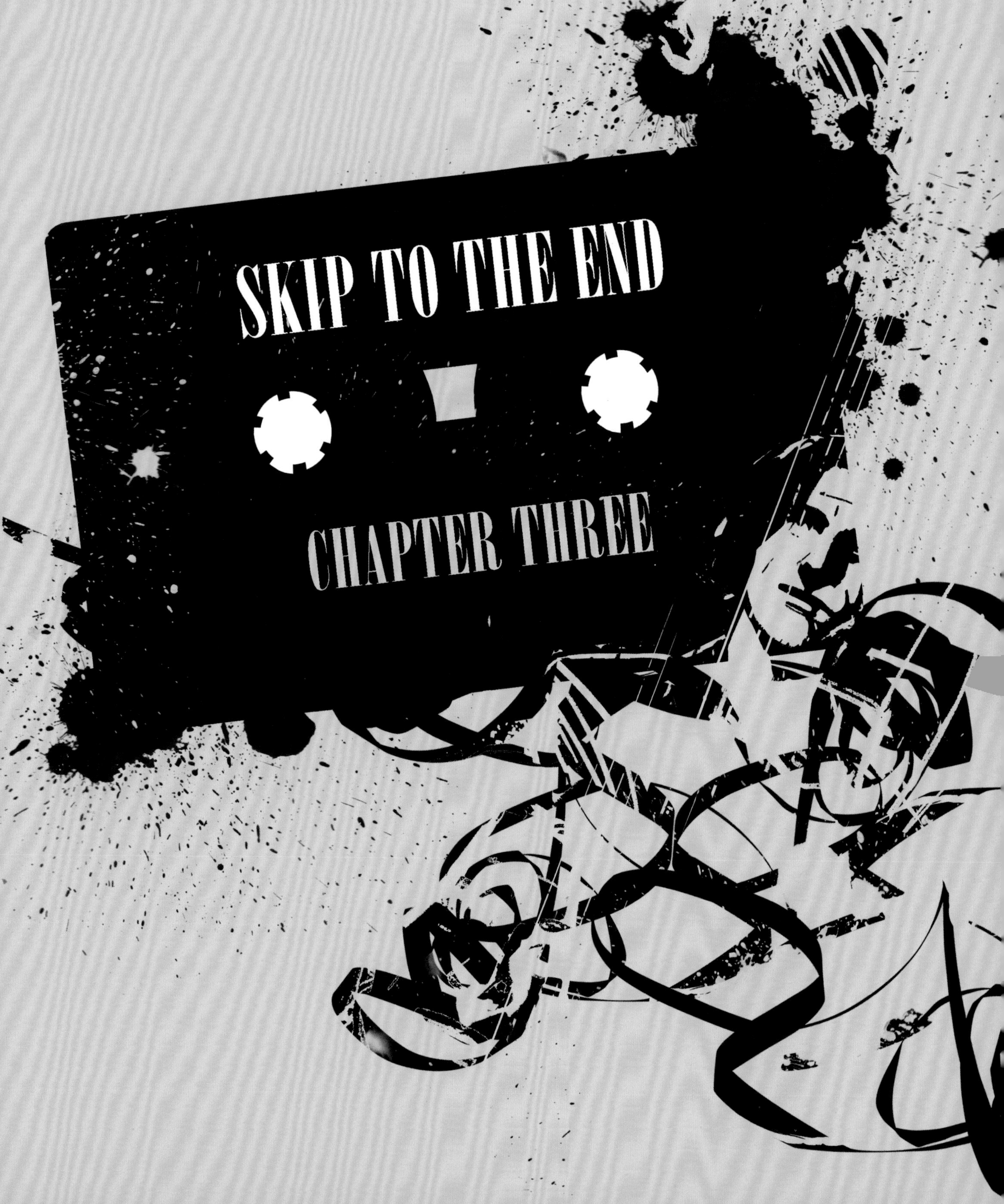
SKIP TO THE END
CHAPTER THREE

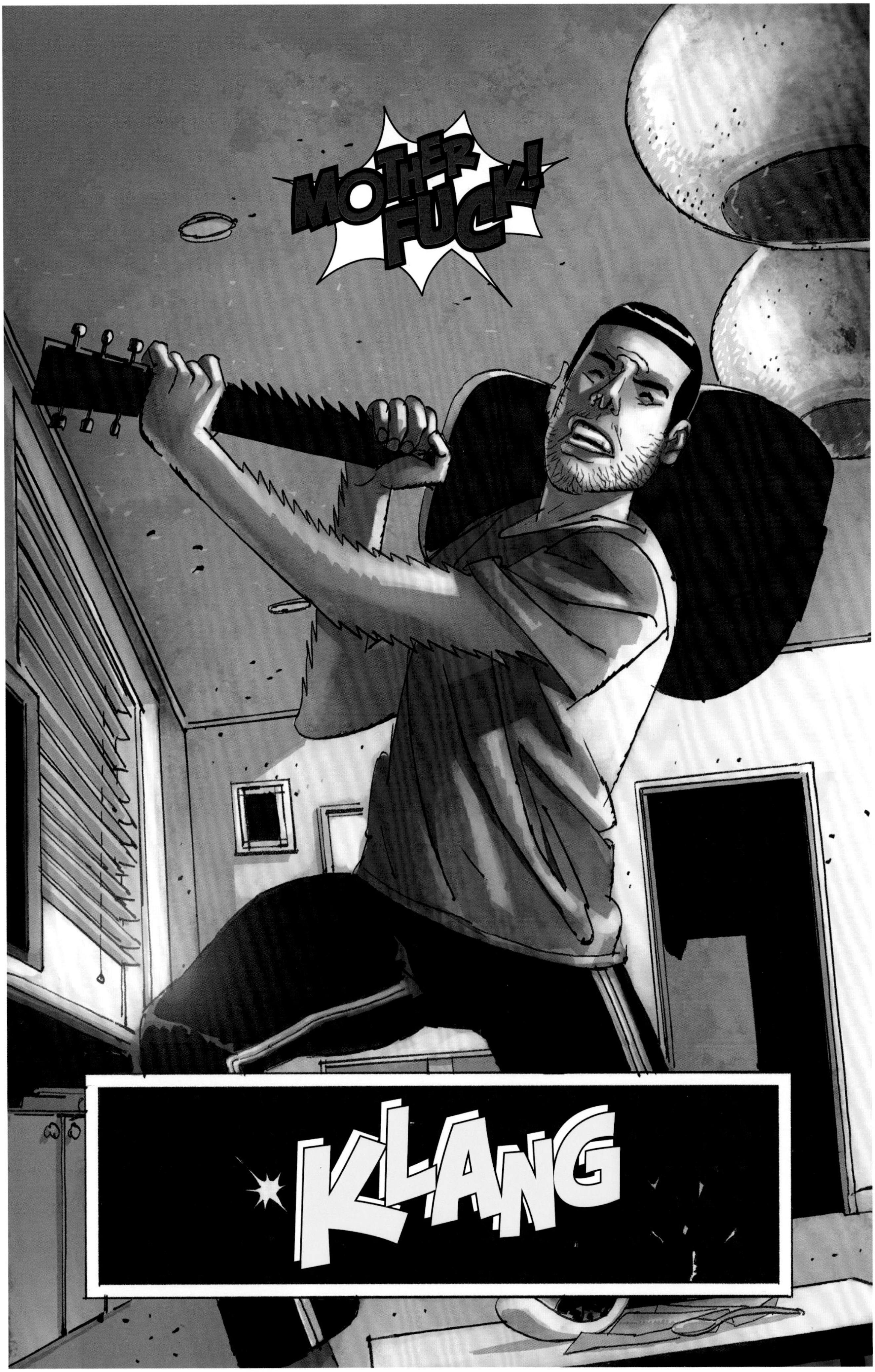
MOTHER FUCK!
KLANG

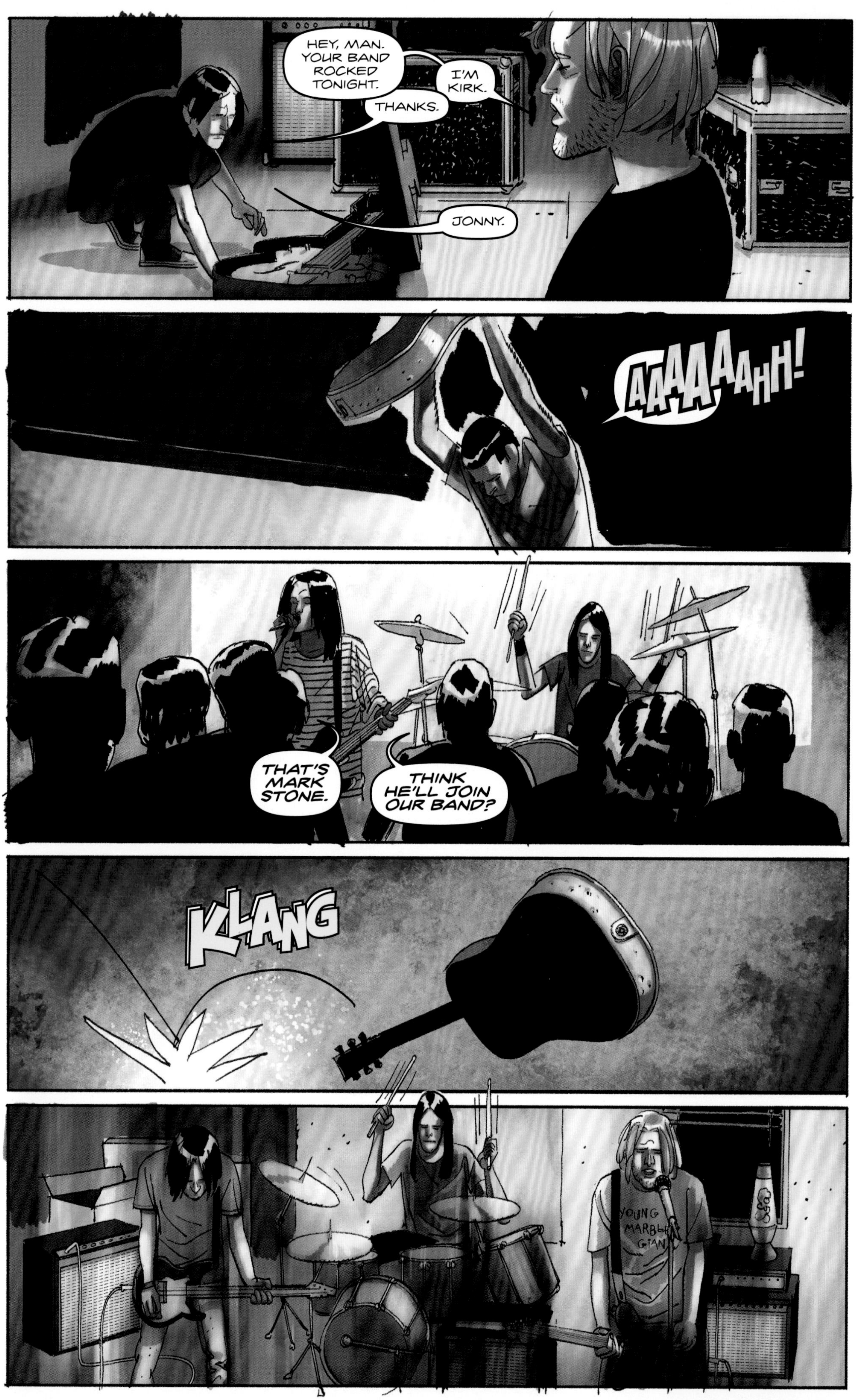
HEY, MAN. YOUR BAND ROCKED TONIGHT.
I'M KIRK.
THANKS.
JONNY.
AAAAAAHH!
THAT'S MARK STONE.
THINK HE'LL JOIN OUR BAND?
KLANG
YOUNG MARBLE GIANTS

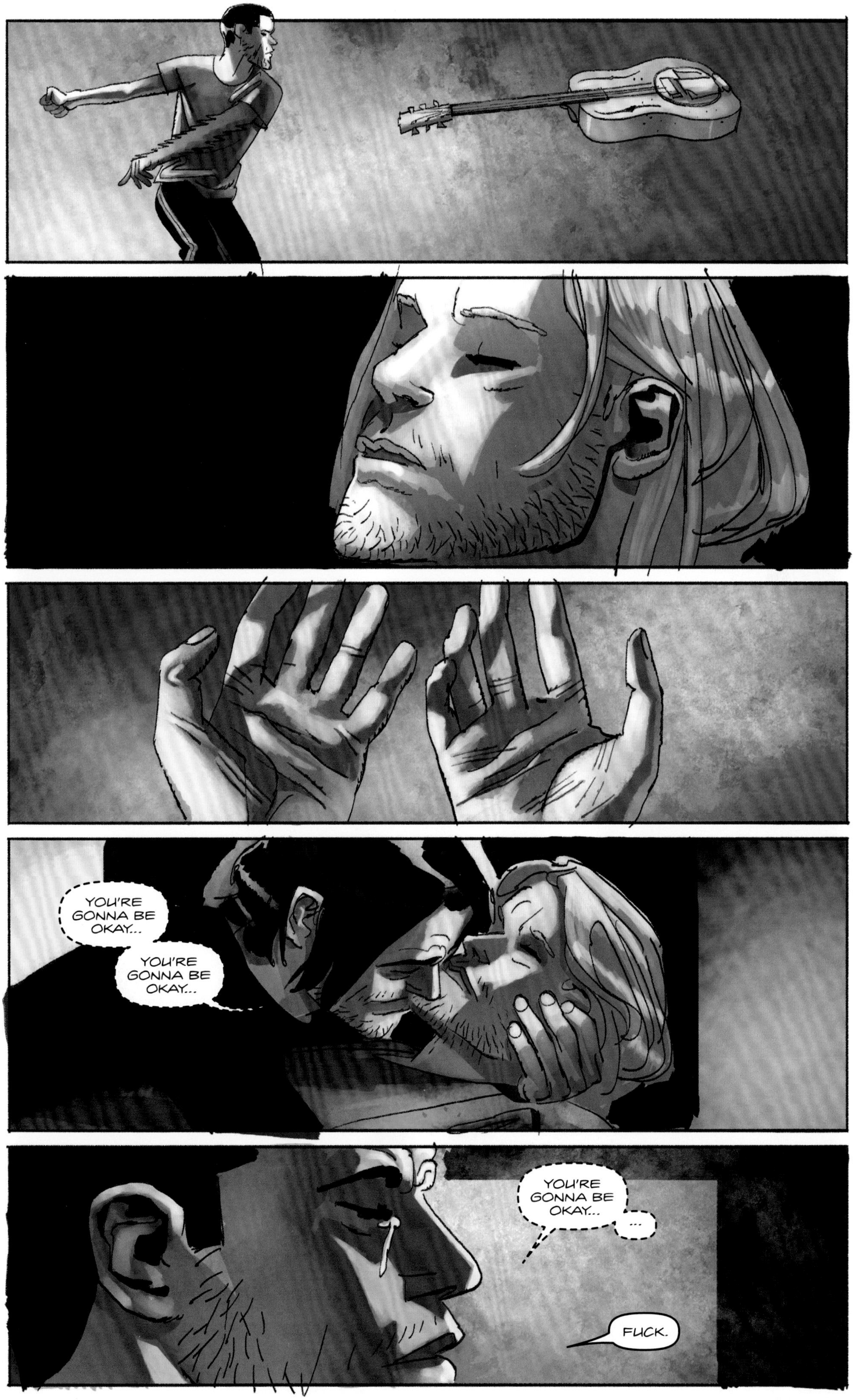
YOU'RE GONNA BE OKAY...
YOU'RE GONNA BE OKAY...
YOU'RE GONNA BE OKAY...
...
FUCK.

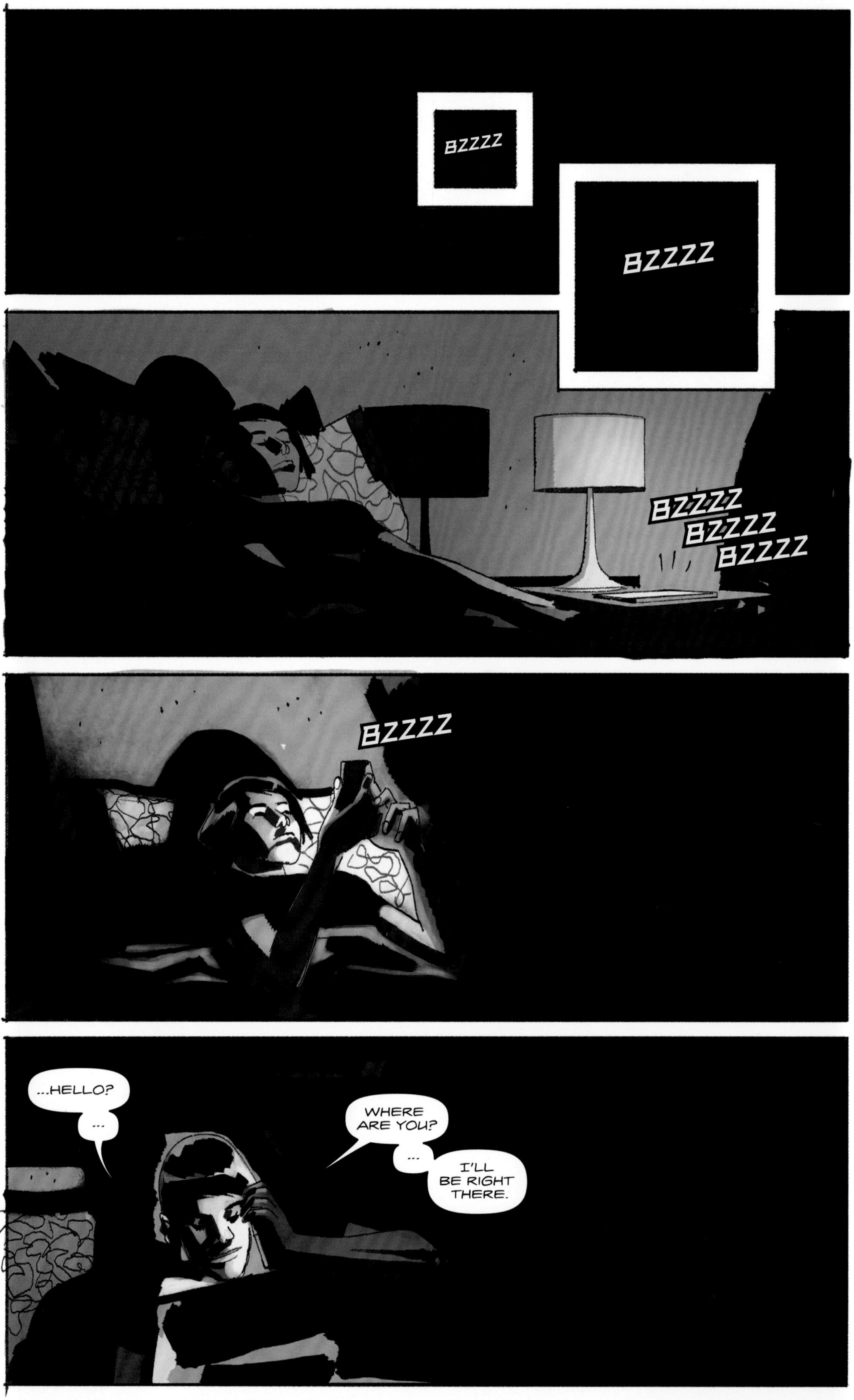
BZZZZ
BZZZZ
BZZZZ
BZZZZ
BZZZZ
BZZZZ
...HELLO?
...
WHERE ARE YOU?
...
I'LL BE RIGHT THERE.

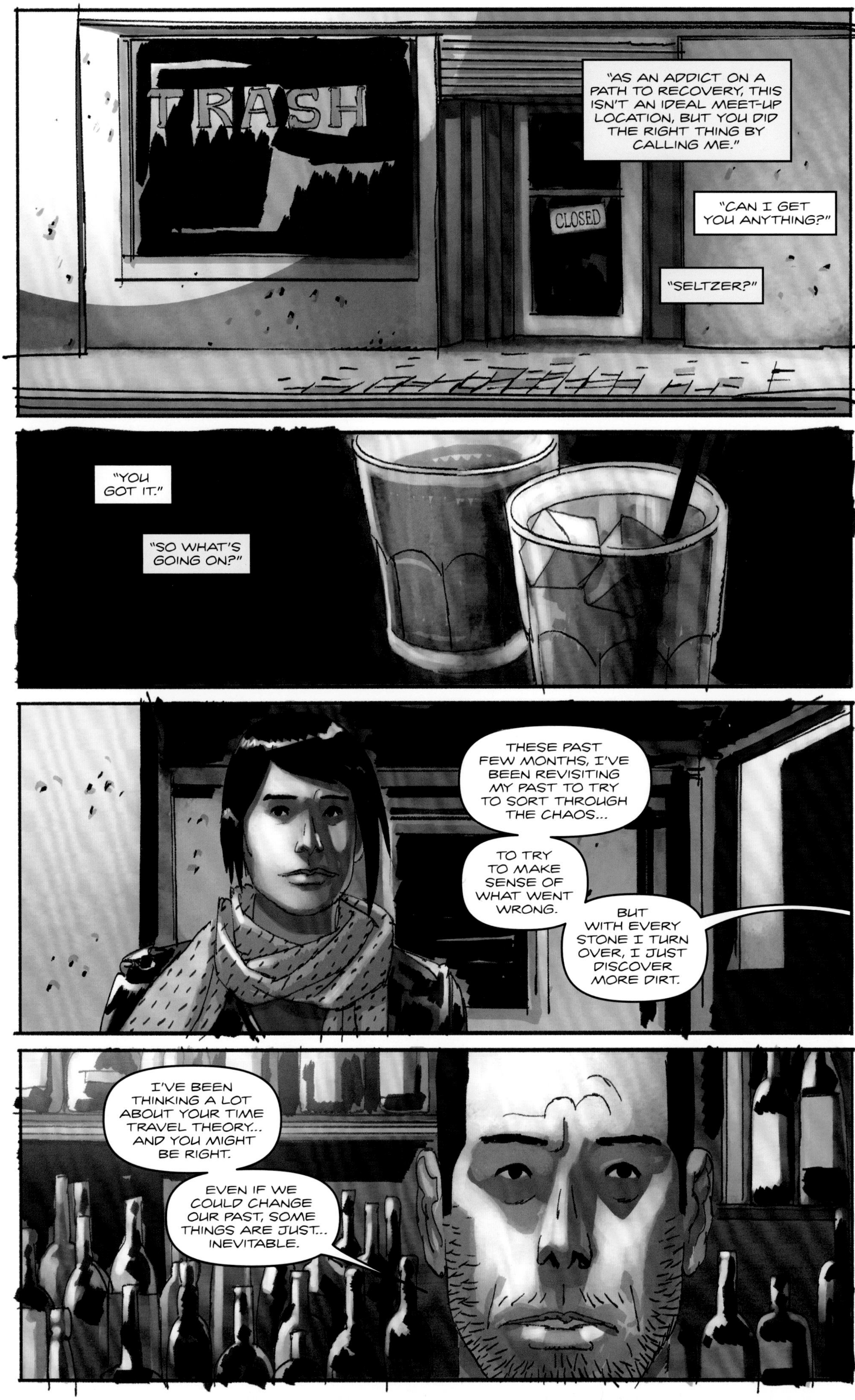
TRASH
"AS AN ADDICT ON A PATH TO RECOVERY, THIS ISN'T AN IDEAL MEET-UP LOCATION, BUT YOU DID THE RIGHT THING BY CALLING ME."
CLOSED
"CAN I GET YOU ANYTHING?"
"SELTZER?"
"YOU GOT IT."
"SO WHAT'S GOING ON?"
THESE PAST FEW MONTHS, I'VE BEEN REVISITING MY PAST TO TRY TO SORT THROUGH THE CHAOS...
TO TRY TO MAKE SENSE OF WHAT WENT WRONG.
BUT WITH EVERY STONE I TURN OVER, I JUST DISCOVER MORE DIRT.
I'VE BEEN THINKING A LOT ABOUT YOUR TIME TRAVEL THEORY... AND YOU MIGHT BE RIGHT.
EVEN IF WE COULD CHANGE OUR PAST, SOME THINGS ARE JUST... INEVITABLE.

I'VE LOST MY BEST FRIEND IN MORE WAYS THAN ONE AND TONIGHT...

I WANTED... NO, NEEDED TO CHASE THE DRAGON.

YOU DIDN'T THOUGH. THAT'S WORTH FOCUSING ON. AND SOMETIMES THE INEVITABLE CAN ACTUALLY BE VIEWED POSITIVELY. US MEETING IS A GOOD EXAMPLE.

CLOSURE IS A DELICATE PROCESS THAT OFTEN GETS NEGLECTED, *ESPECIALLY* AFTER A TRAUMATIC EVENT.

AT THIS STAGE OF YOUR REHABILITATION, IT'S IMPERATIVE THAT YOU DON'T SUBSTITUTE ONE ADDICTION FOR ANOTHER.

HOWEVER, SOMETIMES IT'S JUST A MATTER OF *PERSPECTIVE*...

TELL YOU WHAT, IF THINKING ABOUT YOUR BEST FRIEND IS WHAT'LL GIVE YOU CLOSURE, WHY DWELL ON THE WHAT IFS?

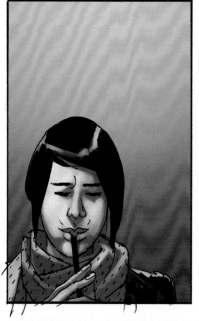

TELL ME SOMETHING YOU KNOW TO BE TRUE AND GOOD ABOUT HIM.

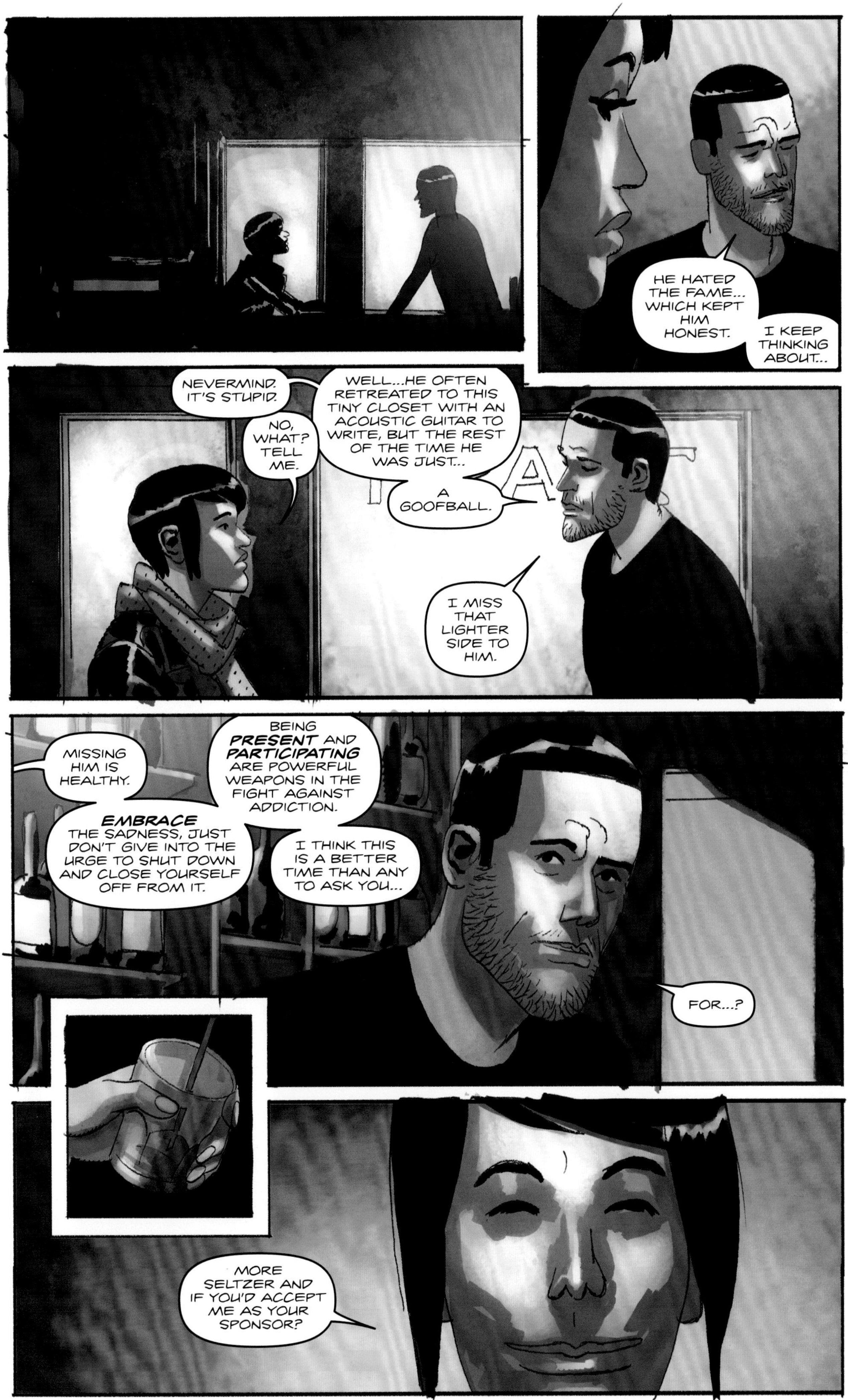
HE HATED THE FAME... WHICH KEPT HIM HONEST.
I KEEP THINKING ABOUT...
NEVERMIND. IT'S STUPID.
NO, WHAT? TELL ME.
WELL...HE OFTEN RETREATED TO THIS TINY CLOSET WITH AN ACOUSTIC GUITAR TO WRITE, BUT THE REST OF THE TIME HE WAS JUST...
A GOOFBALL.
I MISS THAT LIGHTER SIDE TO HIM.
MISSING HIM IS HEALTHY.
BEING PRESENT AND PARTICIPATING ARE POWERFUL WEAPONS IN THE FIGHT AGAINST ADDICTION.
EMBRACE THE SADNESS, JUST DON'T GIVE INTO THE URGE TO SHUT DOWN AND CLOSE YOURSELF OFF FROM IT.
I THINK THIS IS A BETTER TIME THAN ANY TO ASK YOU...
FOR...?
MORE SELTZER AND IF YOU'D ACCEPT ME AS YOUR SPONSOR?

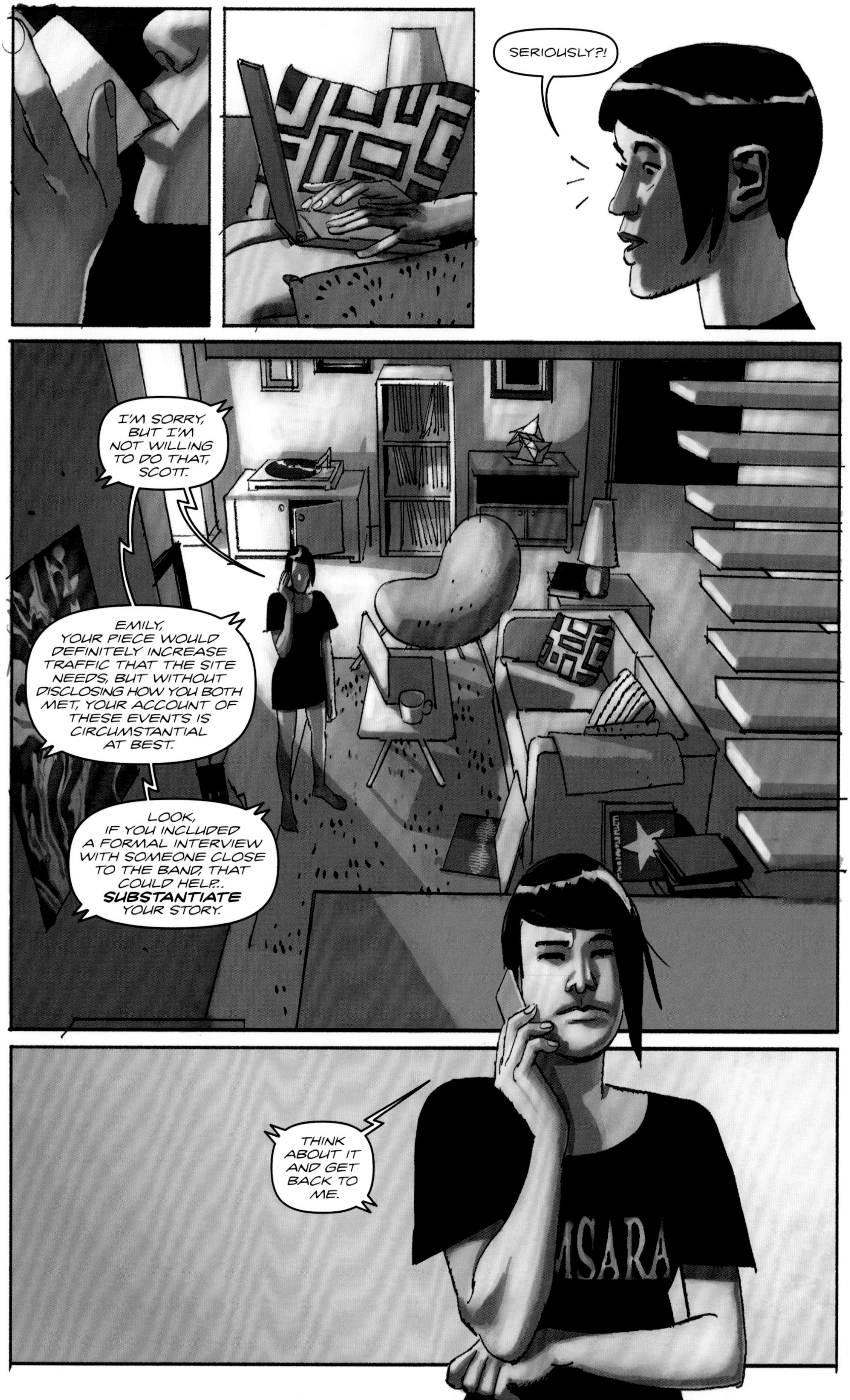
SERIOUSLY?!
I'M SORRY, BUT I'M NOT WILLING TO DO THAT, SCOTT.
EMILY, YOUR PIECE WOULD DEFINITELY INCREASE TRAFFIC THAT THE SITE NEEDS, BUT WITHOUT DISCLOSING HOW YOU BOTH MET, YOUR ACCOUNT OF THESE EVENTS IS CIRCUMSTANTIAL AT BEST.
LOOK, IF YOU INCLUDED A FORMAL INTERVIEW WITH SOMEONE CLOSE TO THE BAND, THAT COULD HELP... **SUBSTANTIATE** YOUR STORY.
THINK ABOUT IT AND GET BACK TO ME.
MSARA

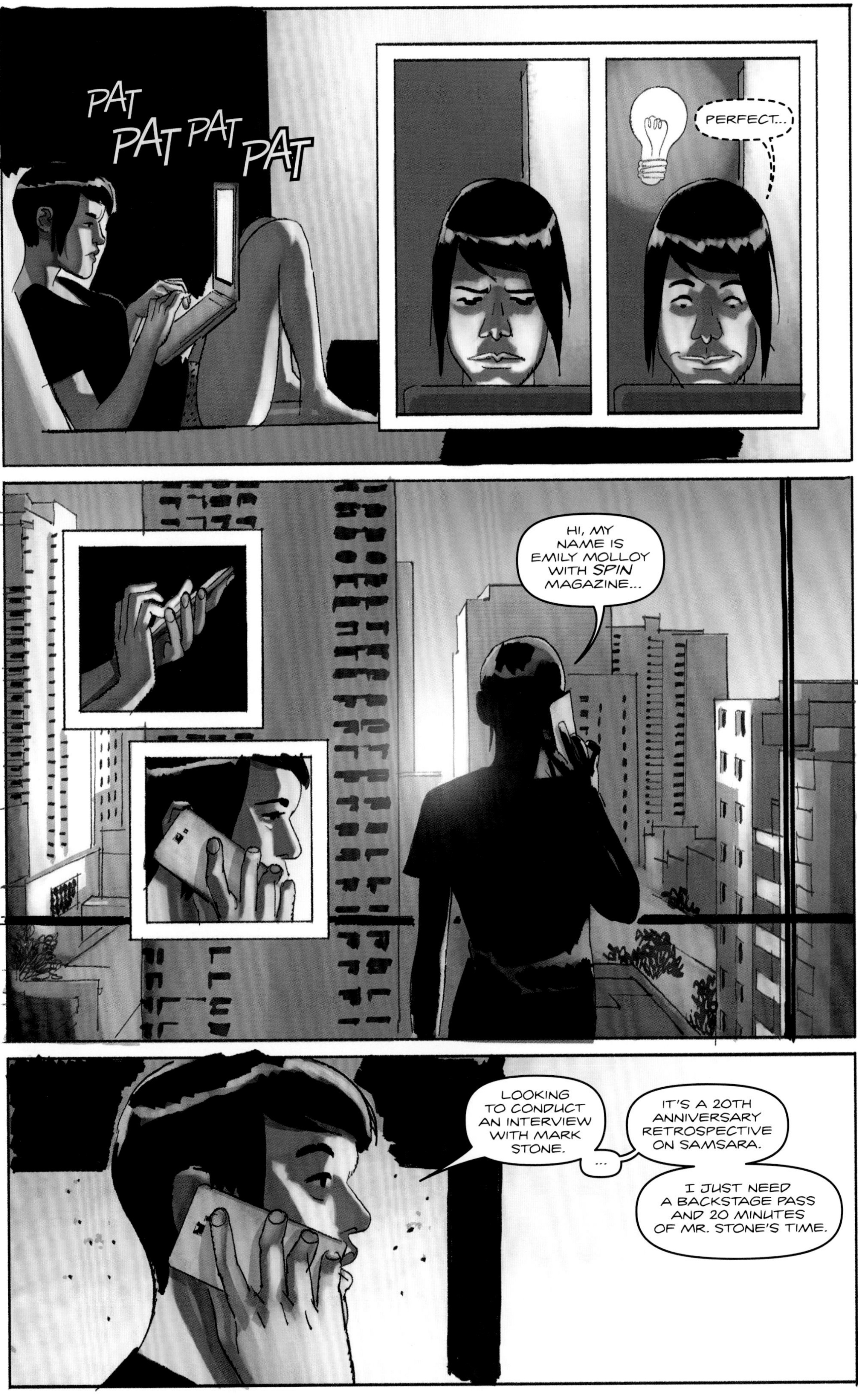
PAT
PAT PAT PAT PAT
PERFECT...
HI, MY NAME IS EMILY MOLLOY WITH SPIN MAGAZINE...
LOOKING TO CONDUCT AN INTERVIEW WITH MARK STONE.
...
IT'S A 20TH ANNIVERSARY RETROSPECTIVE ON SAMSARA.
I JUST NEED A BACKSTAGE PASS AND 20 MINUTES OF MR. STONE'S TIME.

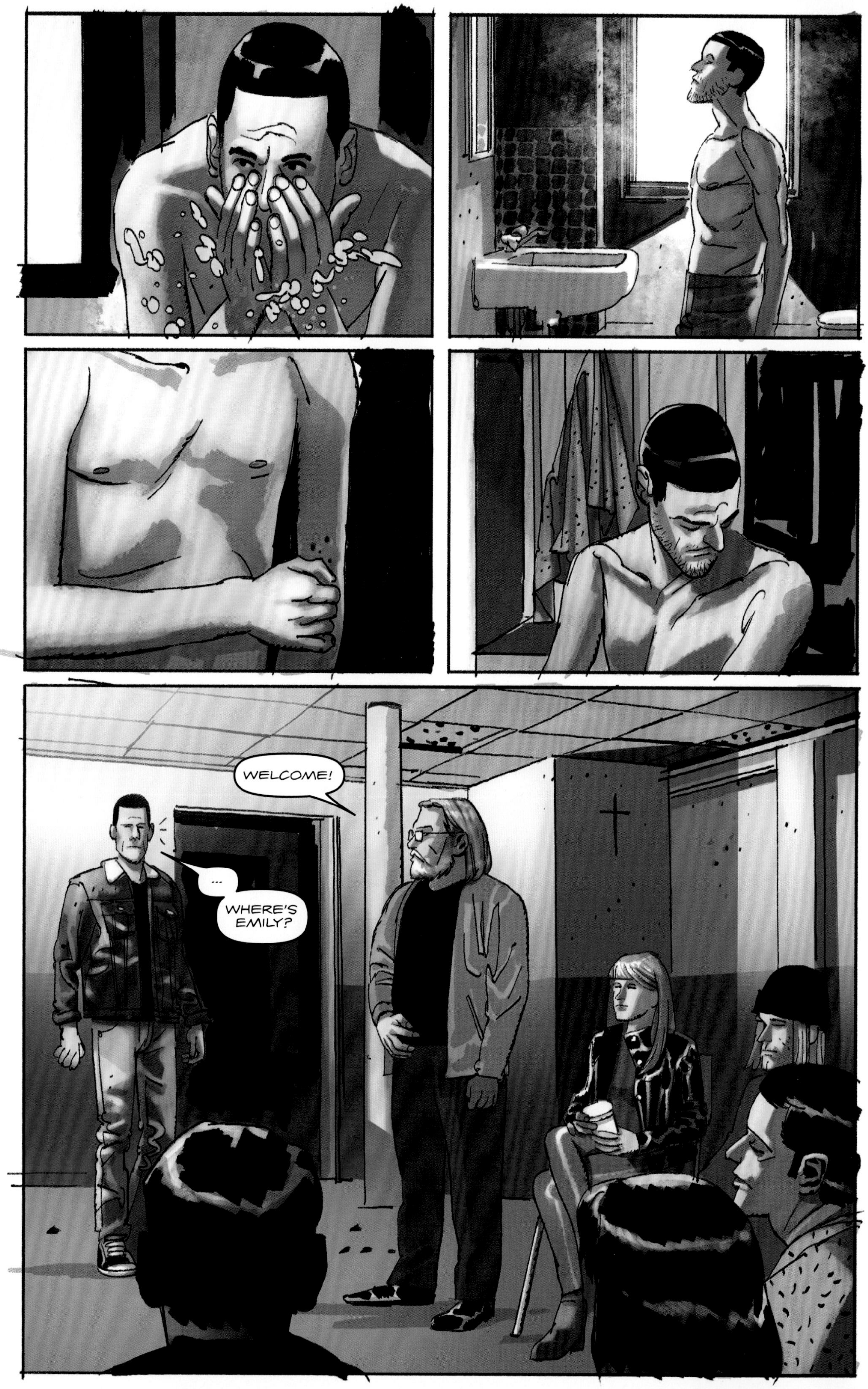
WELCOME!
...
WHERE'S EMILY?

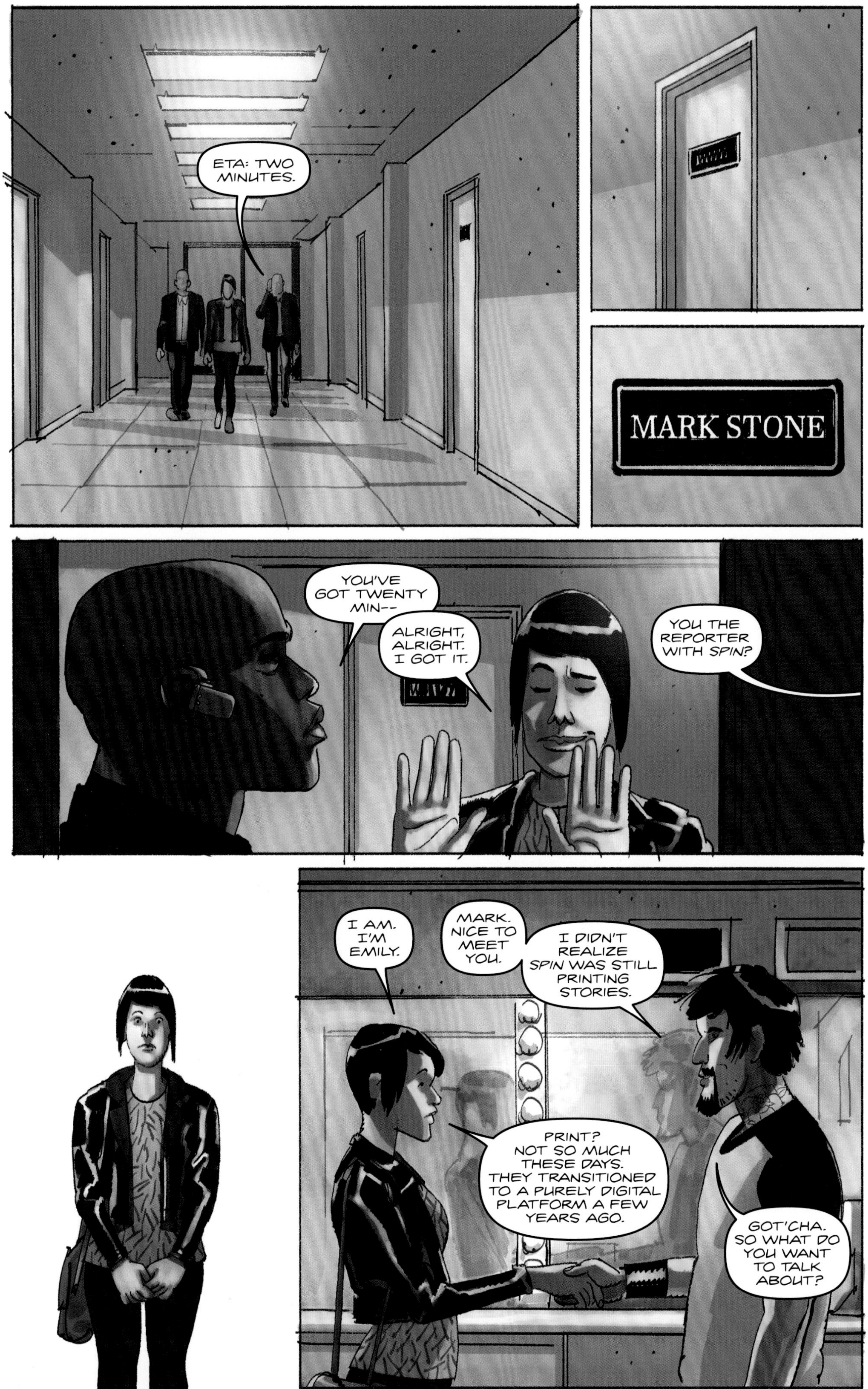
ETA: TWO MINUTES.
MARK STONE
YOU'VE GOT TWENTY MIN--
ALRIGHT, ALRIGHT. I GOT IT.
YOU THE REPORTER WITH *SPIN*?
I AM. I'M EMILY.
MARK. NICE TO MEET YOU.
I DIDN'T REALIZE *SPIN* WAS STILL PRINTING STORIES.
PRINT? NOT SO MUCH THESE DAYS. THEY TRANSITIONED TO A PURELY DIGITAL PLATFORM A FEW YEARS AGO.
GOT'CHA. SO WHAT DO YOU WANT TO TALK ABOUT?

"WELL, I'M CURRENTLY WRITING UP A 20TH ANNIVERSARY RETROSPECTIVE ON SAMSARA, FOCUSING ON THE INFLUENCE THEY HAD DURING THEIR BRIEF BUT BRIGHT EXISTENCE."

"IF YOU DON'T MIND, I WAS HOPING TO STROLL DOWN MEMORY LANE WITH YOU?"

"SURE, WHERE DO YOU WANT TO START?"

"AT THE BEGINNING. I UNDERSTAND YOU WERE SORT OF DISCOVERED BY THE BAND. HOW'D THAT HAPPEN?"

YEAH, I WAS ACTUALLY IN ANOTHER BAND WHEN KIRK AND JONNY CAME KNOCKIN'.

THEY HAD JUST LOST THEIR DRUMMER TO CREATIVE DIFFERENCES, I THINK.

MY BAND WAS ON THE SKIDS, TOO, AND BEFORE I KNEW IT, I WAS BEING ASKED TO JOIN SAMSARA IN SEATTLE.

WITH A COUPLE HUNDRED BUCKS AND SOME BAGS OF CLOTHES, I FIGURED, "WHAT THE HELL? WHY NOT?" SO I DID.

"AND SAMSARA'S HIT SONG 'SKIP TO THE END' WAS BORN."

"THAT'S RIGHT. THEY RELEASED THAT FIRST ALBUM THROUGH SUB POP IN THE SUMMER OF '89 AND RECORDED THE THING FOR LIKE SIX HUNDRED BUCKS."

"THOUGH I DIDN'T JOIN THEM UNTIL THE FALL OF 1990."

"ONLY SIX HUNDRED BUCKS?! TALK ABOUT PASSIONATE. YOU GUYS MUST HAVE BEEN CLOSE."

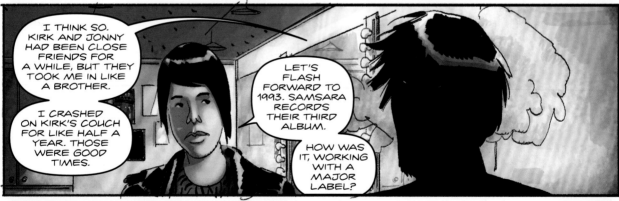

I THINK SO. KIRK AND JONNY HAD BEEN CLOSE FRIENDS FOR A WHILE, BUT THEY TOOK ME IN LIKE A BROTHER.

I CRASHED ON KIRK'S COUCH FOR LIKE HALF A YEAR. THOSE WERE GOOD TIMES.

LET'S FLASH FORWARD TO 1993. SAMSARA RECORDS THEIR THIRD ALBUM.

HOW WAS IT, WORKING WITH A MAJOR LABEL?

SAMSARA

SKIP TO THE END

"IT WAS GREAT. AFTER THE FIRST ALBUM HIT, WE STARTED GETTING OFFERS AND DECIDED TO GO WITH DGC BECAUSE THEY OFFERED US THE MOST CREATIVE CONTROL."

"WHAT WAS YOUR RELATIONSHIP LIKE WITH KIRK AND JONNY BY THEN?"

"..."

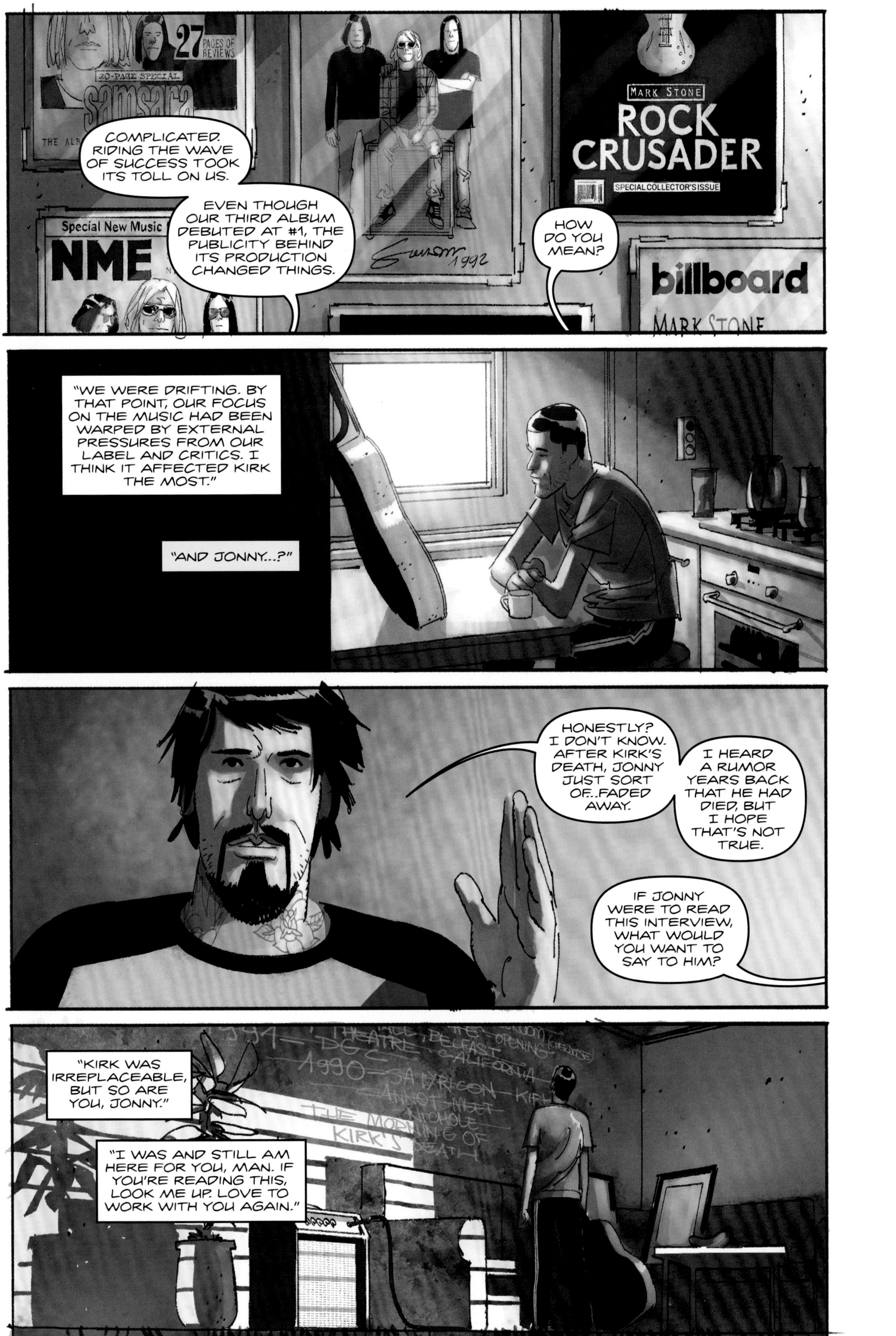
27 PAGES OF REVIEWS
20-PAGE SPECIAL
samsara
MARK STONE
ROCK CRUSADER
SPECIAL COLLECTOR'S ISSUE
COMPLICATED. RIDING THE WAVE OF SUCCESS TOOK ITS TOLL ON US.
EVEN THOUGH OUR THIRD ALBUM DEBUTED AT #1, THE PUBLICITY BEHIND ITS PRODUCTION CHANGED THINGS.
Special New Music
NME
HOW DO YOU MEAN?
billboard
MARK STONE
"WE WERE DRIFTING. BY THAT POINT, OUR FOCUS ON THE MUSIC HAD BEEN WARPED BY EXTERNAL PRESSURES FROM OUR LABEL AND CRITICS. I THINK IT AFFECTED KIRK THE MOST."
"AND JONNY...?"
HONESTLY? I DON'T KNOW. AFTER KIRK'S DEATH, JONNY JUST SORT OF...FADED AWAY.
I HEARD A RUMOR YEARS BACK THAT HE HAD DIED, BUT I HOPE THAT'S NOT TRUE.
IF JONNY WERE TO READ THIS INTERVIEW, WHAT WOULD YOU WANT TO SAY TO HIM?
"KIRK WAS IRREPLACEABLE, BUT SO ARE YOU, JONNY."
"I WAS AND STILL AM HERE FOR YOU, MAN. IF YOU'RE READING THIS, LOOK ME UP. LOVE TO WORK WITH YOU AGAIN."

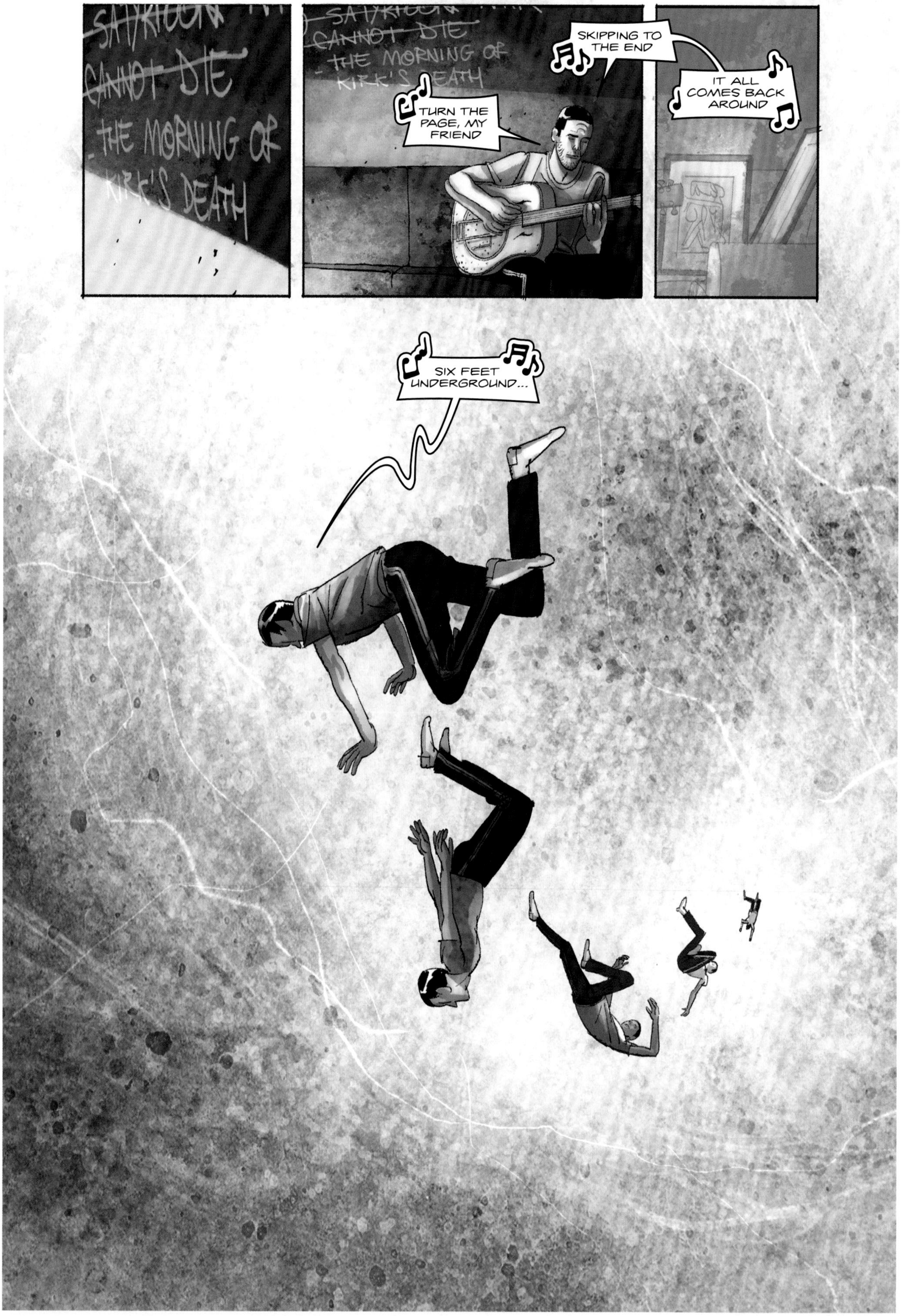
CANNOT DIE
- THE MORNING OF KIRK'S DEATH
TURN THE PAGE, MY FRIEND
SKIPPING TO THE END
IT ALL COMES BACK AROUND
SIX FEET UNDERGROUND...

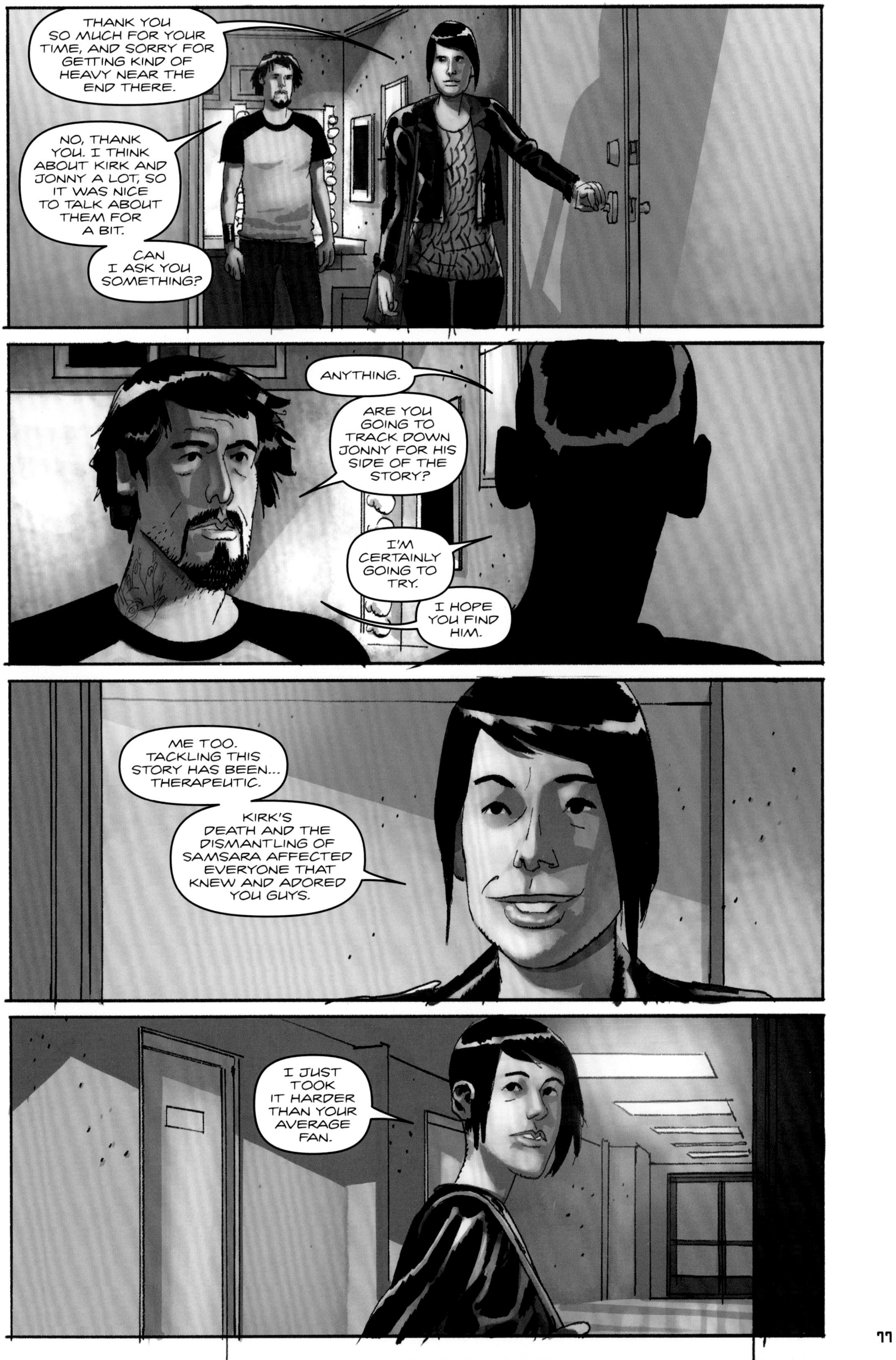
THANK YOU SO MUCH FOR YOUR TIME, AND SORRY FOR GETTING KIND OF HEAVY NEAR THE END THERE.
NO, THANK YOU. I THINK ABOUT KIRK AND JONNY A LOT, SO IT WAS NICE TO TALK ABOUT THEM FOR A BIT.
CAN I ASK YOU SOMETHING?
ANYTHING.
ARE YOU GOING TO TRACK DOWN JONNY FOR HIS SIDE OF THE STORY?
I'M CERTAINLY GOING TO TRY.
I HOPE YOU FIND HIM.
ME TOO. TACKLING THIS STORY HAS BEEN... THERAPEUTIC.
KIRK'S DEATH AND THE DISMANTLING OF SAMSARA AFFECTED EVERYONE THAT KNEW AND ADORED YOU GUYS.
I JUST TOOK IT HARDER THAN YOUR AVERAGE FAN.

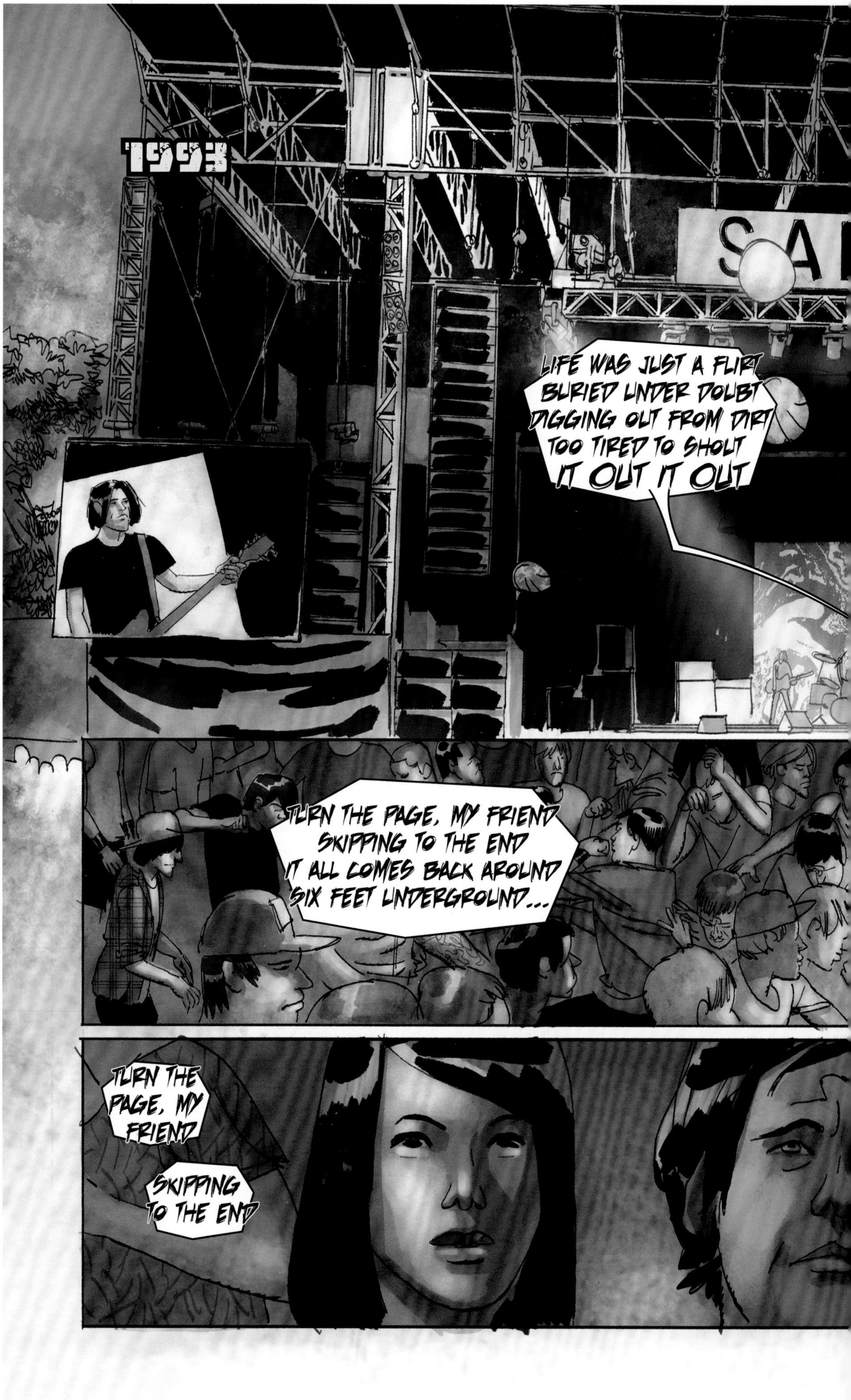
1993
LIFE WAS JUST A FLIRT
BURIED UNDER DOUBT
DIGGING OUT FROM DIRT
TOO TIRED TO SHOUT
IT OUT IT OUT
TURN THE PAGE, MY FRIEND
SKIPPING TO THE END
IT ALL COMES BACK AROUND
SIX FEET UNDERGROUND...
TURN THE PAGE, MY FRIEND
SKIPPING TO THE END

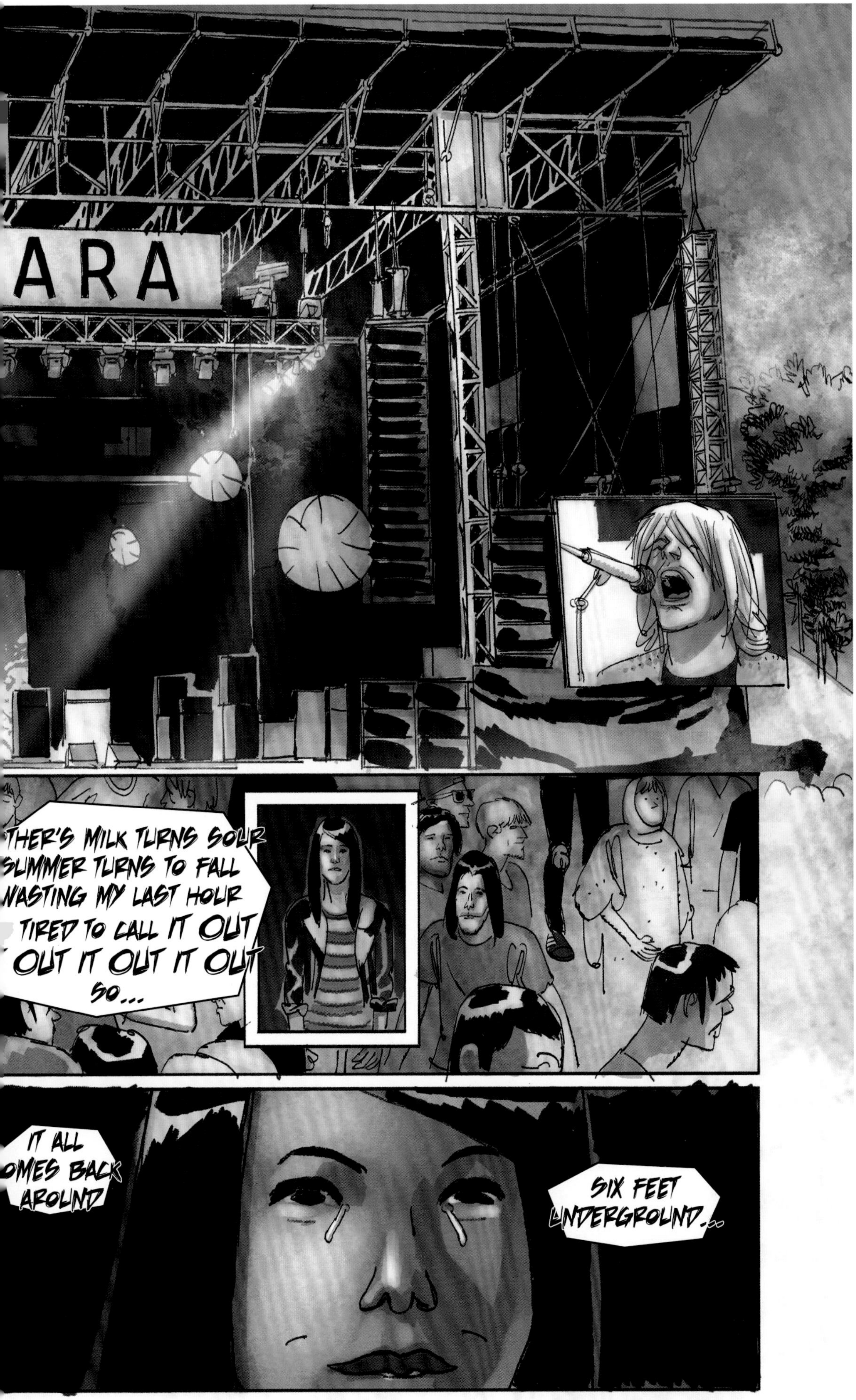
ARA
THER'S MILK TURNS SOUR
SUMMER TURNS TO FALL
WASTING MY LAST HOUR
TIRED TO CALL IT OUT
OUT IT OUT IT OUT
SO...
IT ALL
OMES BACK
AROUND
SIX FEET
UNDERGROUND..

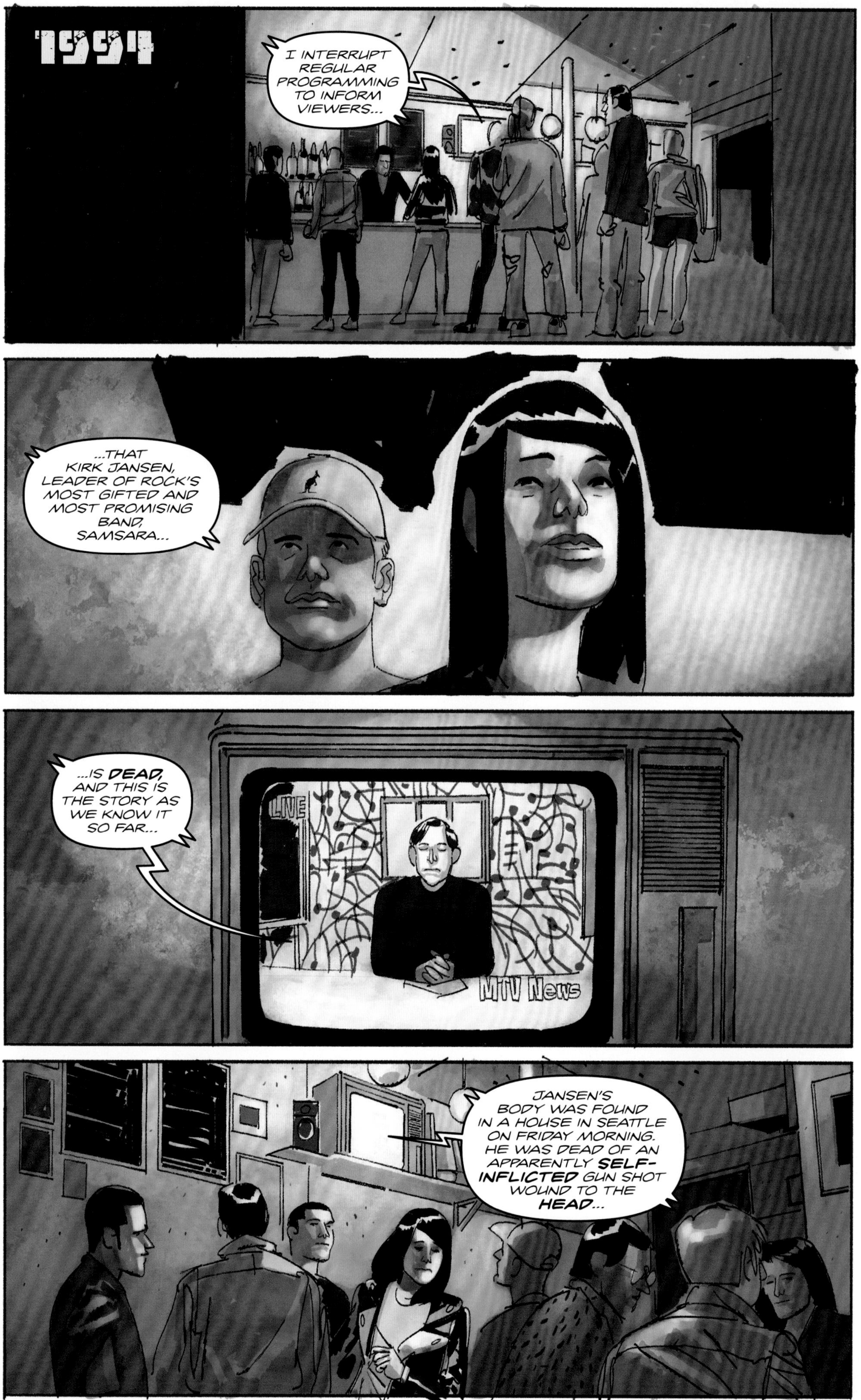
1994
I INTERRUPT REGULAR PROGRAMMING TO INFORM VIEWERS...
...THAT KIRK JANSEN, LEADER OF ROCK'S MOST GIFTED AND MOST PROMISING BAND, SAMSARA...
...IS **DEAD,** AND THIS IS THE STORY AS WE KNOW IT SO FAR...
LIVE
MTV News
JANSEN'S BODY WAS FOUND IN A HOUSE IN SEATTLE ON FRIDAY MORNING. HE WAS DEAD OF AN APPARENTLY **SELF-INFLICTED** GUN SHOT WOUND TO THE **HEAD...**

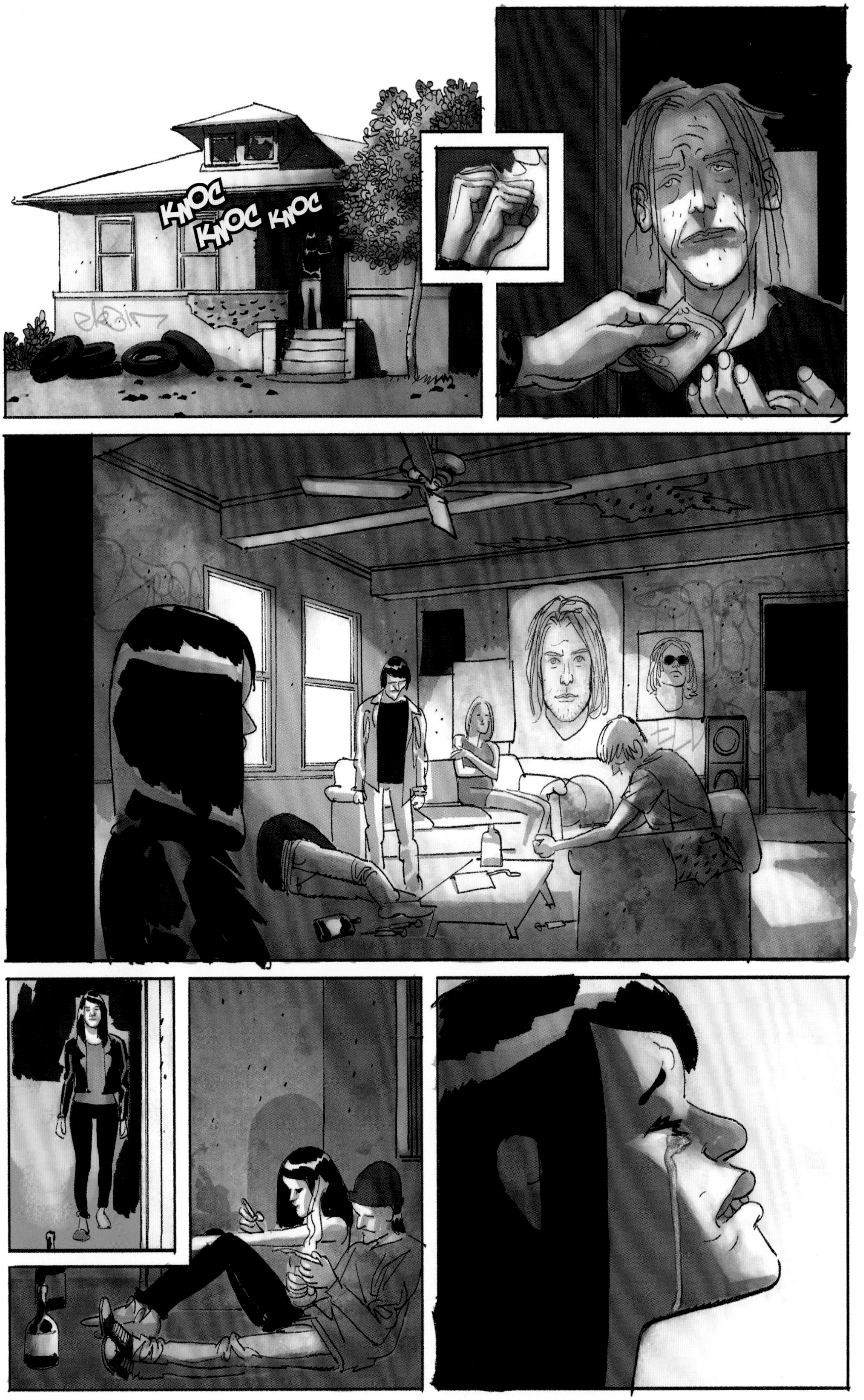
KNOC
KNOC KNOC

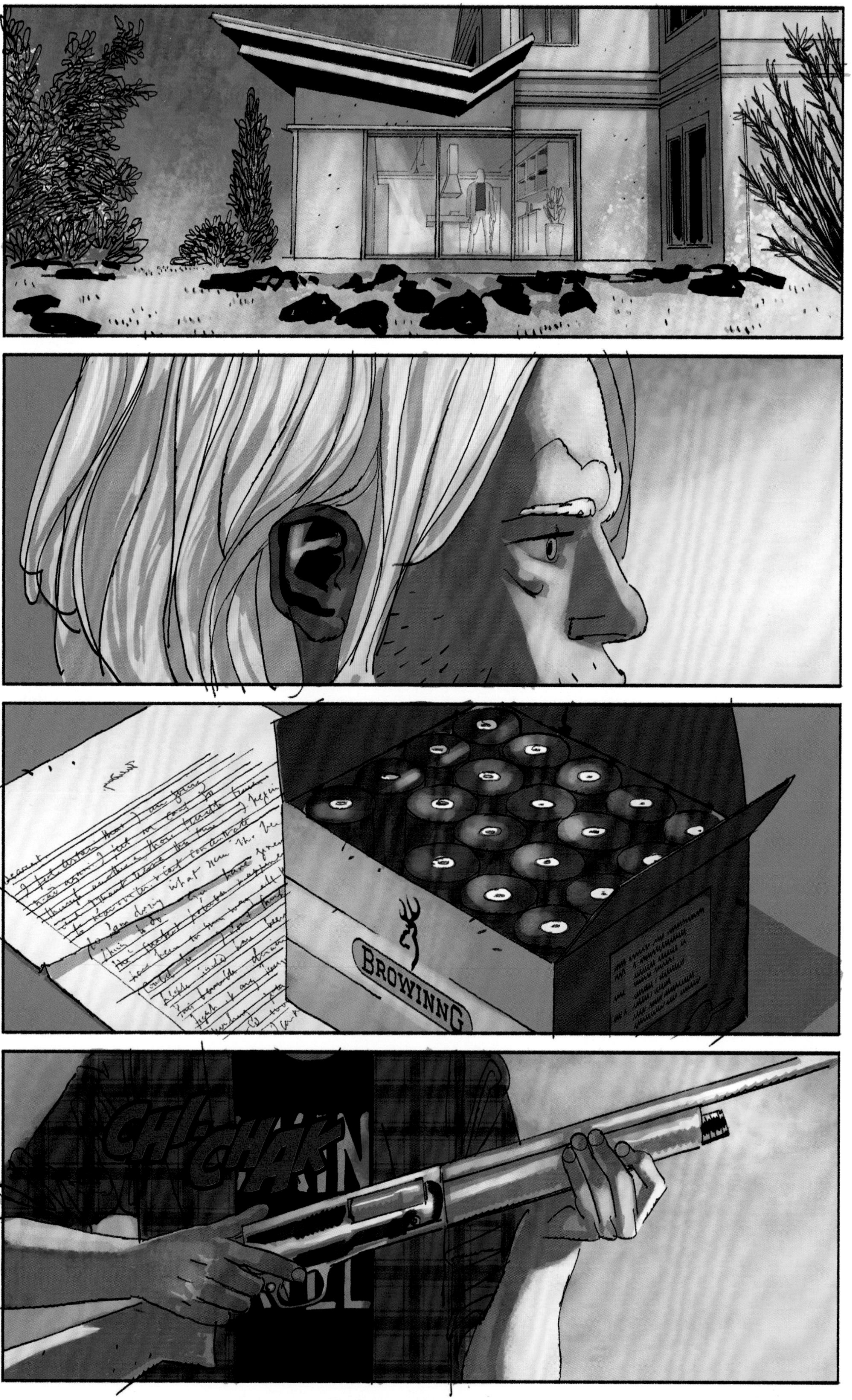
BROWINNG
CHI-CHAK

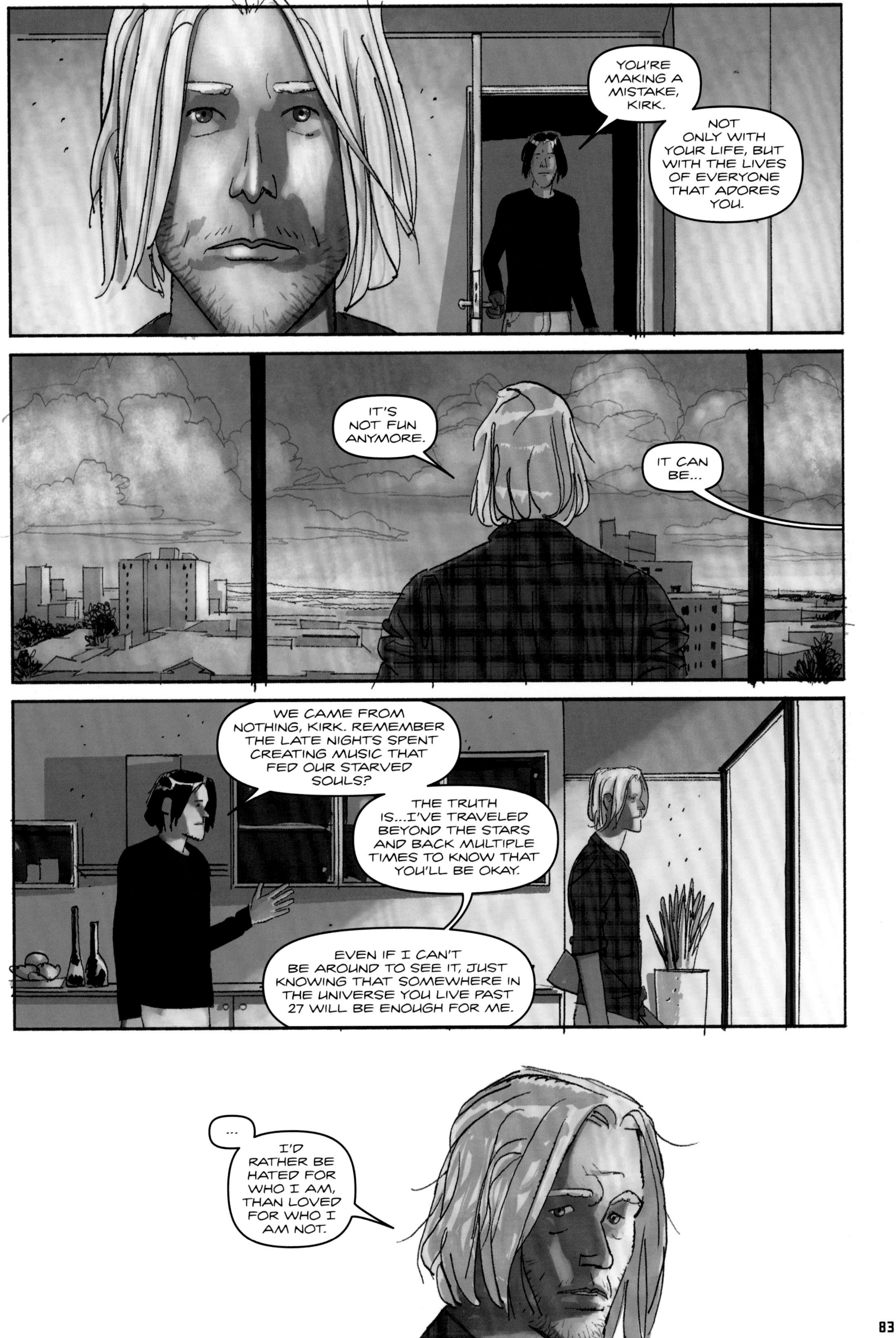
YOU'RE MAKING A MISTAKE, KIRK.
NOT ONLY WITH YOUR LIFE, BUT WITH THE LIVES OF EVERYONE THAT ADORES YOU.
IT'S NOT FUN ANYMORE.
IT CAN BE...
WE CAME FROM NOTHING, KIRK. REMEMBER THE LATE NIGHTS SPENT CREATING MUSIC THAT FED OUR STARVED SOULS?
THE TRUTH IS...I'VE TRAVELED BEYOND THE STARS AND BACK MULTIPLE TIMES TO KNOW THAT YOU'LL BE OKAY.
EVEN IF I CAN'T BE AROUND TO SEE IT, JUST KNOWING THAT SOMEWHERE IN THE UNIVERSE YOU LIVE PAST 27 WILL BE ENOUGH FOR ME.
...
I'D RATHER BE HATED FOR WHO I AM, THAN LOVED FOR WHO I AM NOT.

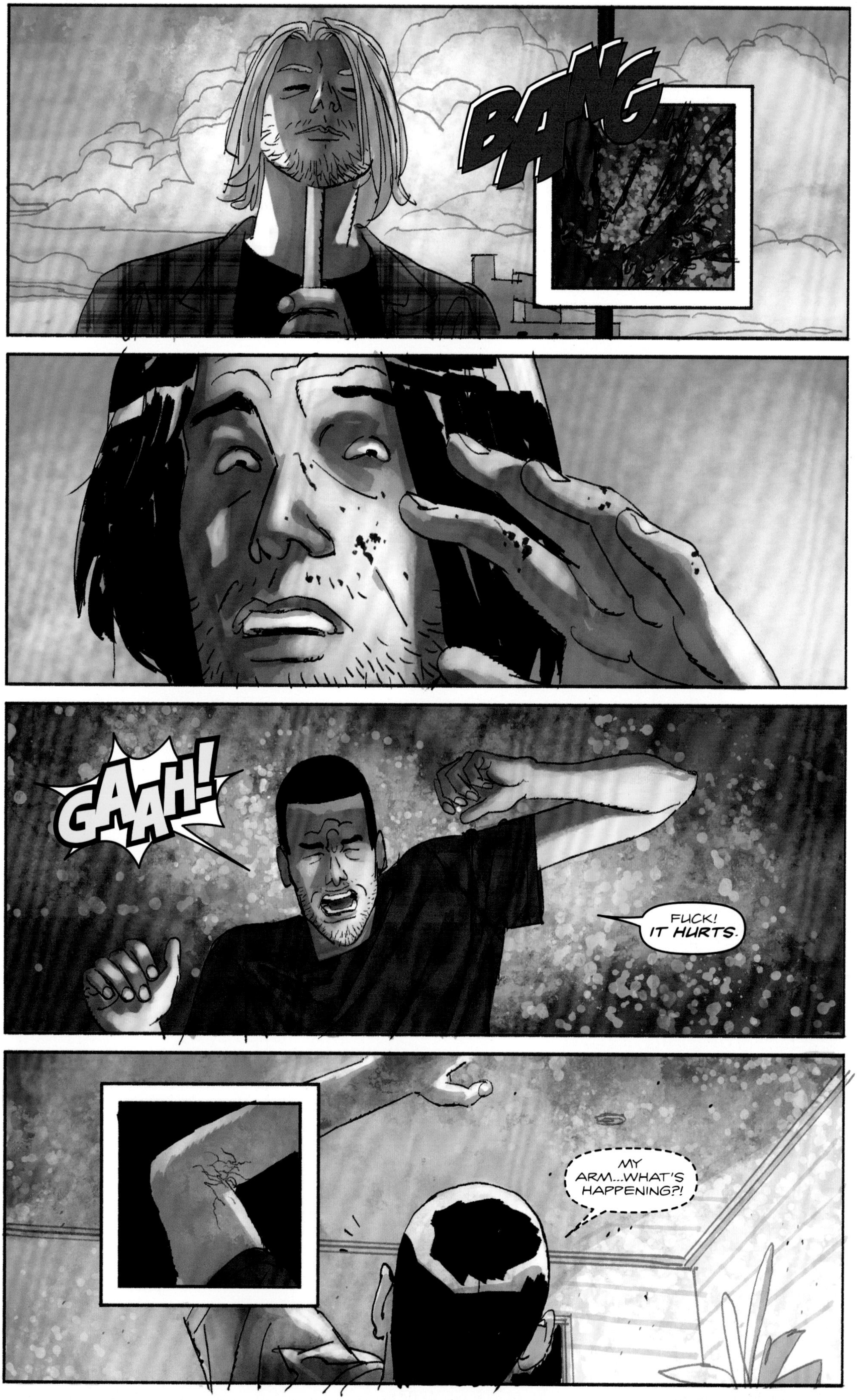
BANG
GAAH!
FUCK! IT HURTS.
MY ARM...WHAT'S HAPPENING?!

SKIP TO THE END

CHAPTER FOUR

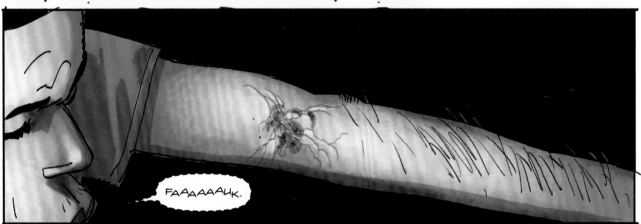

FAAAAAAUK.

YOU DESERVE THIS...

YOU *FUCKING* DESERVE THIS.

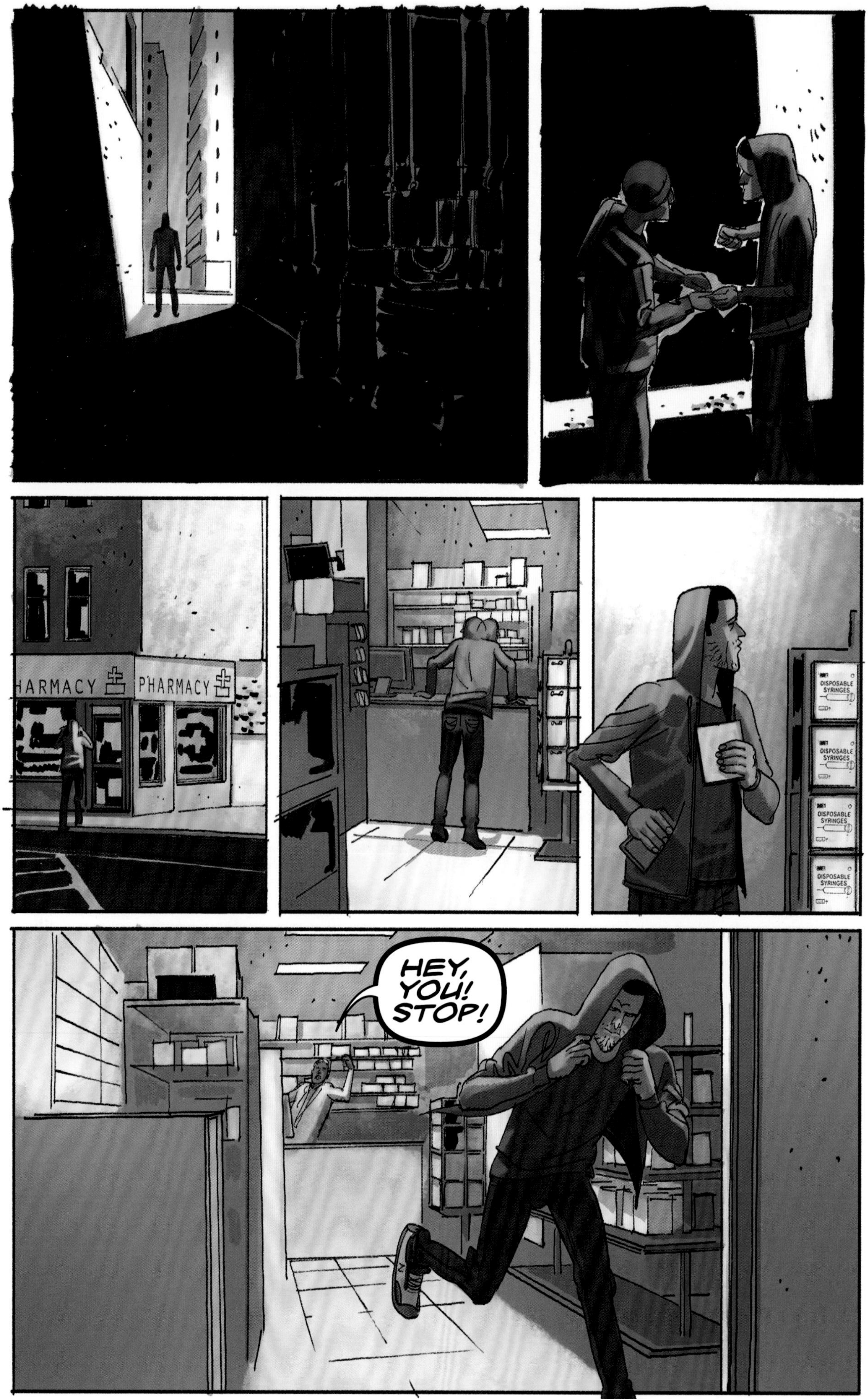
PHARMACY
PHARMACY
DISPOSABLE SYRINGES
DISPOSABLE SYRINGES
DISPOSABLE SYRINGES
DISPOSABLE SYRINGES
HEY, YOU! STOP!

FLINK

YOU *DESERVE* THIS...

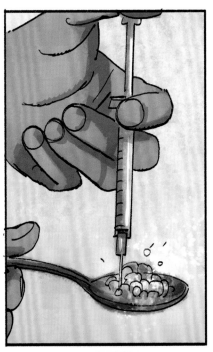

YOU DESERVE *THIS*...

MMM...

JUST A TASTE...

KNOC
KNOC
KNOC

JONNY...?

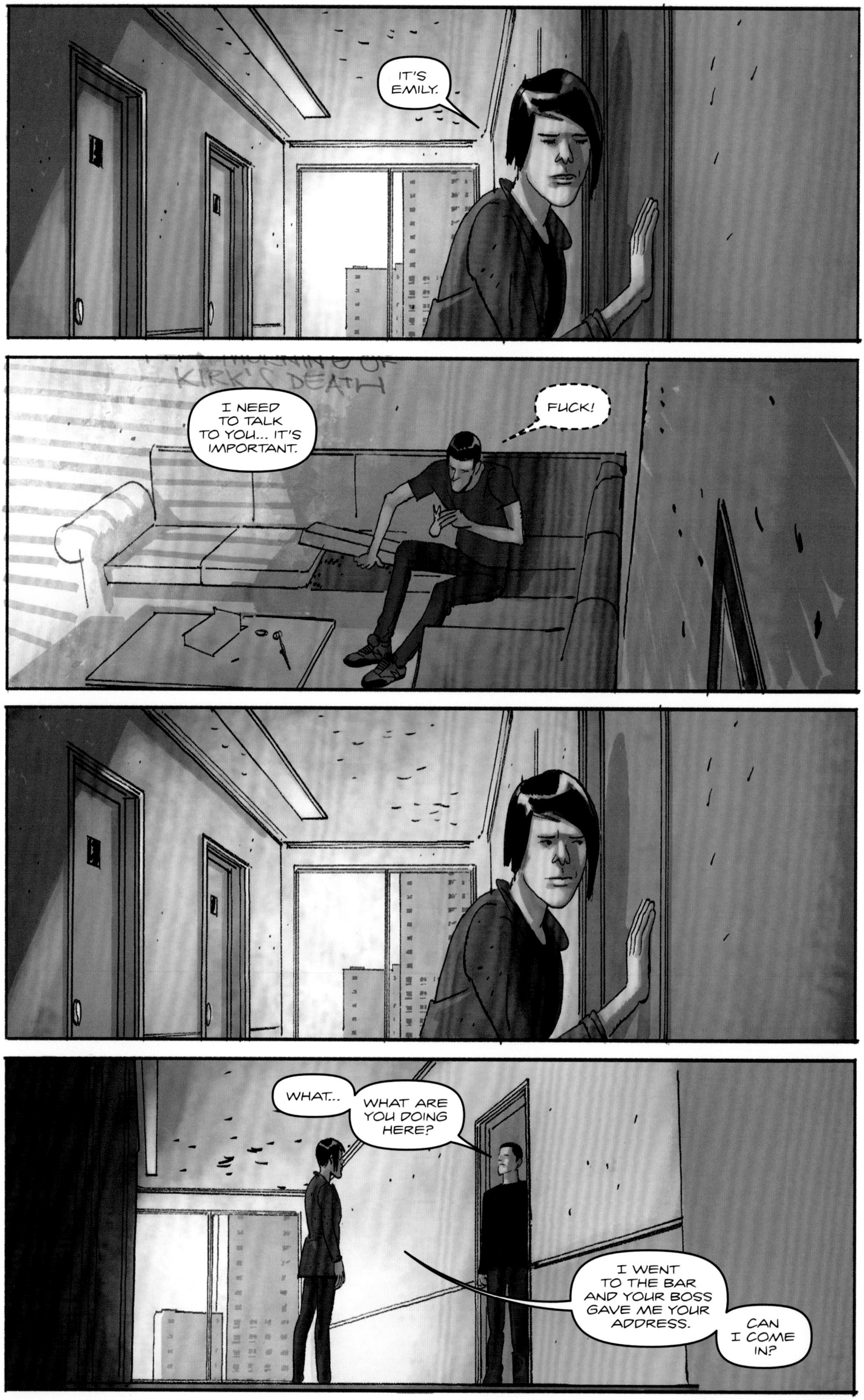
IT'S EMILY.
I NEED TO TALK TO YOU... IT'S IMPORTANT.
FUCK!
WHAT...
WHAT ARE YOU DOING HERE?
I WENT TO THE BAR AND YOUR BOSS GAVE ME YOUR ADDRESS.
CAN I COME IN?

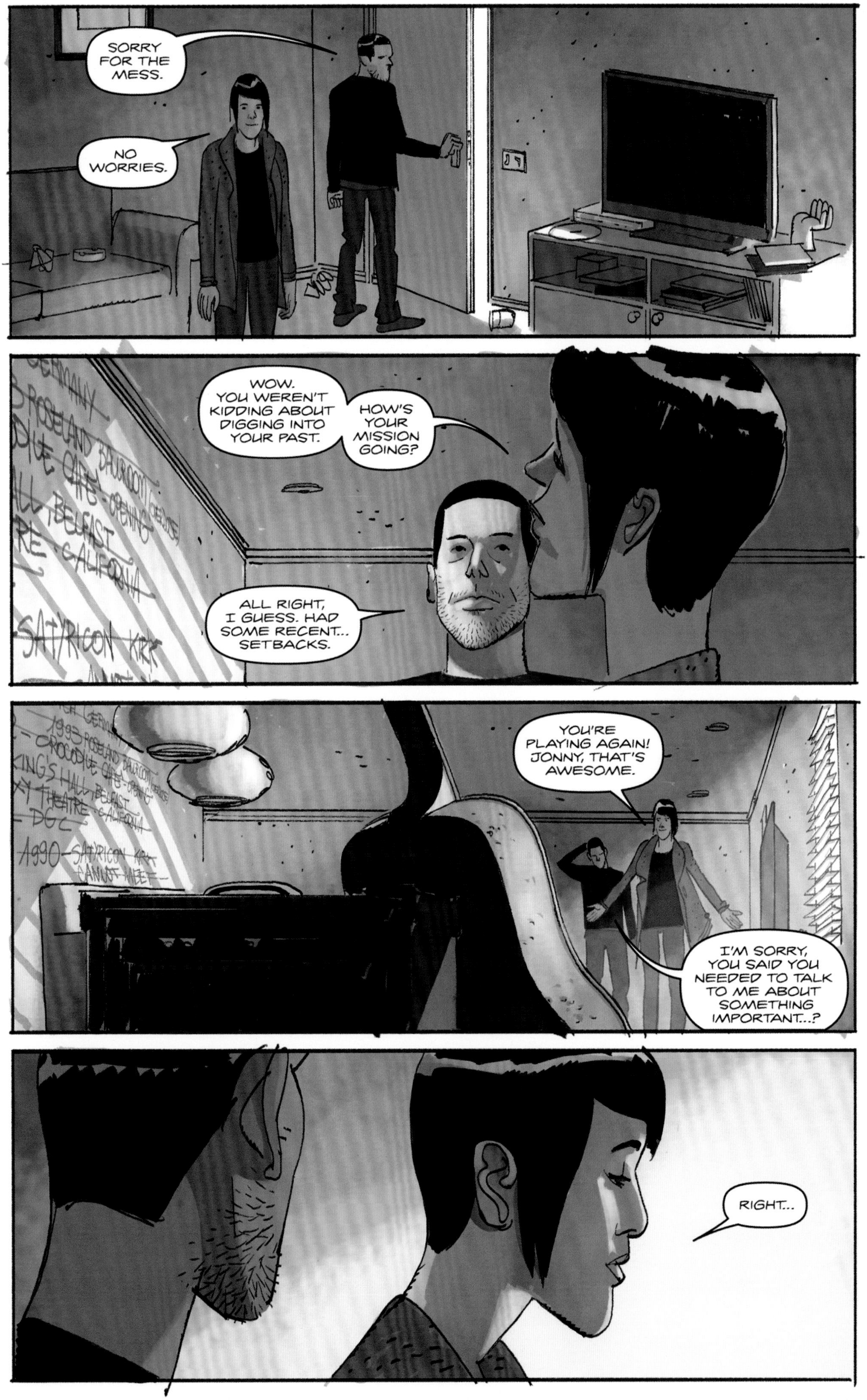
SORRY FOR THE MESS.
NO WORRIES.
WOW. YOU WEREN'T KIDDING ABOUT DIGGING INTO YOUR PAST.
HOW'S YOUR MISSION GOING?
ALL RIGHT, I GUESS. HAD SOME RECENT... SETBACKS.
YOU'RE PLAYING AGAIN! JONNY, THAT'S AWESOME.
I'M SORRY, YOU SAID YOU NEEDED TO TALK TO ME ABOUT SOMETHING IMPORTANT...?
RIGHT...

REMEMBER OUR FIRST CONVERSATION AT MERCHANT'S?

WHEN WE DISCUSSED OUR PASSIONS?

...YEAH.

WELL, OUR PASSIONS SORT OF *PARALLEL* EACH OTHER.

YOU SEE, I'M A FREELANCE JOURNALIST...

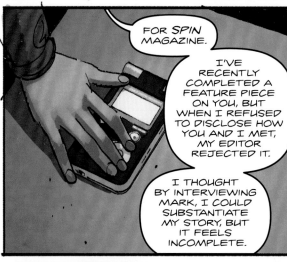

FOR *SPIN* MAGAZINE.

I'VE RECENTLY COMPLETED A FEATURE PIECE ON YOU, BUT WHEN I REFUSED TO DISCLOSE HOW YOU AND I MET, MY EDITOR REJECTED IT.

I THOUGHT BY INTERVIEWING MARK, I COULD SUBSTANTIATE MY STORY, BUT IT FEELS INCOMPLETE.

YOU... SPOKE TO MARK?

I KNOW THIS LOOKS BAD... LIKE REALLY BAD. BUT YOU NEED TO KNOW SOMETHING ABOUT ME.

TO SAY I WAS A SAMSARA FAN WOULD BE A GROSS UNDERSTATEMENT. TRUTH IS...

I *ADORED* YOU GUYS. YOUR MUSIC WAS SO FUCKING SPECIAL.

KIRK'S DEATH...DRUGS WERE THE ONLY THING THAT COULD NUMB MY PAIN, BUT THEN I FOUND GROUP.

YOUR PAIN? *YOUR* PAIN?!

HE WAS MY BEST FRIEND, EMILY! MY LIFE ISN'T FUCKING ENTERTAINMENT!

IS THAT WHY YOU WANTED TO BE MY SPONSOR? TO GET EVEN MORE DIRT ON ME?!

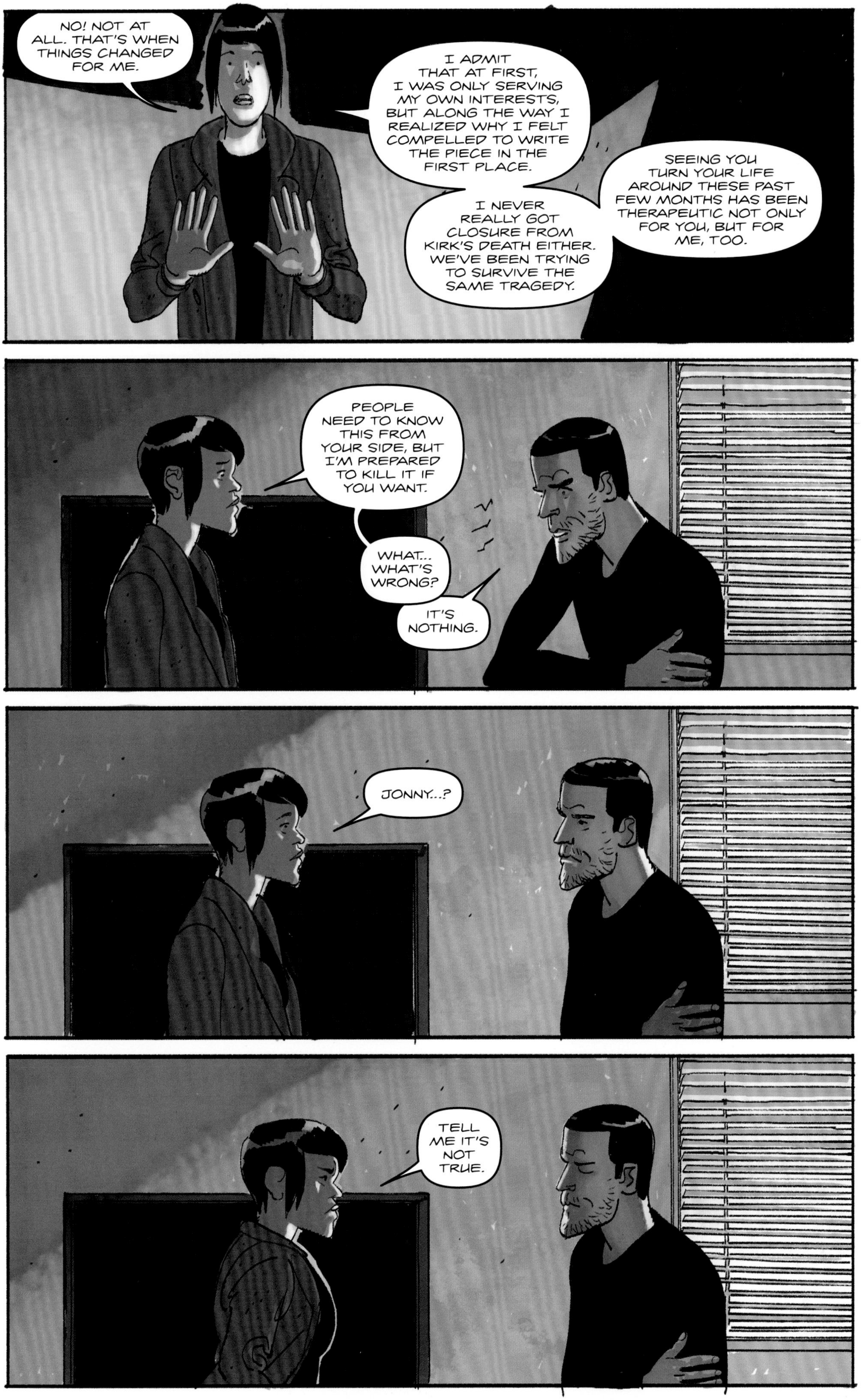
NO! NOT AT ALL. THAT'S WHEN THINGS CHANGED FOR ME.
I ADMIT THAT AT FIRST, I WAS ONLY SERVING MY OWN INTERESTS, BUT ALONG THE WAY I REALIZED WHY I FELT COMPELLED TO WRITE THE PIECE IN THE FIRST PLACE.
I NEVER REALLY GOT CLOSURE FROM KIRK'S DEATH EITHER. WE'VE BEEN TRYING TO SURVIVE THE SAME TRAGEDY.
SEEING YOU TURN YOUR LIFE AROUND THESE PAST FEW MONTHS HAS BEEN THERAPEUTIC NOT ONLY FOR YOU, BUT FOR ME, TOO.
PEOPLE NEED TO KNOW THIS FROM YOUR SIDE, BUT I'M PREPARED TO KILL IT IF YOU WANT.
WHAT... WHAT'S WRONG?
IT'S NOTHING.
JONNY...?
TELL ME IT'S NOT TRUE.

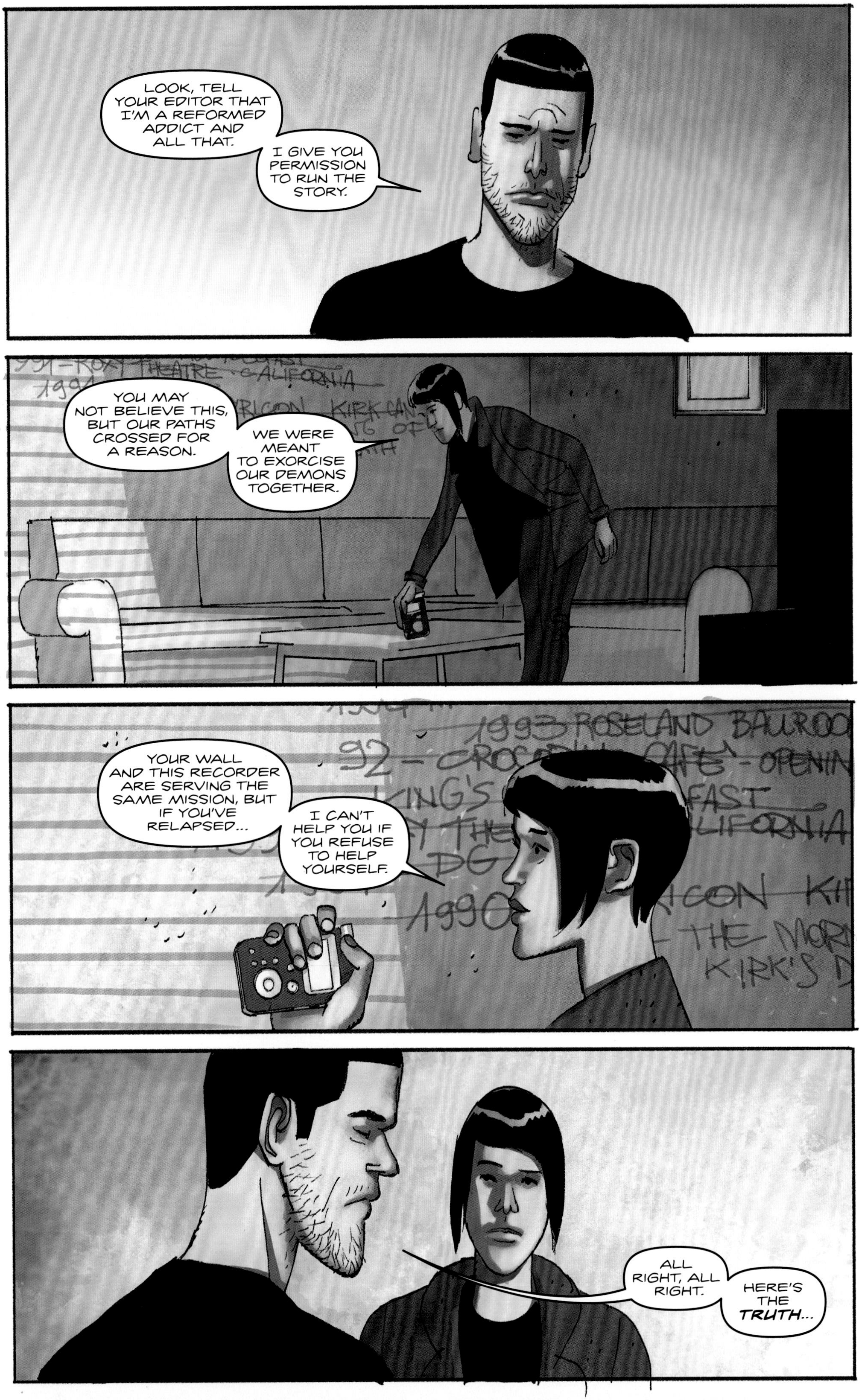
LOOK, TELL YOUR EDITOR THAT I'M A REFORMED ADDICT AND ALL THAT.
I GIVE YOU PERMISSION TO RUN THE STORY.
YOU MAY NOT BELIEVE THIS, BUT OUR PATHS CROSSED FOR A REASON.
WE WERE MEANT TO EXORCISE OUR DEMONS TOGETHER.
YOUR WALL AND THIS RECORDER ARE SERVING THE SAME MISSION, BUT IF YOU'VE RELAPSED...
I CAN'T HELP YOU IF YOU REFUSE TO HELP YOURSELF.
ALL RIGHT, ALL RIGHT.
HERE'S THE *TRUTH*...

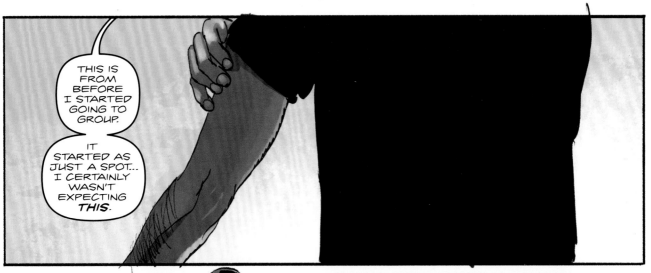

THIS IS FROM BEFORE I STARTED GOING TO GROUP.

IT STARTED AS JUST A SPOT... I CERTAINLY WASN'T EXPECTING **THIS**.

JESUS, JONNY...YOU NEED TO SEE A DOCTOR.

I WILL...

BUT FIRST I HAVE SOMETHING TO TELL YOU.

MY MISSION GOING BACK INTO MY PAST HASN'T BEEN **FIGURATIVE**... IT'S BEEN **LITERAL**.

THIS GUITAR IS CAPABLE OF TIME TRAVEL.

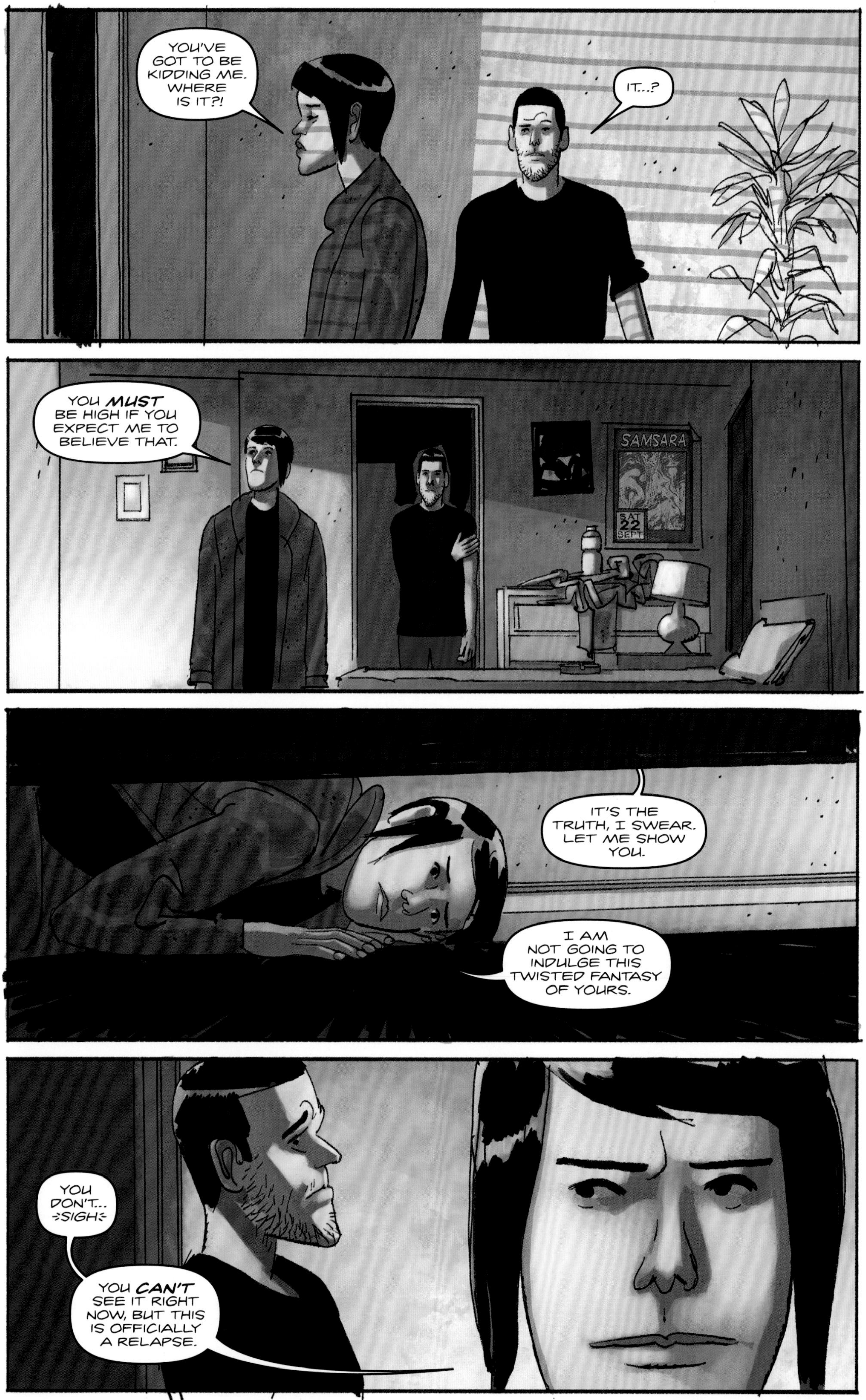
YOU'VE GOT TO BE KIDDING ME. WHERE IS IT?!
IT...?
YOU MUST BE HIGH IF YOU EXPECT ME TO BELIEVE THAT.
SAMSARA
SAT 22 SEPT
IT'S THE TRUTH, I SWEAR. LET ME SHOW YOU.
I AM NOT GOING TO INDULGE THIS TWISTED FANTASY OF YOURS.
YOU DON'T... SIGH
YOU CAN'T SEE IT RIGHT NOW, BUT THIS IS OFFICIALLY A RELAPSE.

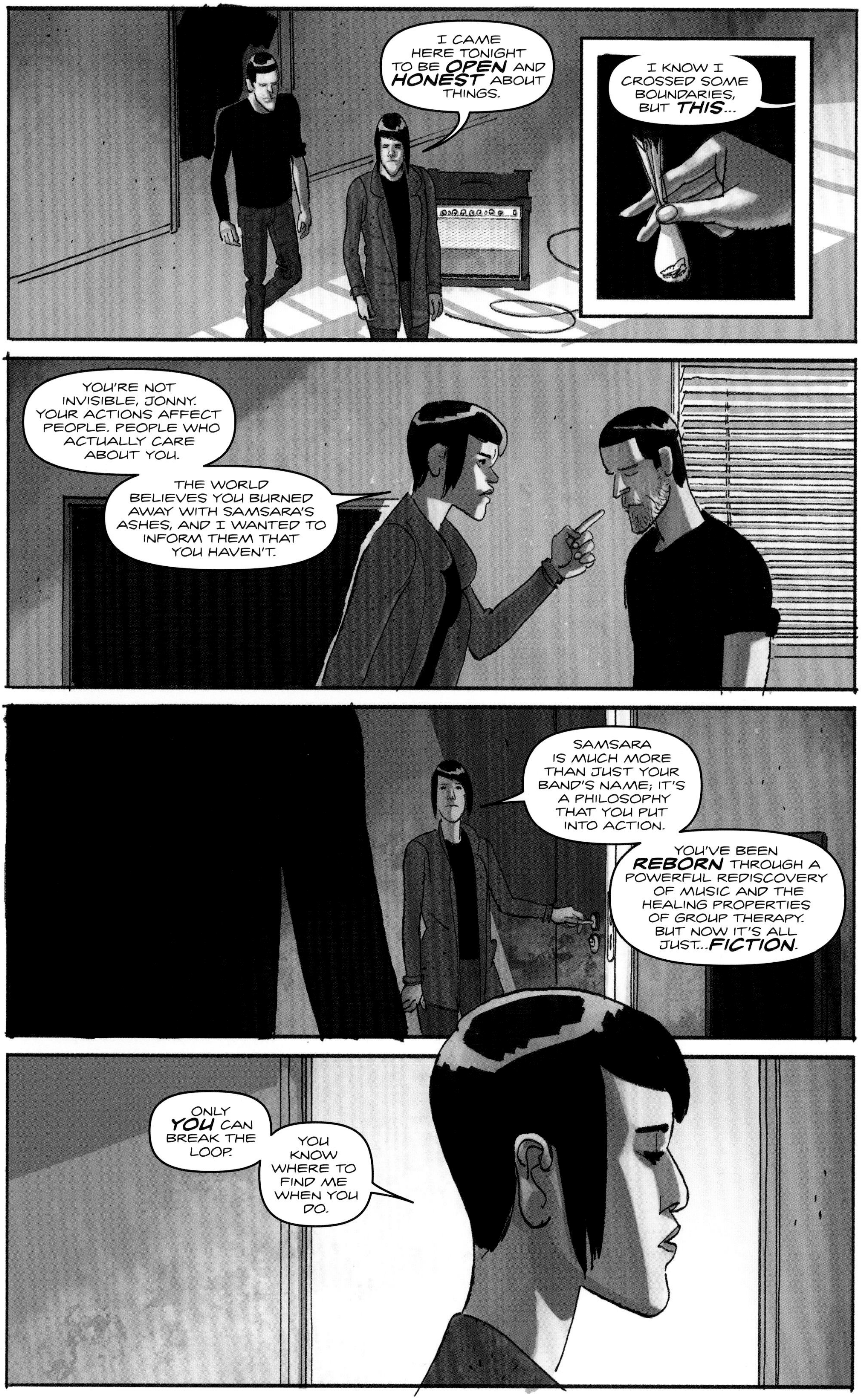
I CAME HERE TONIGHT TO BE OPEN AND HONEST ABOUT THINGS.
I KNOW I CROSSED SOME BOUNDARIES, BUT THIS...
YOU'RE NOT INVISIBLE, JONNY. YOUR ACTIONS AFFECT PEOPLE. PEOPLE WHO ACTUALLY CARE ABOUT YOU.
THE WORLD BELIEVES YOU BURNED AWAY WITH SAMSARA'S ASHES, AND I WANTED TO INFORM THEM THAT YOU HAVEN'T.
SAMSARA IS MUCH MORE THAN JUST YOUR BAND'S NAME; IT'S A PHILOSOPHY THAT YOU PUT INTO ACTION.
YOU'VE BEEN REBORN THROUGH A POWERFUL REDISCOVERY OF MUSIC AND THE HEALING PROPERTIES OF GROUP THERAPY. BUT NOW IT'S ALL JUST...FICTION.
ONLY YOU CAN BREAK THE LOOP.
YOU KNOW WHERE TO FIND ME WHEN YOU DO.

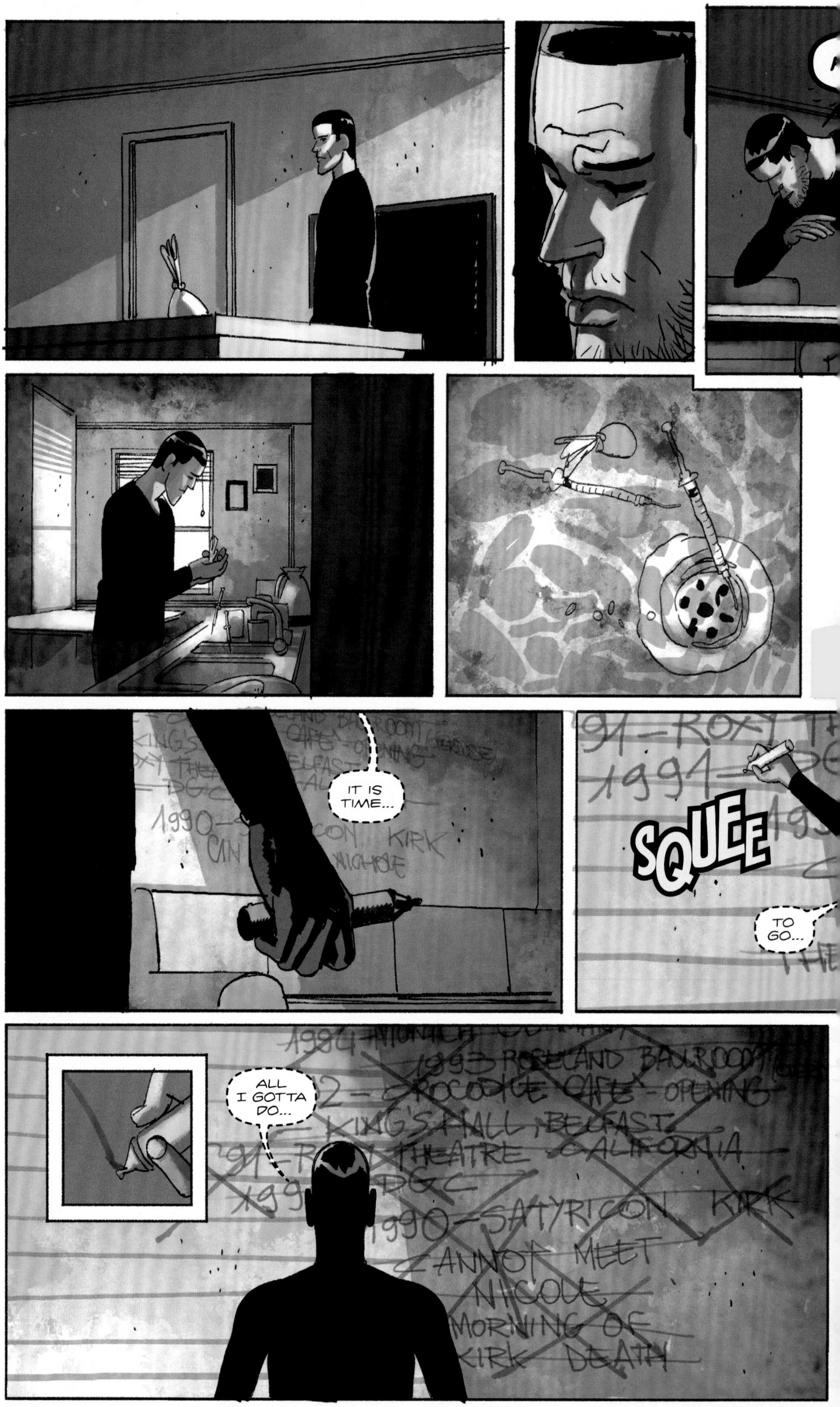
IT IS TIME...
SQUEEE
TO GO...
ALL I GOTTA DO...
1993 ROSELAND BALLROOM
KING'S HALL BELFAST
THEATRE CALIFORNIA
DGC
1990-SATYRICON KIRK
CANNOT MEET
NICOLE
MORNING OF
KIRK DEATH

KLIK

ONLY YOU CAN BREAK...THE LOOP.

I THINK...

SQUEEEEEE

AND STAY GONE.

LOOP THE PLAYBACK.

SQUESQUEE-FK SQUEEFK SQLQUEE-FK SQUEEK

FIONA'S HAIR SALON

I'LL SEE YOU SOON, KIRK.

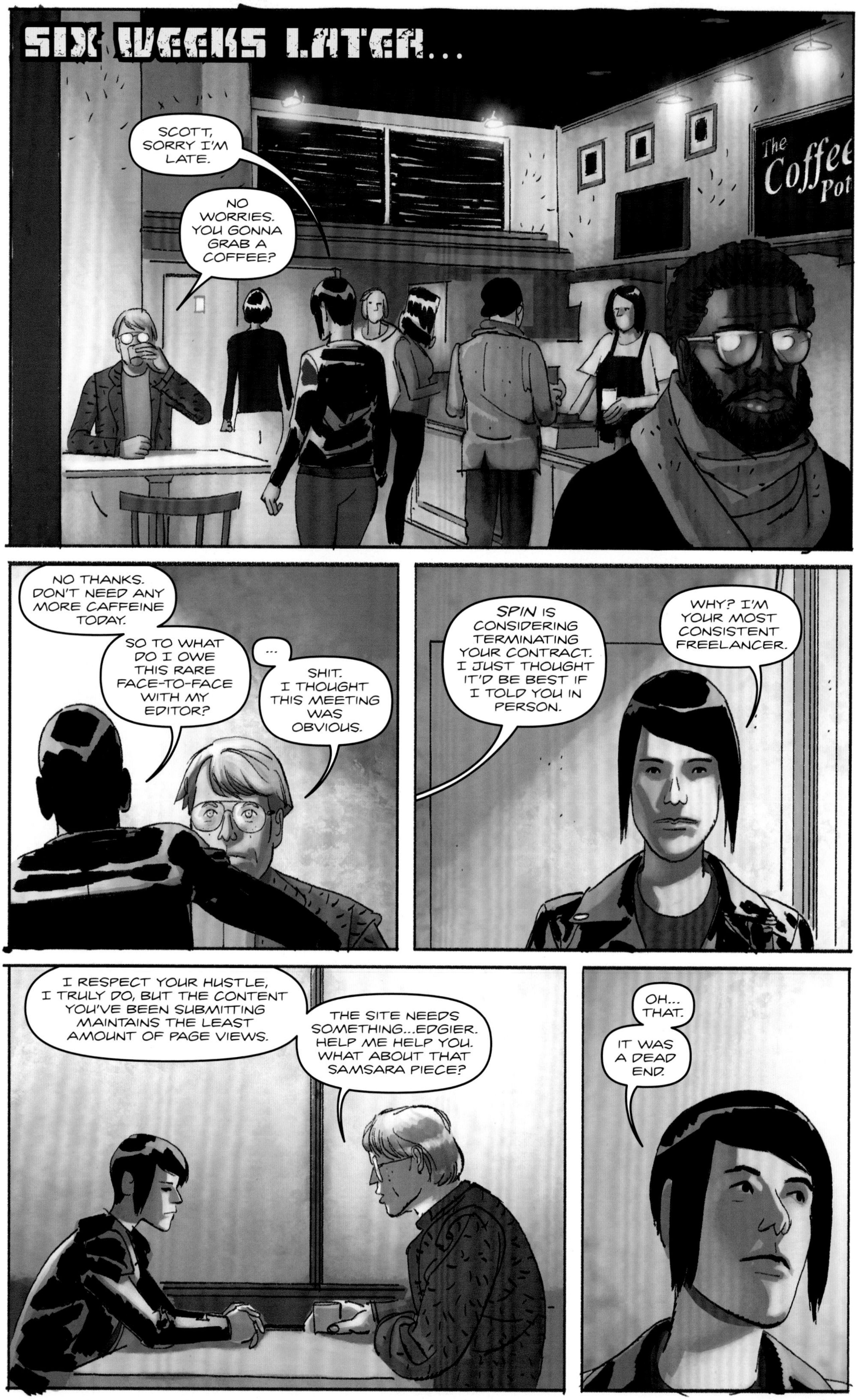
SIX WEEKS LATER...
SCOTT, SORRY I'M LATE.
NO WORRIES. YOU GONNA GRAB A COFFEE?
The Coffee Pot
NO THANKS. DON'T NEED ANY MORE CAFFEINE TODAY.
SO TO WHAT DO I OWE THIS RARE FACE-TO-FACE WITH MY EDITOR?
...
SHIT. I THOUGHT THIS MEETING WAS OBVIOUS.
SPIN IS CONSIDERING TERMINATING YOUR CONTRACT. I JUST THOUGHT IT'D BE BEST IF I TOLD YOU IN PERSON.
WHY? I'M YOUR MOST CONSISTENT FREELANCER.
I RESPECT YOUR HUSTLE, I TRULY DO, BUT THE CONTENT YOU'VE BEEN SUBMITTING MAINTAINS THE LEAST AMOUNT OF PAGE VIEWS.
THE SITE NEEDS SOMETHING...EDGIER. HELP ME HELP YOU. WHAT ABOUT THAT SAMSARA PIECE?
OH... THAT.
IT WAS A DEAD END.

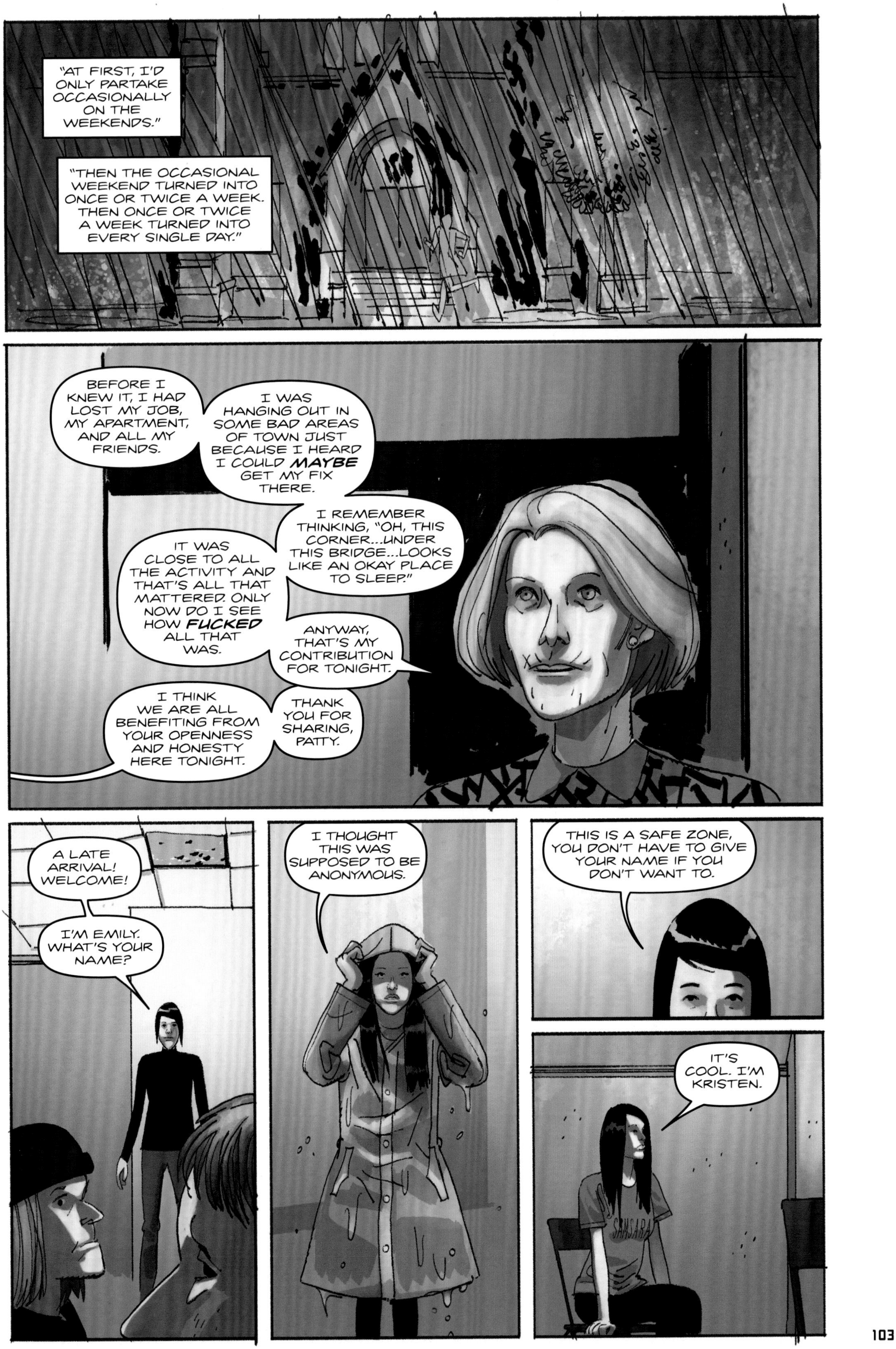
"AT FIRST, I'D ONLY PARTAKE OCCASIONALLY ON THE WEEKENDS."
"THEN THE OCCASIONAL WEEKEND TURNED INTO ONCE OR TWICE A WEEK. THEN ONCE OR TWICE A WEEK TURNED INTO EVERY SINGLE DAY."
BEFORE I KNEW IT, I HAD LOST MY JOB, MY APARTMENT, AND ALL MY FRIENDS.
I WAS HANGING OUT IN SOME BAD AREAS OF TOWN JUST BECAUSE I HEARD I COULD ***MAYBE*** GET MY FIX THERE.
I REMEMBER THINKING, "OH, THIS CORNER...UNDER THIS BRIDGE...LOOKS LIKE AN OKAY PLACE TO SLEEP."
IT WAS CLOSE TO ALL THE ACTIVITY AND THAT'S ALL THAT MATTERED. ONLY NOW DO I SEE HOW ***FUCKED*** ALL THAT WAS.
ANYWAY, THAT'S MY CONTRIBUTION FOR TONIGHT.
THANK YOU FOR SHARING, PATTY.
I THINK WE ARE ALL BENEFITING FROM YOUR OPENNESS AND HONESTY HERE TONIGHT.
A LATE ARRIVAL! WELCOME!
I'M EMILY. WHAT'S YOUR NAME?
I THOUGHT THIS WAS SUPPOSED TO BE ANONYMOUS.
THIS IS A SAFE ZONE, YOU DON'T HAVE TO GIVE YOUR NAME IF YOU DON'T WANT TO.
IT'S COOL. I'M KRISTEN.
SAMSARA

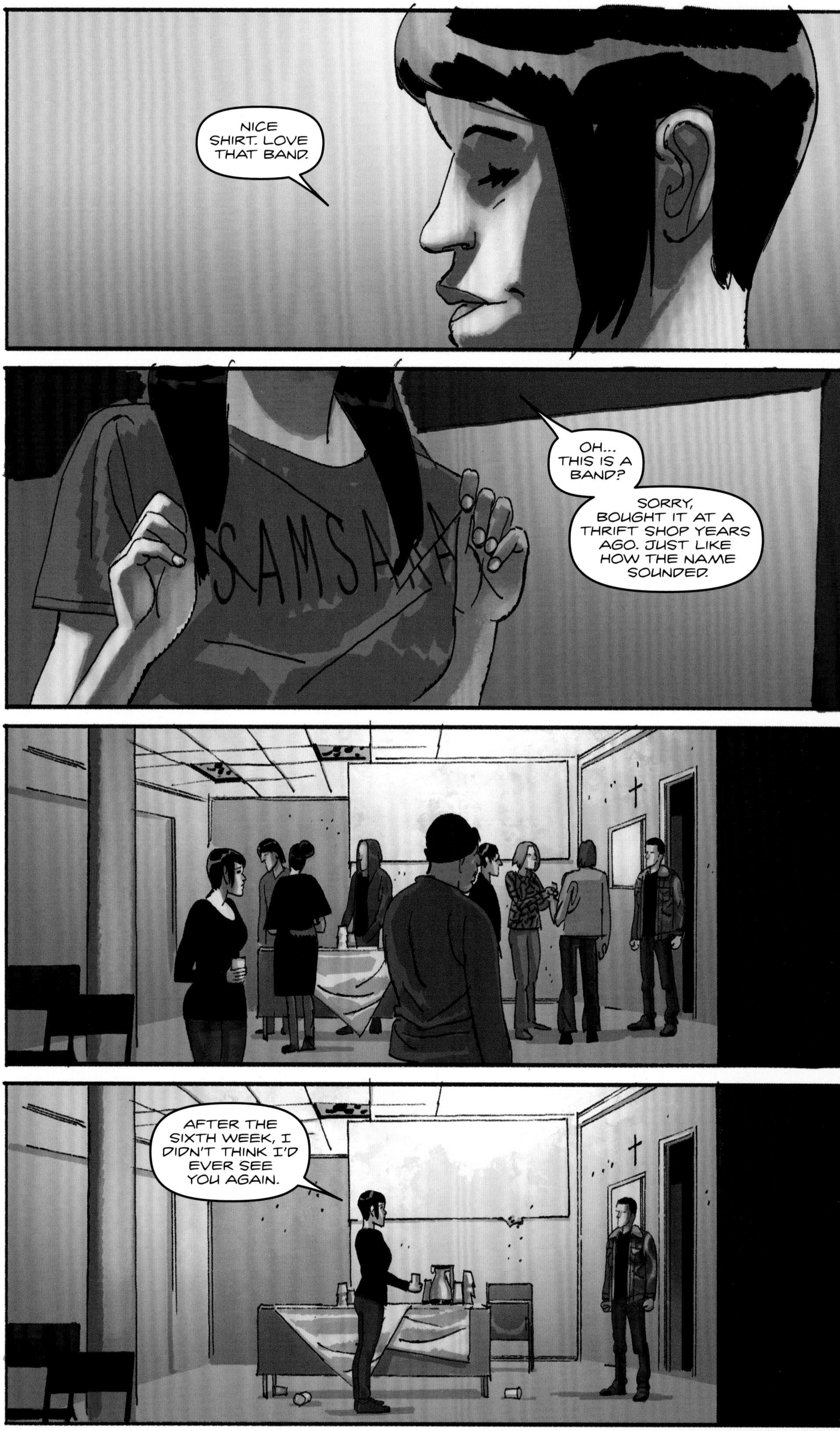
NICE SHIRT. LOVE THAT BAND.
SAMSARA
OH... THIS IS A BAND?
SORRY, BOUGHT IT AT A THRIFT SHOP YEARS AGO. JUST LIKE HOW THE NAME SOUNDED.
AFTER THE SIXTH WEEK, I DIDN'T THINK I'D EVER SEE YOU AGAIN.

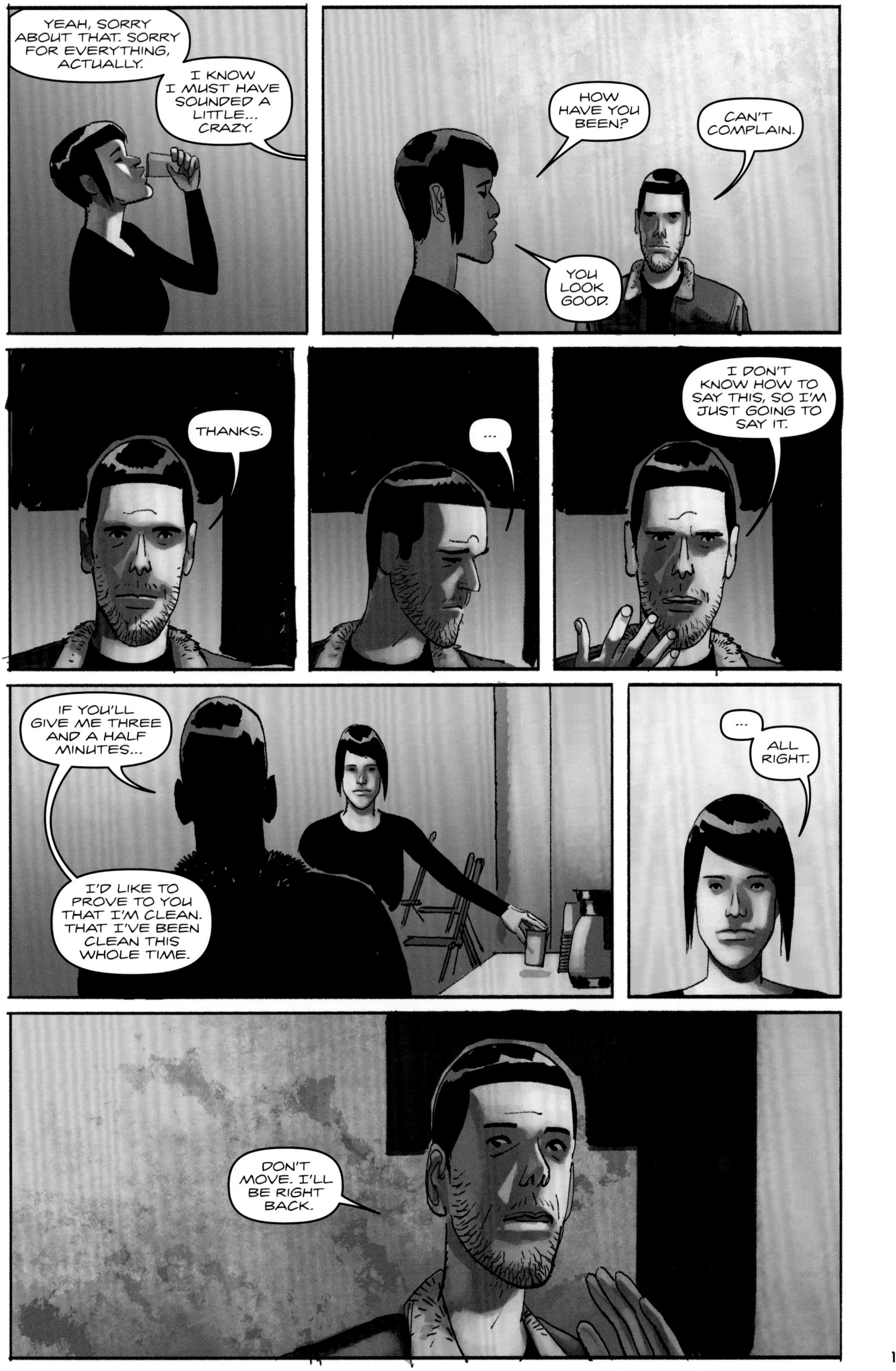
YEAH, SORRY ABOUT THAT. SORRY FOR EVERYTHING, ACTUALLY.
I KNOW I MUST HAVE SOUNDED A LITTLE... CRAZY.
HOW HAVE YOU BEEN?
CAN'T COMPLAIN.
YOU LOOK GOOD.
THANKS.
...
I DON'T KNOW HOW TO SAY THIS, SO I'M JUST GOING TO SAY IT.
IF YOU'LL GIVE ME THREE AND A HALF MINUTES...
I'D LIKE TO PROVE TO YOU THAT I'M CLEAN. THAT I'VE BEEN CLEAN THIS WHOLE TIME.
...
ALL RIGHT.
DON'T MOVE. I'LL BE RIGHT BACK.

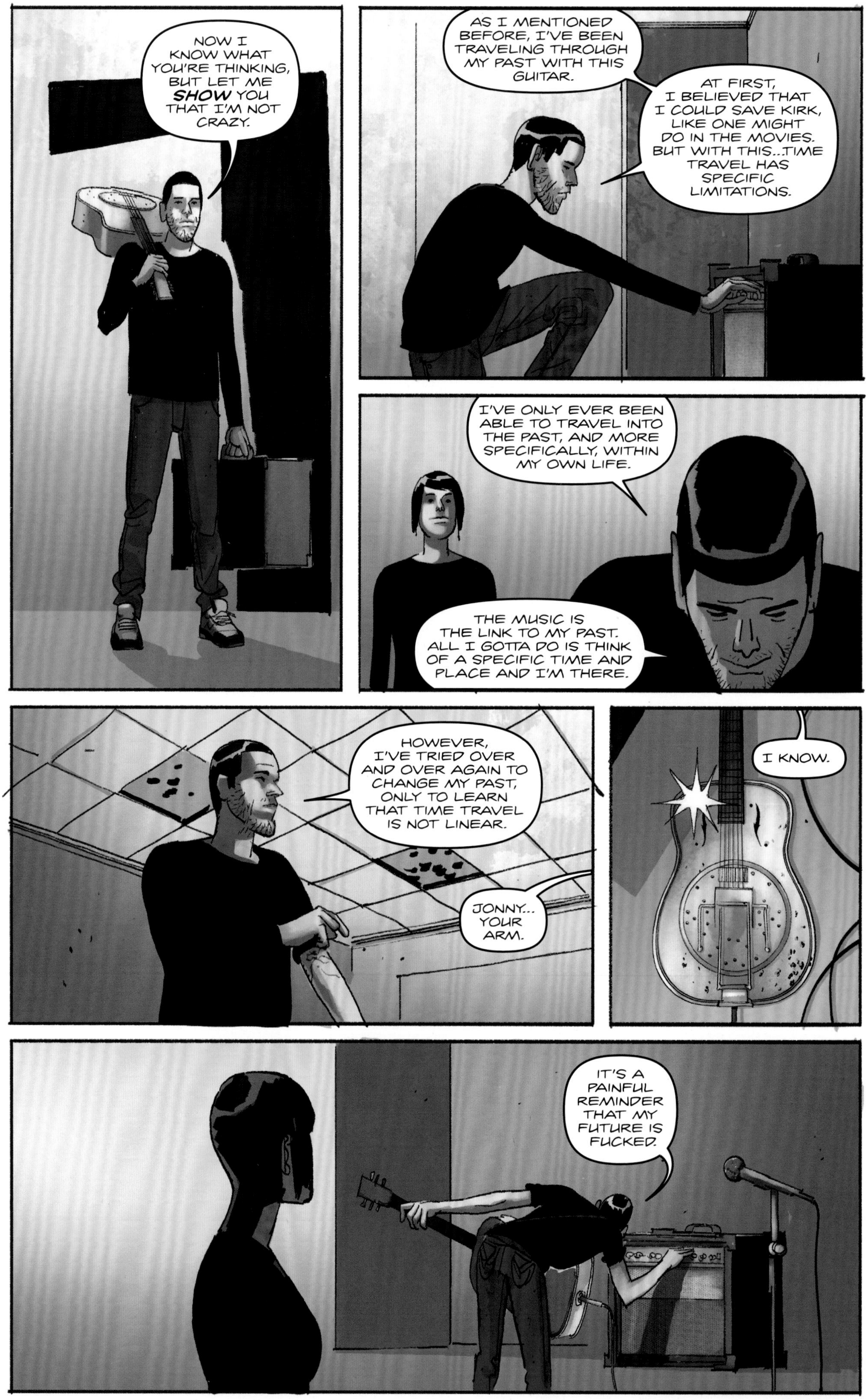
NOW I KNOW WHAT YOU'RE THINKING, BUT LET ME **SHOW** YOU THAT I'M NOT CRAZY.
AS I MENTIONED BEFORE, I'VE BEEN TRAVELING THROUGH MY PAST WITH THIS GUITAR.
AT FIRST, I BELIEVED THAT I COULD SAVE KIRK, LIKE ONE MIGHT DO IN THE MOVIES. BUT WITH THIS...TIME TRAVEL HAS SPECIFIC LIMITATIONS.
I'VE ONLY EVER BEEN ABLE TO TRAVEL INTO THE PAST, AND MORE SPECIFICALLY, WITHIN MY OWN LIFE.
THE MUSIC IS THE LINK TO MY PAST. ALL I GOTTA DO IS THINK OF A SPECIFIC TIME AND PLACE AND I'M THERE.
HOWEVER, I'VE TRIED OVER AND OVER AGAIN TO CHANGE MY PAST, ONLY TO LEARN THAT TIME TRAVEL IS NOT LINEAR.
JONNY... YOUR ARM.
I KNOW.
IT'S A PAINFUL REMINDER THAT MY FUTURE IS FUCKED.

LOOK, I KNOW HOW CRAZY THIS ALL SOUNDS. I DIDN'T BELIEVE IT THE FIRST TIME I ACCIDENTALLY MADE THE JUMP.
WHEN I REALIZED WHAT THIS GUITAR IS CAPABLE OF, I THOUGHT IT WAS A SOLUTION TO ALL OF MY PROBLEMS, BUT IT WASN'T.
AFTER A LIFETIME OF FAILED ATTEMPTS TO SAVE KIRK, I WAS CONVINCED THIS THING WAS A CURSE. THAT WAS UNTIL...
I MET YOU.
BY HELPING ME UNDERSTAND HOW MY PAIN WORKS, YOU HELPED ME UNDERSTAND HOW THIS GUITAR WORKS.
I CAME HERE TONIGHT TO SAY THANK YOU... THANK YOU FOR PROVIDING ME A SPACE TO HEAL, FREE OF JUDGEMENT.
YOU WERE RIGHT ABOUT A MULTIVERSE AND ABOUT ME.
I HAVE BEEN REBORN...
JUST ON THE WRONG PLANE OF MY EXISTENCE.

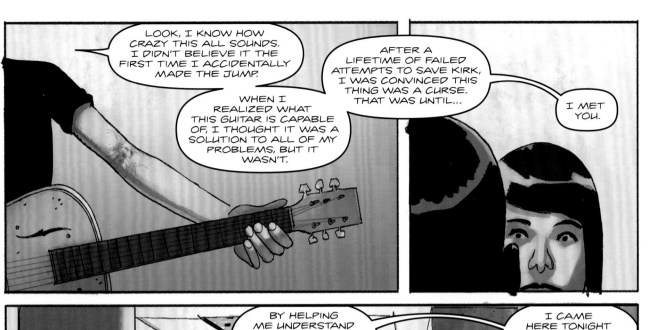

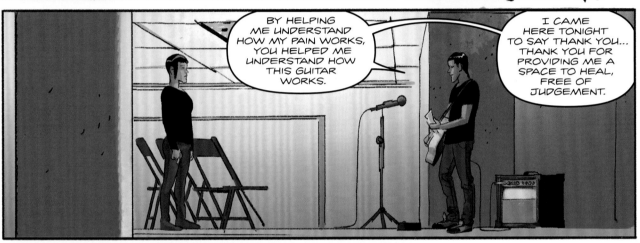

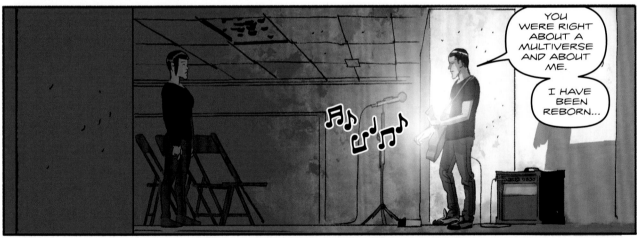

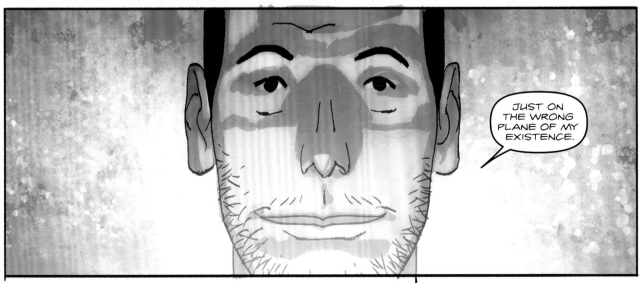

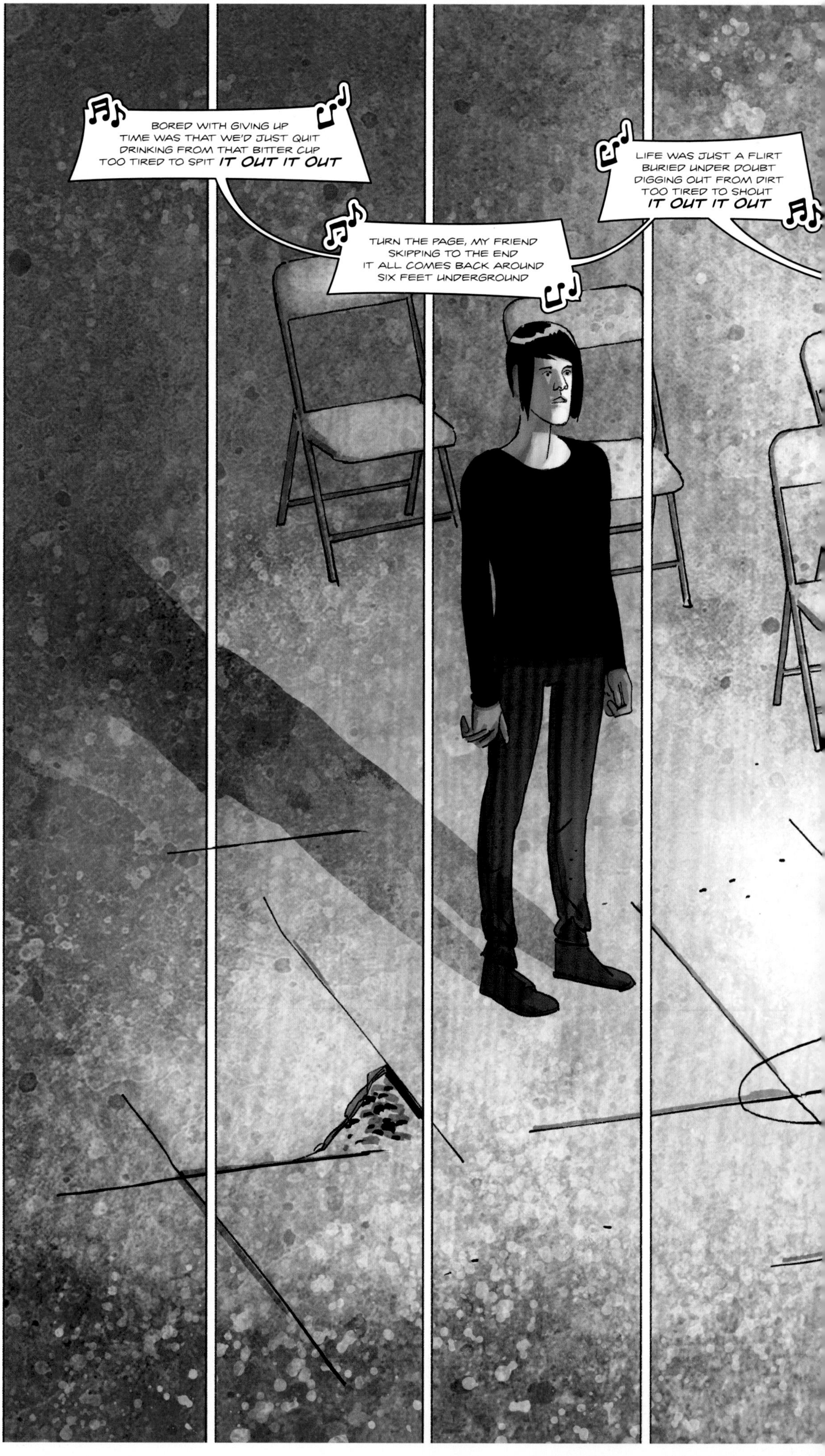
BORED WITH GIVING UP
TIME WAS THAT WE'D JUST QUIT
DRINKING FROM THAT BITTER CUP
TOO TIRED TO SPIT IT OUT IT OUT
TURN THE PAGE, MY FRIEND
SKIPPING TO THE END
IT ALL COMES BACK AROUND
SIX FEET UNDERGROUND
LIFE WAS JUST A FLIRT
BURIED UNDER DOUBT
DIGGING OUT FROM DIRT
TOO TIRED TO SHOUT
IT OUT IT OUT

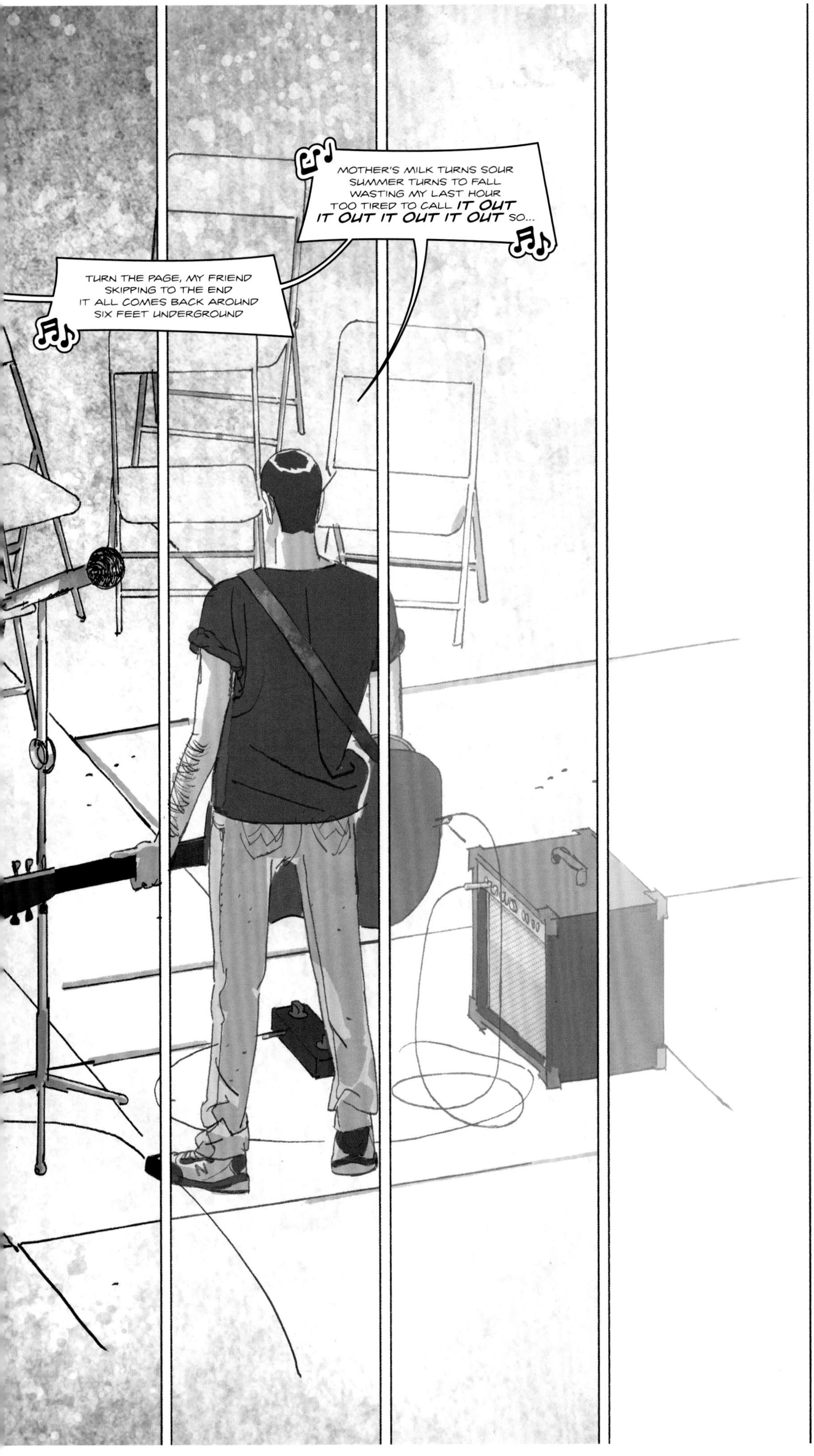
TURN THE PAGE, MY FRIEND SKIPPING TO THE END IT ALL COMES BACK AROUND SIX FEET UNDERGROUND
MOTHER'S MILK TURNS SOUR SUMMER TURNS TO FALL WASTING MY LAST HOUR TOO TIRED TO CALL IT OUT IT OUT IT OUT IT OUT SO...

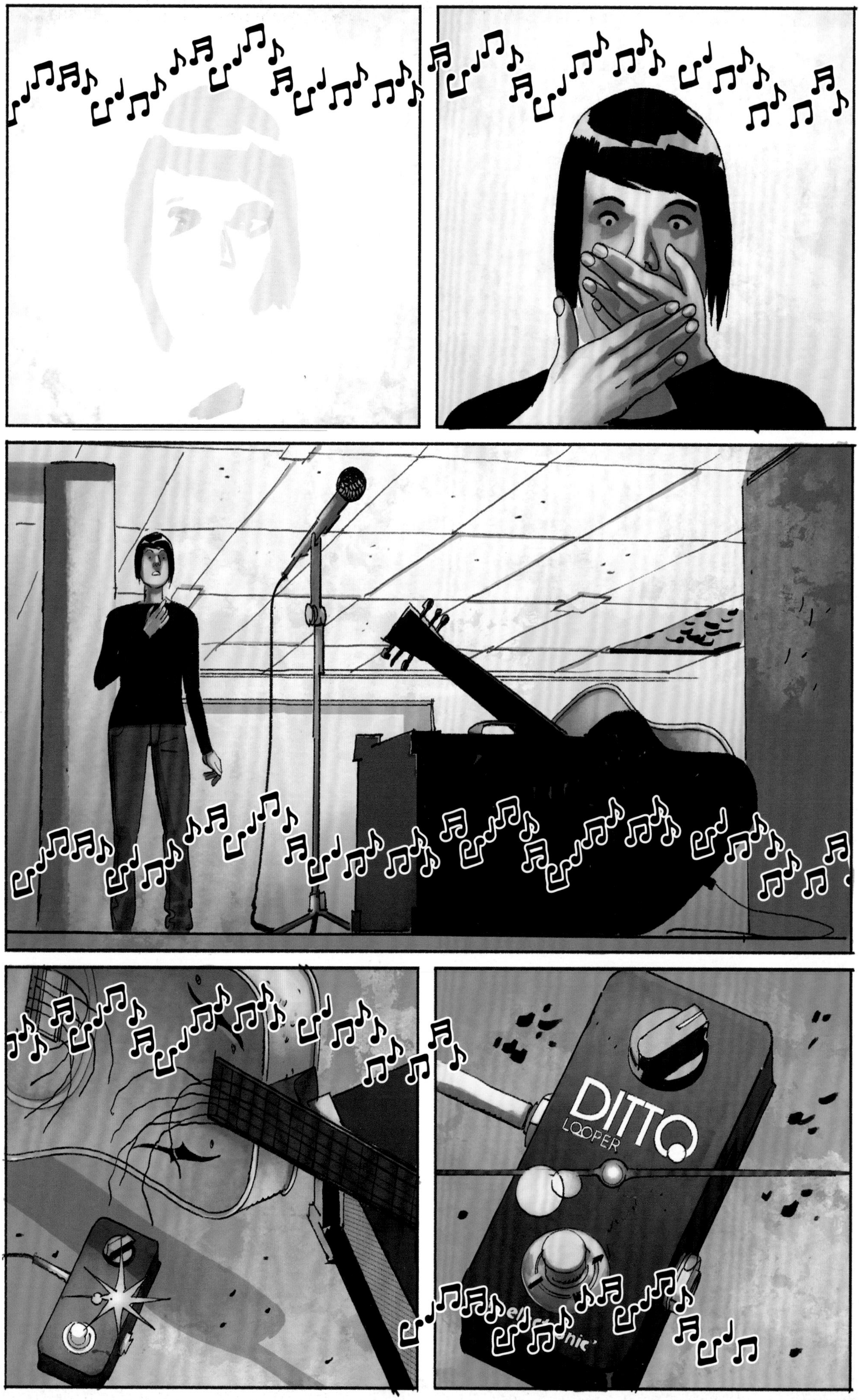
DITTO
LOOPER

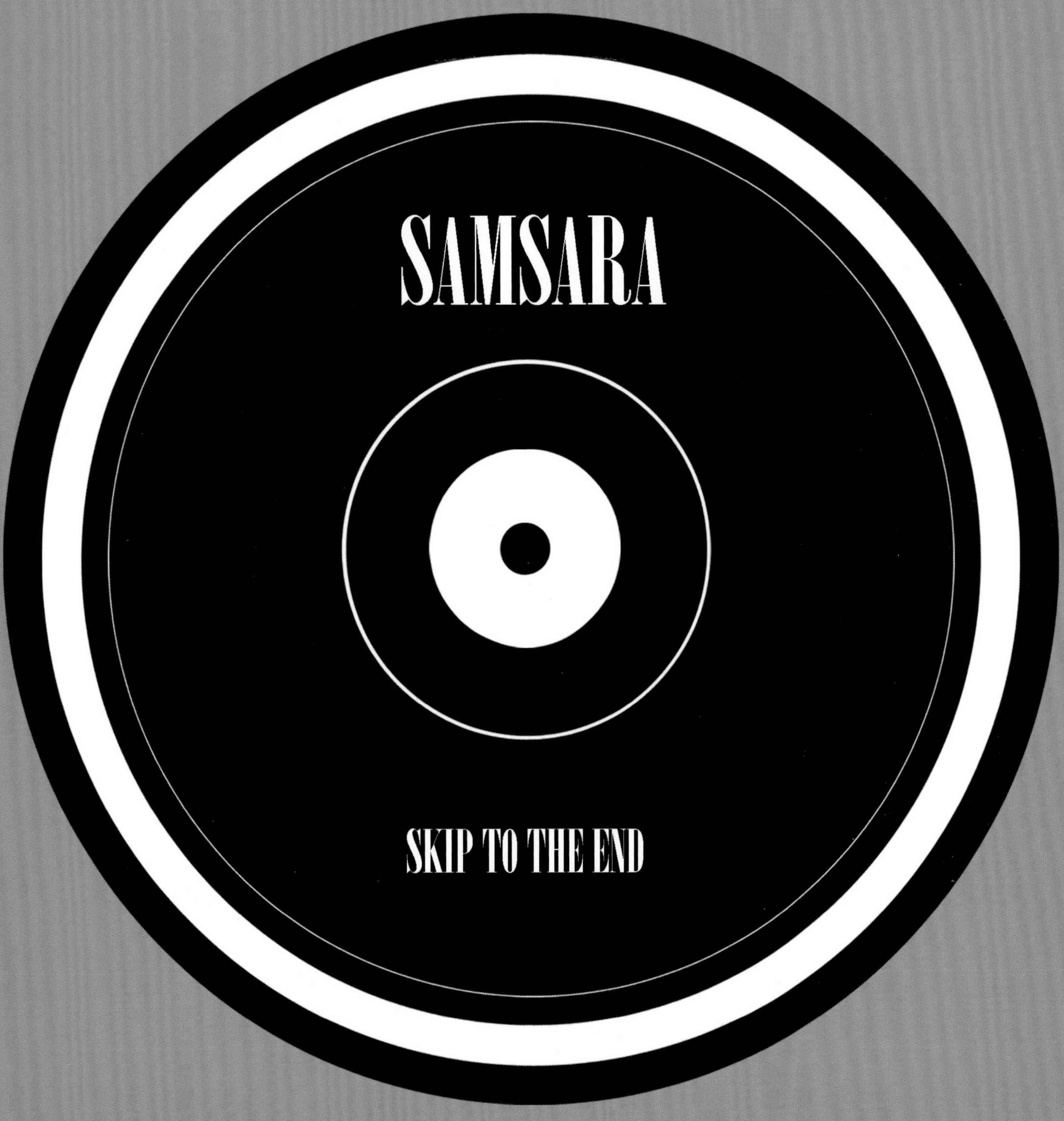
SAMSARA
SKIP TO THE END

An Imprint of Insight Editions
PO Box 3088
San Rafael, CA 94912
www.insightcomics.com

Find us on Facebook:
www.facebook.com/InsightEditionsComics

Follow us on Twitter:
@insightcomics

Follow us on Instagram:
@Insight_Comics

Library of Congress Cataloging-in-Publication Data available.

ISBN: 978-1-68383-439-7

Publisher: Raoul Goff
Associate Publisher: Vanessa Lopez
Art Director: Chrissy Kwasnik
Executive Editor: Mark Irwin
Managing Editor: Alan Kaplan
Editorial Assistant: Holly Fisher
Senior Production Editor: Elaine Ou
Production Manager: Greg Steffen

ROOTS of PEACE REPLANTED PAPER

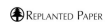

Insight Editions, in association with Roots of Peace, will plant two trees for each tree used in the manufacturing of this book. Roots of Peace is an internationally renowned humanitarian organization dedicated to eradicating land mines worldwide and converting war-torn lands into productive farms and wildlife habitats. Roots of Peace will plant two million fruit and nut trees in Afghanistan and provide farmers there with the skills and support necessary for sustainable land use.

Manufactured in China by Insight Editions

10 9 8 7 6 5 4 3 2 1

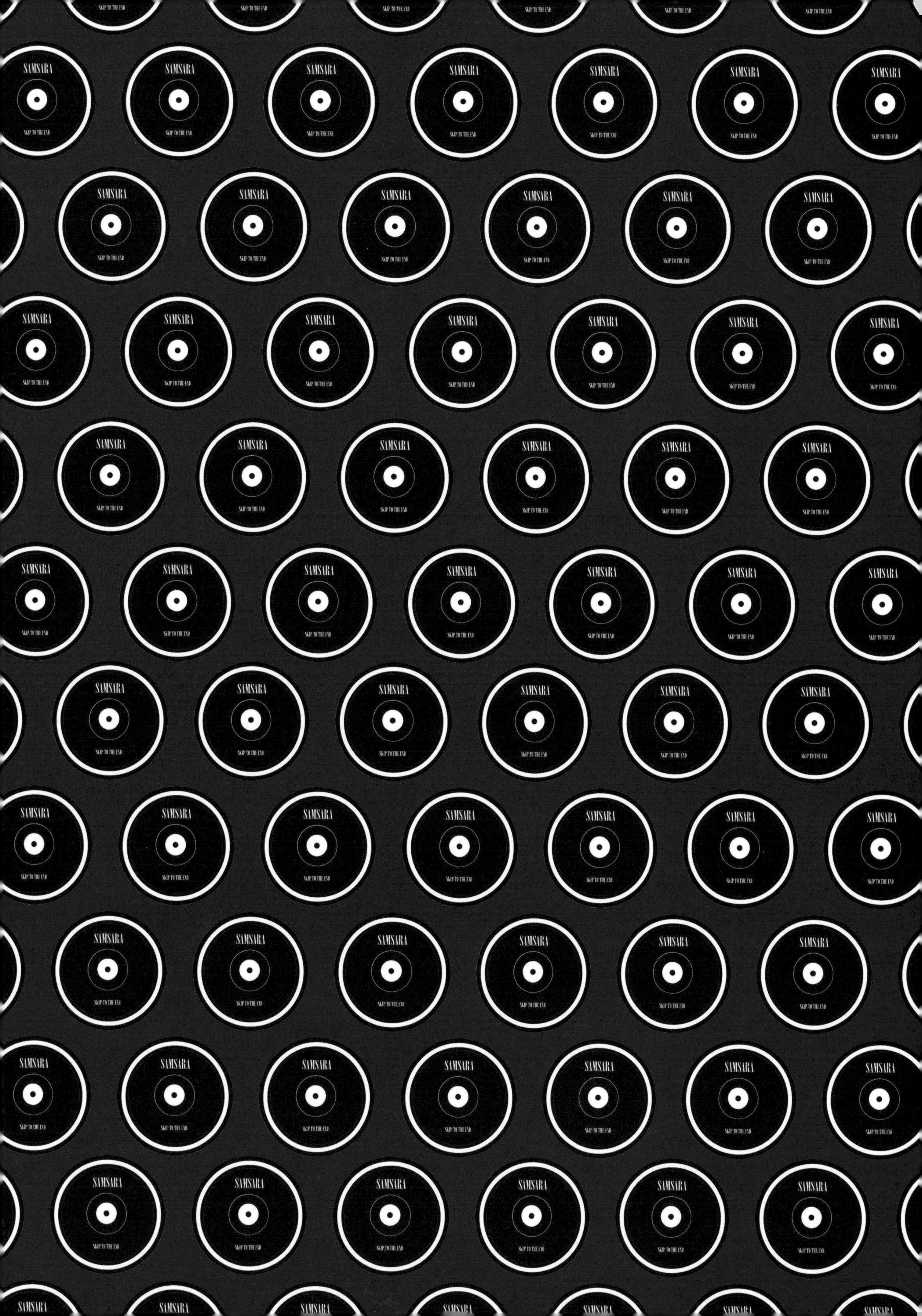
SAMSARA
SKIP TO THE END

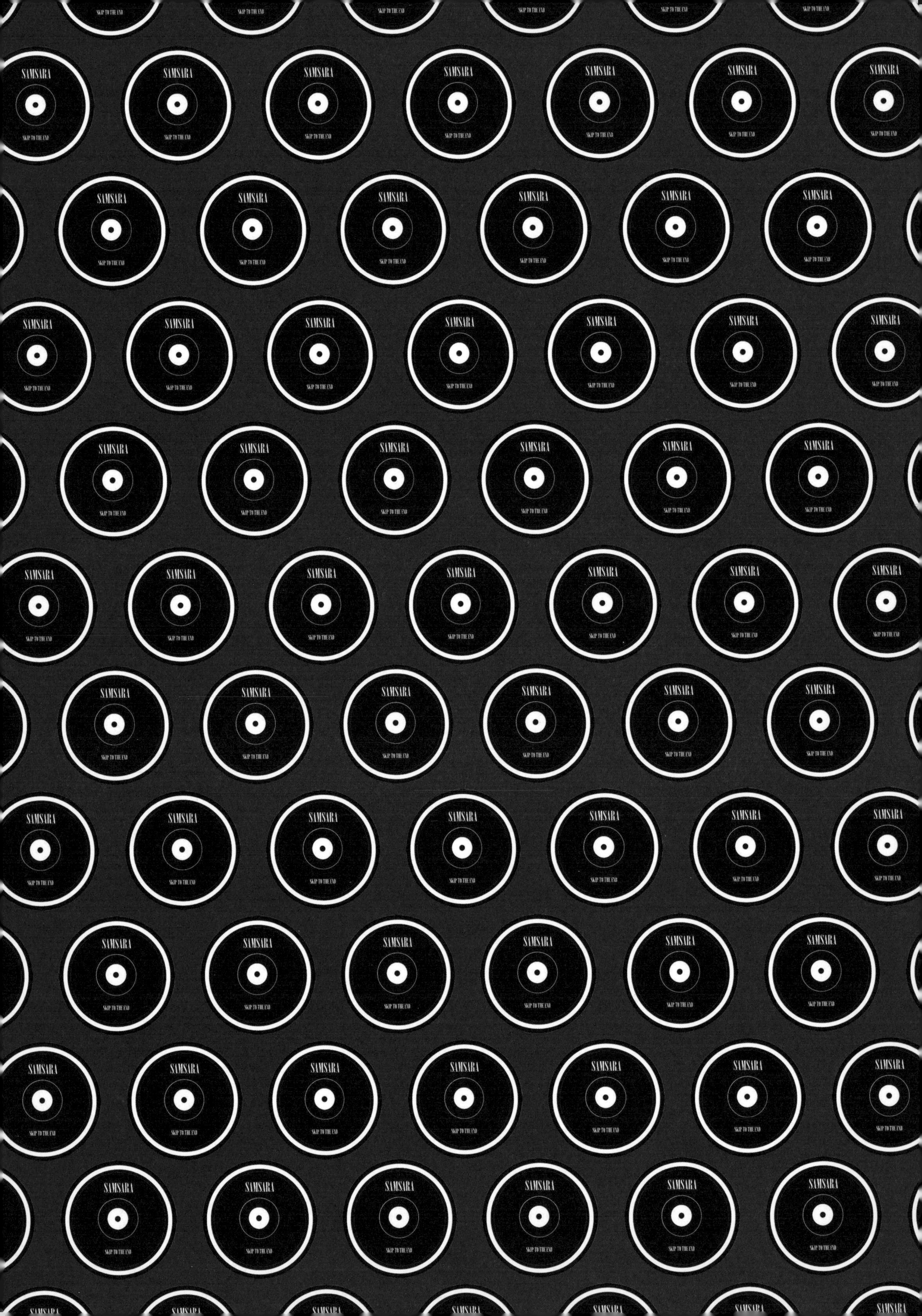
SAMSARA
SKIP TO THE END